The Stone
OF DESTINY

The Stone OF DESTINY

JIM WARE

David C Cook®

transforming lives together

THE STONE OF DESTINY
Published by David C Cook
4050 Lee Vance View
Colorado Springs, CO 80918 U.S.A.

David C Cook Distribution Canada
55 Woodslee Avenue, Paris, Ontario, Canada N3L 3E5

David C Cook U.K., Kingsway Communications
Eastbourne, East Sussex BN23 6NT, England

David C Cook and the graphic circle C logo
are registered trademarks of Cook Communications Ministries.

This story is a work of fiction. All characters and events are
the product of the author's imagination. Any resemblance
to any person, living or dead, is coincidental.

Genesis 28:10–12, 16, 18–19 in chapter 23 are taken from the King James
Version of the Bible. (Public Domain.) The first segment of Deuteronomy
26:5 in chapter 9 is taken from the *New American Standard Bible,* ©
Copyright 1960, 1995 by The Lockman Foundation. Used by permission.
The second segment of Deuteronomy 26:5 is taken from *The Holy Bible,
English Standard Version.* Copyright © 2000; 2001 by Crossway Bibles, a
division of Good News Publishers. Used by permission. All rights reserved.

LCCN 2010942615
ISBN 978-1-4347-6464-5
eISBN 978-1-4347-0363-7

The Team: John Blase, Andrew Meisenheimer, Amy
Kiechlin, Caitlyn York, Karen Athen.
Cover Illustrations: Luke Flowers Design, Luke Flowers, © David C Cook.

Printed in the United States of America
First Edition 2011

1 2 3 4 5 6 7 8 9 10

123010

To Joni,

who never stopped believing in the story

CONTENTS

Part 3

PROLOGUE

October 31, ———

    J. 2. P. Izaak
    Institute of Linguistics
    Santa Piedra, California

Only a few moments are left to me now. While time remains, I will make my last confession.

I will confess that I was not expecting to see her again.

I will confess that I did not think it possible.

Until quite recently, much as I admired the philosophy expounded in the books that bear their names, I had given little serious thought to the actual, literal existence of such persons. The uncanny thing, the thing that even now I find hard to believe, is that each one eventually answered my call: Hermes, Stephanos, Jabir; Scot, Flamel, Paracelsus. And then finally, she came to me as well. From somewhere out of the unknown they responded to my burning curiosity. They showed me wisdom and granted my pleas for power. Higher and higher, step by step, they lifted me up along the ascending stairway of knowledge.

But not without cost. She in particular demanded compensation. In exchange for her favors, she placed me under oath to seek the thing she seeks. She charged me to tell her at once if ever I should discover the smallest clue as to its whereabouts.

And now, against all odds, that clue has actually fallen into my hands. It came to me when I least expected it. Why, I cannot say; how, I dare not.

This, too, I must confess.

But I will also confess that, having what she wants, I am at last resolved to keep it from her. Though she torment me, yet will I keep the secret. She knows all this, of course. She knows that I know. And yet she does not know exactly what I know. My suspicion is that she thinks I know much more than I do. And so she returns to claim her due.

Something approaches through the darkness, a swirling spot of deeper blackness rising up against the night sky across La Coruna Inlet. Out of the iron heart of the gray sea mist, it advances—a swelling shadow, a dark man-shape, a lumbering giant looming over the sleeping town. A vast hand sweeps upward over the stony slope above the shore.

I can see it all from my window here at the Institute.

The Board of Regents will be astonished to learn that such experiments were being conducted under their very noses. For this I bear a burden of sincere remorse. I realize that activities of this nature do not normally figure into the routine of a linguist and teacher of language.

But words are powerful things, and the quest for deeper meanings sometimes produces unintended results.

To my young son I bequeath what remains of the Great Work. My books and instruments—pestle and mortar, hermetic jars and alembics, scissors, shovels, bottles, spoons, and pans—must go to him as soon as he is old enough to learn their uses. May he succeed where I have failed. May he climb the stairway of wisdom. May he learn more than I have been able to learn about the appropriate way to blend knowledge and light. At the top of that ladder stands the door to Power. All the Power of the stars. Of this I remain convinced.

I could say more, but I dare not linger. From the room across the hall come sounds of shattering glass. An intangible, invisible, yet palpable, presence pauses at the door. The shadows in the corners grow deeper.

Now that it comes to it, I confess a desperate and sickening desire to escape the trial of this last encounter.

Now that it comes to it, I confess—

Part 1

Chapter One

RIGHT FIELD

Morgan Izaak hated Santa Piedra Middle School—he loathed physical education; he detested competitive games like football, soccer, and baseball and the twisted social caste system that was founded upon them; and most of all, he resented the people who had somehow been granted the power to use these instruments of torture to oppress him and make his life wretched.

What could a boy like Morgan do against that kind of power? Nothing. Not for the time being, anyway. But one of these days, he would throw off the shackles of his bondage; one of these days he'd wield a power greater than anything they'd ever imagined. One of these days he'd show them all.

He'd do it through *alchemy*.

Mercury, sulphur, salt.

It was a warm, dreamy afternoon in early spring, and Morgan was standing out in deep right field, his skinny legs spread wide apart, his lanky arms akimbo. Over and over again he rehearsed the formula to himself: *Mercury, sulphur, salt*. Sticking his forefinger into his mouth, he picked a scrap of lettuce from his braces—the last remains of lunch—and spat on the ground. Lazily he swung his fielder's glove at a passing fly and breathed out a prayer that the ball wouldn't come his way. *Good thing nobody ever hits to right field*, he thought. *Mercury, sulphur, salt …*

> *Not the substances themselves, but their essential qualities … essential qualities extracted from the raw materials … One primal element … in it all the power of the stars….*

Off in the distance the game was dragging on, but Morgan hadn't the slightest notion of the inning or the score. His mind was fixed upon weightier matters: mineral spirits and elemental emanations; earth, air, fire, and water; the power of the stars and the unity of all things; freedom and release. He yawned. He stretched. He kicked idly at a dandelion that had pushed its way up through a tussock of tough crabgrass.

Then he turned and stared out to the west.

Across the field, past the chain-link fence, over the tops of the dark green pines and cypresses that covered the seaward slope beyond the schoolyard, he could see the afternoon sunlight glinting on the blue face of La Coruna Inlet. *Like gold*, he thought with a smile. Essence of gold. Again his mind drifted off into dreams of power—power to turn lead or tin into gold. Power to *change* things. *Mercury, sulphur, salt.*

"Hey, batta, batta, batta! *Swing*, batta, *swing!*"

Dimly, gradually, the remote shouts of his classmates elbowed their way back in among the jumble of his wandering thoughts. He glanced at the infield and frowned. Shoving a clump of yellow hair out of his eyes, he lifted his face to the sky and squinted. The sun was sailing far out over the ocean, and there was a damp, salty fragrance in the air—a sure sign that the sea-fog would soon be washing ashore down on Front Street.

It must be past three o'clock by now, he thought impatiently. *It has to be!* He pursed his lips, closed his eyes, and pictured himself leaning over the stained and mottled workbench in his lab, adjusting the Bunsen burner, leafing through the pages of a dusty old copy of Paracelsus.

> *Recombine the essences in an alembic over a*
> *flame of very low heat.… Fixed principle …*
> *Volatile principle … Quintessence of earth.…*

Crack!

Only in the vaguest way was he aware of it: the sharp report of a bat and ball connecting somewhere, followed by the scuffle of running feet and the swelling babble of urgent voices raised in anxious shouts.

"Right field!" someone shouted.

"Wake up, Izaak!"

"Oh no!" breathed Morgan. They were calling his name! Was it the ball? Could it be? He shook himself, spun around, and feverishly searched the bright expanse of the sky. Blinded by the sun, he pawed the air helplessly with his glove.

Whoosh! A blast of wind like a passing truck.

17

Whump! A stunning blow to his abdomen, like the kick of a mule directly to the solar plexus.

Morgan gasped. He clutched his stomach. Stars clouded his vision. He saw a baseball drop to the ground at his feet. Then numb, dumb, and deflated, he doubled over and collapsed into the sweetly fragrant turf, straining for air, staring in wide-eyed shock at the grass-stained toes of his tennis shoes.

In the next moment his teammates gathered in a huddle above his head. Lower and lower they bent over him, a confused mass of dark shapes, blocking out the sunlight. A hand seized him roughly by the shoulder, ripping the sleeve of his new blue Oxford shirt. Someone yanked him mercilessly to his feet. He blinked, staggered, and swayed.

"Idiot!"

For all his dizziness, he couldn't help but recognize the voice of Baxter Knowles, captain of the team. "What have you been *doing* out here, Izaak? Daydreaming?"

Morgan lurched and retched and tried to speak but found he couldn't utter a sound. The muscles of his chest were completely paralyzed. There wasn't a single molecule of air left in his lungs, and he felt helpless to refill them no matter how hard he tried. Steadying himself as best he could, he gazed mutely from one end of the semicircle of hostile faces to the other while the scene oscillated, blurred, and spun crazily before his eyes.

"We've had it with you, Izaak!" Baxter said, glaring at him from under the bill of a San Francisco Giants baseball cap. "You're out of the game!" Baxter's face was red and glistening with perspiration. "Nick, you'll just have to cover center *and* right. We don't have a chance with *him* on the team!"

Murmurs of assent all around. Baxter let go of Morgan's shirt and turned away. Morgan crumpled into the grass like an old rag doll.

"Next time ask the Wizard for a *brain,* Strawhead!" Baxter said over his shoulder as the rest of the team followed him back to the infield.

"Robot-Mouth!" said another boy.

"Freckle-Nose!" added a third.

Morgan squeezed his eyes shut. He wanted desperately to yell something back at them. He wanted to tell them that he that he was *glad* to be out of the game. Most of all, he wanted to slay Baxter with a swift, rapierlike insult—to blow him and all his kind clean off the face of the earth. But he couldn't. He was absolutely powerless. He didn't even have the breath to moan or groan. And so, still struggling for air, he rolled over on his side, gripped his abdomen, and slipped back into the laboratory inside his mind.

The fusing of these materials into a new and unknown substance … the single substance of which all material is composed … yielding in the end a fine white powder … a powder with transmutative properties … in it—

all the power of the stars …

Chapter Two

THE TOWER LAB

The tall Gothic tower of St. Halistan's Church rose blue-gray and hazy in the gathering mist as Morgan came trudging up Iglesia Street. Upon reaching home—a white stucco duplex that he and his mother shared with the Ariello family—he cast an anxious glance at the darkened window. *I hope Mom's feeling better this afternoon,* he thought.

He hated to keep her waiting alone in an empty house, especially when she wasn't well. But he couldn't neglect his work, not now, not when he'd been making such encouraging progress. To tell her what he was up to was out of the question. So he let her believe that he'd been helping George Ariello around the church every day after school. That way, she didn't worry, and he didn't feel quite so guilty.

It was a harmless deception.

Besides, he had the consolation of knowing that once his experiments succeeded he'd be in a position to offer her some real help. With the Elixir, he'd be able to cure her every ailment. Smiling at the thought, he stepped carefully over the gaping cracks in the ancient sidewalk where the roots of an old jacaranda tree had pushed the pavement up into a steep little hill of broken concrete. Then he jumped off the curb and dashed across the street to the double oak doors at the base of the square stone tower.

Slinging his backpack over his left shoulder, Morgan seized the brass handle and opened the massive door. From within came the sweet tones of a violin. He had heard the tune many times before—a sad old Irish air called "The May Morning Dew." Almost involuntarily he paused for a moment to listen. Then he poked his head inside and squinted up through the confused jumble of light and shadow on the tower staircase.

At the top of the first flight, sitting on the last stone step below the first wooden landing, was a slim girl with a fiddle under her chin. At the sound of Morgan's steps, she lowered the instrument, shook a strand of copper-colored hair out of her face, and turned to him. Of all the striking things about her remarkable appearance, her eyes were the most remarkably striking of all, for they were of two very different colors. The right one, in keeping with her dark olive complexion, was a lustrous brown, but the left was sky blue—a blue so pale and clear that it seemed almost luminous in the dim and shifting light.

"Hey, Eny," said Morgan.

"Hullo, Morgan," she replied. "How's your day?"

Eny, the only child of George and Moira Ariello, St. Halistan's resident caretakers, spent a big part of her free time here on the tower stairs. The stairwell was one of her favorite haunts—the place to which she most naturally resorted when she wasn't at home or in school or down by the sea caves of La Punta Lira. Here she would sit almost every afternoon, reading or playing her violin. When she grew tired of stories or music, she would lift her face to the light and ponder the tall, arched stained-glass window above the landing: a colorful, jewel-like depiction of angels ascending and descending between heaven and earth on Jacob's golden ladder.

"My day?" said Morgan in answer to her question. "The usual. Baxter Knowles is still Baxter Knowles."

Besides his mother, Eny was the one person in the world with whom Morgan felt he could speak freely and openly. She could be dreamy and quiet, but she was also an unfailingly good listener. Though nearly two years his junior, she was practically Morgan's only friend. He thought of her as his *soror mystica*—the "mystical sister" every good alchemist needs to assist him in the Great Work.

"Anyway," he continued as he came clumping up the stairs, "I didn't come to talk about Baxter. There's something I want to show you. Up in my lab. Come with me?"

Without a word she laid the fiddle gently in its case and leaned it in a corner on the landing. Then she followed him up two flights of creaking wooden stairs until they reached a small green door on a dingy gray-carpeted landing. Morgan fumbled in the pocket of his brown corduroys, pulled out a little brass key, and unlocked the door. Inside lay a bare atticlike room where a rickety wooden ladder led to a square opening in the ceiling. Quickly he scaled the steps and flung open the trap door.

Slanting bars of fading gray afternoon light met his eyes as he entered the lofty, airy, cube-shaped chamber above. Each of the room's four mortared stone walls was pierced by two tall, slatted Gothic windows, through which the damp sea-mist flowed unhindered. Morgan climbed up, drawing Eny behind him, and threw his backpack down on a white Formica-topped workbench that spanned the entire length of the west wall. Switching on a green-shaded desk lamp, he pulled up an old cane chair and motioned to Eny to sit down.

"Messy as ever," she said absently. "What have you been doing up here?" She buttoned her brown woolen sweater up to the chin, shivering in the damp, chill air. Then she pulled a dusty old book off a shelf that hung precariously over the workbench and sat down to examine it. "What's *Iliaster?*" she asked.

Morgan glanced in her direction. "Careful with that! It was my dad's. Paracelsus. *The Philosophy of Theophrastus Concerning the Generations of the Elements.* Very rare. Really old and fragile. And you know what I'm working on. The same thing I'm always working on."

She looked up from the book. "Powder?"

"*Transmutative* powder. The Philosophers' Stone. The *Elixir.*"

She wrinkled up her nose. "I don't think you should be playing around with magic, Morgan."

"It's *not* magic! How many times do I have to tell you, Eny? It's *science!* Alchemy! The parent of all sciences! Every major alchemical writer talks about the Philosophers' Stone.

24

Hermes Trismegistus. Paracelsus. Edward Kelly. Armand Barbault. Fulcanelli. It's a transmutative powder. It changes things into other things. Turns lead into gold. They call it the Elixir of Life because it's supposed to have healing properties. *In it all the power of the stars.*"

"If it's a powder, then why do they call it a *stone?*"

He scowled at her. "'Stone' doesn't always have to mean 'big rock.' In this case it obviously refers to a *mineral essence* of some kind. *The One Primal Element.* Paracelsus believed in the virtue of minerals. 'How does a Tree become a Stone, which then becomes a Star?' That's how Fulcanelli put it. That's the riddle of the Philosophers' Stone."

Eny shrugged, shook her head, and turned back to the book.

She was right about the lab, of course. It *was* pure chaos. Morgan knew it. But then he hadn't had time to think about straightening up. The work was going too well. It was intoxicating, consuming—success was so near he could almost taste it. Noisily shoving aside a few bottles, some crusty spoons, and a pile of crumpled papers, he groped around on the bench until his fingers found what he was seeking: two corked test tubes and his *alembic*—a narrow-necked glass jar connected by a thin tube to a small glass globe.

"Here," he said, squaring his shoulders and taking a deep breath. "This is what I wanted to show you." He blew a few strands of yellow hair out of his eyes, picked up the tubes and the alembic, and carried them to a sink in the corner. "I'm getting close, Eny. *Real* close. Watch this."

Biting his lip, Morgan carefully poured the contents of the first tube—a clear scarlet fluid—into the alembic. Then he uncapped the other, which was filled with something that looked like watery milk, and added it to the solution. Silence reigned in the chamber while the milky stuff mingled with the red. As they watched, the mixture turned green, then gold, then orange, then maroon. At last it became a pinkish liquid of a pearled and cloudy consistency.

Morgan felt a smile tugging at the corners of his mouth. The blood was drumming in his ears. "See that?" he said. "That's just the way the books said it should happen!" With the greatest of care he transferred the alembic to the workbench, placed it gingerly over a Bunsen burner, and fired up the flame. Immediately he turned it down to a mere blue flicker. *A flame of very low heat.*

"So how's your mom?" said Eny.

He blinked and looked up at her abruptly. It was just like a girl to bring up a subject like that at a time like this. "Not too good," he said.

"My parents are worried about her."

Morgan grunted and turned back to the Bunsen burner. "I guess they hear all the coughing. The walls are thin enough."

Eny shut *The Philosophy of Theophrastus* with a snap. "Has the doctor said anything new?"

"Nope." Morgan's attention was focused intently on the pink liquid, which was beginning to seethe and roil in the alembic like a tiny tempest.

"And what about your mom? What does *she* think?"

"She says it's all 'in the hands of the Lord.' *I* say it all goes back to that bad case of the flu she had a couple of years ago. She's been coughing ever since. Lately she's had some dizziness, too. And fainting spells. But it's no big deal. She was supposed to see Dr. Vincent again this afternoon."

"So you'll know more when we get home?"

He nodded absently. By this point he was completely immersed in the drama unfolding inside the glass container. Sparks were jumping inside his brain in sympathy with the leaping and popping bubbles in the churning brew. Without shifting his gaze, he beckoned to her with his hand. "Quick, Eny!" he said. "Come look at *this!*"

She was beside him in a moment. The rosy solution was boiling rapidly now, turning over and over inside the alembic, sending up a pale roseate steam into the distillation tube. The steam, in turn, was solidifying into crystals inside the glass, and the crystals were slowly changing color before their very eyes—from pink to orange, from orange to scarlet, from scarlet to purple, from purple to blue.

"It's happening!" shouted Morgan, clapping his hands. "It's happening at last!"

"What's happening?"

"*Mercury, sulphur, and salt* … extracted from common substances—dead leaves, seaweed, dirt, crabgrass—cooked down, hermetically sealed, slowly boiled over and over again. It's supposed to yield what the alchemists called *materia prima*—'prime matter.' And *materia prima,* if it's handled just right, produces the *Stone!* Watch the crystals, Eny! When they turn white, the process is complete!"

Suddenly he felt her grip his arm and squeeze it tightly. "Morgan!" she shouted. He jerked his head around and saw that her eyes were wide with alarm.

"What's wrong?" he said. "There's nothing to be afraid of! Just think—"

A flash like blue lightning illuminated the room. With one ear Morgan heard the blast of an explosion and the crash of breaking glass, with the other the piercing wail of Eny's scream. A sharp, searing pain slashed him along the right side of his face. He fell down into darkness.

When at last he was able to raise himself on one elbow, he glanced around at the wreckage and caught sight of Eny, unhurt but trembling, hunched up against the opposite wall. The last dim shafts of a fog-muffled sunset were streaming in through the windows and piercing the clouds of smoke that filled the room. He jumped up, filled a bucket at the sink, and doused the little yellow flames that were dancing along the edge of his workbench. Then he collapsed into the cane chair and put a hand to his cheek.

It burned like fire.

"You won't tell your parents, will you?" pleaded Morgan as he and Eny parted ways in front of the white stucco duplex. "I don't know what I'd do if your dad made me shut down the lab!" George Ariello wielded absolute sway over every square inch of St. Halistan's. It was he who had granted Morgan use of the tower chamber in the first place.

"He won't," said Eny. "Not yet, anyway. Not unless Reverend Alcuin finds out about it. Or unless I happen to change my mind." Shivering in the evening fog, she clasped her violin tightly under her arm and frowned. There was a strange, distant expression on her face. Her one blue eye seemed to glow in the gathering darkness. "Besides, you've got bigger things to worry about right now."

"What do you mean?"

She shrugged. "You'd better go in and put something on that burn," she said. "G'night." With a faint smile, she turned and went in the door on the left.

Morgan stood staring after her. "Bigger things to worry about," he muttered. He could hear the voices of George and Moira Ariello raised in a vigorous exchange as the door closed behind his friend. *Sounds like she's got worries of her own,* he thought. Turning to the right, he slipped quietly into his own half of the duplex, determined to avoid his mother until he'd had a chance to change and wash up.

Morgan knew something was not right the minute he set foot inside the apartment. All was dark; all was quiet. At this time of day, Mom ought to have been in the kitchen getting dinner on the table. Hadn't she come back from the doctor yet? He paused to listen; reached up to flip on a light; then stopped, baffled at his own hesitancy to disrupt the dim gray silence.

At the end of the front hallway he could see a dull light flickering among the lilies on the living room wallpaper. Approaching on tiptoe, he held his breath and stuck his head into the room. There was a fire on the hearth. In front of it, humped over on the worn green sofa, the red-orange glow of the flames caught like a halo in her angel-fine hair, sat his mother. Her back was to him, and her head was in her hands. Except for the crackling of the flames and the ticking of the clock on the mantel, the room was deathly still.

"What is it, Mom?" he said, his voice barely more than a whisper. "Is something wrong?"

She turned. It was hard to tell in the glare of the firelight, but he thought her eyes looked red. She tried to smile, but her hand trembled as she held it out to him. "Cancer," was all she said.

The sea-fog heaved and shifted on the breeze, then divided and parted, revealing the pale sheen of the moon rippling on the surface of La Coruna Inlet. Morgan stood at his bedroom window, his forehead pressed against the glass. The midnight stars glinted in the dark spaces between the scattering shreds of mist. He clenched his fists and bit his lip.

Elixir of life. In it all the power of the stars. I'll start over again. Tomorrow.

Drawing the curtains, he collapsed into bed and pulled the covers up over his head.

Chapter Three

MADAME MEDEA

Ruddy sunlight played in bright liquid ripples across the shop windows as Morgan and Eny shuffled down Front Street the following afternoon. Across the road lay the windswept beach, a silvery crescent of California coastline, glittering with sand and shells. On their right marched the painted storefronts of Santa Piedra's Old Towne district, a bougainvillea-shaded row of eateries and curiosity shops. Morgan took a deep breath, ran his fingers through his unruly yellow hair, and stole a glance at his companion. He had chosen this way home from school—the *long* way—on purpose. He was looking for a chance to talk.

"It must have been methane," he said.

"Methane?" Eny clutched her schoolbooks closer and regarded him out of the corner of her eye.

"It's the only possible explanation. Somehow or other, I produced methane yesterday afternoon. 'Swamp gas.' Highly flammable."

She turned just long enough to look at him curiously. Then they walked on in silence beneath the cool shadows of the curbside ficus trees.

Normally Morgan would have avoided this part of town at this time of day. Not that he disliked the seashore or the shops; in spite of all the commercialization, Old Towne retained an atmosphere that he found almost irresistible: the air of a whaling village mingled with the romance of a colonial Spanish pueblo. Still, he could never forget that this entire piece of real estate was owned by the Knowles empire. Every single establishment along Front Street—from La Coruna Gifts and Cards to the Knowles Book Knoll to Uncle Pritchard's Restaurant—all of it belonged to Baxter's father. Morgan couldn't pass this way without feeling as if Baxter himself might emerge from one of those doors at any moment.

"I don't know anything about methane," Eny said at last. "But whatever you did, you better not do it again. If my dad finds out, he'll be mad. He has enough trouble with fire inspectors."

"That's why I need your help," said Morgan.

"What do you mean?"

He stopped and faced her. "I mean I've *got* to do it again. At least I have to try. And since I can't guarantee how it will turn out, I'll need you to help cover for me. In case of mishaps."

She squinted at him in the glare of the westering sun. "Why is this white powder so important to you, Morgan? Is this about Baxter Knowles?"

"No!" he said, reddening. "It's not that at all. It's something much more important." He hesitated. "It's my mom."

Her eyes were fixed on his. He knew she was waiting for an explanation. A hot, burning sensation rose up the back of

32

his neck. He fumbled and bit his lip. "It's cancer," he said at last. "She's got cancer."

Eny's eyes grew large and round. She dropped her books on a nearby bench. "Cancer?"

Morgan nodded.

Her face darkened. "But we've been praying for her every day, my dad and me. Is she scared?"

"She's worried. I can tell. I think she'd been crying before I came in last night. But she just smiles and tells me everything will be okay. She says God is taking care of her."

Eny shook her head. "I just can't believe it," she said.

"I won't believe it!" said Morgan. "And I *won't* let it happen. That's why I've got to go back into the lab. Don't you see? It's more crucial than ever now. The Elixir of Life is the only way to—"

He stopped in midsentence. Just above Eny's head, swinging gently in the sea breeze, hung a signboard he'd never seen before: an intricately carved and newly painted sign that dangled from a twisted, rusty rod of black wrought iron. It bore the emblem of a white hand on a black field. Beneath the hand, in curled and gilded letters, were the words MADAME MEDEA'S:

Coffee House
Metaphysical Gifts
Palm Readings
Consultations in the Alchemical Arts

"What's wrong?" said Eny, tilting her head back in an effort to see what he was gaping at. "You look like you've seen a ghost!"

Morgan tossed his schoolbooks down beside Eny's. "I've never seen this place before."

"It wasn't here yesterday," she said, wrinkling her nose. "At least I don't think so. That's kind of creepy."

Morgan approached the shop window and peered inside. It was cluttered with a bewildering miscellany of merchandise. There were candles and wind chimes, ribbons and streamers, gold chains and strings of bright beads. There were copper pots and silver dishes, teakettles and coffee grinders, bottles and jars of green and blue glass. Of special interest was a set of alembics and glass tubes of various sizes and a collection of dusty old books in worn leather covers. Painted across the window itself, in a double-arched semicircle of Gothic letters, was the motto,

That which is above is as that which is below,
And that which is below is as that which is
above.

"*Consultations in the Alchemical Arts,*" muttered Morgan, glancing up at the sign again. "I don't know much about prayer, Eny, but this might be the answer! Let's find out."

He grabbed her by the arm and thrust his way into the shop.

A tiny brass bell tinkled above their heads as the door clicked shut behind them. The next moment they were enveloped in a silence as deep and thick as the velvety purple carpet beneath their feet. Morgan took a few tentative steps forward, then stopped and looked around.

The interior of the shop was darker than he had expected. As his eyes adjusted to the dimness, he gradually became aware that the place was filled with rows of haphazard wooden shelves and aisles of dusty glass cases, all of them crammed with more of the same kind of stuff he'd seen in the window: pestles and mortars, snips and shears, pokers and tongs, shovels and bellows, jars of crystals, astrolabes, scales, censers, double boilers, ceramic pots. Everywhere were bottles filled with tinctures of every possible color—gold, green, azure, carnelian, purple, violet, mustard yellow. An umbrella stand stood just inside the entrance, housing a random collection of parasols, canes, and walking sticks.

Morgan looked up. From the rafters dangled shaggy bundles of fragrant herbs and common garden weeds: dandelion, horsetail, dill, scouring rush, sweet marjoram, lemon balm, lavender, plantain. Dark tapestries hung along the walls, one of them bearing a picture of a flaming bird in a Greek temple on a pyramid of seven tiers. Each of the pyramid's seven terraces was clearly labeled: *Calcination, Dissolution, Separation, Conjunction, Fermentation, Distillation, Coagulation*. Beneath the picture, embroidered in letters of gold, were the words *The Ladder of the Wise*.

Along the left side of the room ran a dark oak counter bearing a silvery espresso machine. Above this rose yet another bank of shelves, stocked to the ceiling with multicolored bottles of flavored syrups and jars of aromatic coffee beans. The air was filled with an extravagant mixture of wild, contradictory aromas, rich, pungent, sweet, and spicy. Three small round tables were jammed into a corner beside the counter, each of them surrounded by three black wrought-iron chairs. Soothing harp music floated through a narrow doorway at the back of the room, where Morgan could see a faint, flickering yellow light filtering through a screen of wooden beads.

"And how might we be serving you, young miss and young mister?"

Startled, Morgan whipped around to find a strange little man standing at his elbow, his nose long and crooked, his chin sharp and stubbly, his head as bald as an egg except for a fringe of gray hair that ran from ear to ear round the back of his skull. His large gray eyes gleamed like stars from beneath his bushy gray eyebrows. His shabby black coat was tattered and worn, and his brown woolen pants had holes at the knees. From his belt hung a lumpy satchel of soft leather, like an old drawstring purse.

"Is it a cup of hot brew you'd be after?" said the little man in answer to Morgan's surprised stare. "Or a book, perhaps? A bell or a candle?"

"Is this—*your* store?" stammered Morgan, gaping at the pinched and wrinkled face.

"Mine?" The little man's eyes twinkled. "*Mine*, he wants to know, Falor!"

At that, a second person, broad of girth, heavy of body, and so huge that he had to stoop to get through the doorway, emerged from behind the curtain of clacking beads. His shaved head was small and round, his right eye was covered with a patch, and his greasy black suit appeared to be at least two sizes too small. He said nothing but glared at them coldly out of his one good eye.

"Na, na," laughed the little man. "It's not *my* shop, nor none of *his,* either. We're both of us hired men. That's Falor, son of Balor," he added, jabbing a thumb across the room at his mountainous colleague.

Morgan felt Eny clutching his arm. "Falor, son of Balor?" she whispered. "Is this some kind of a joke?"

"And I'm called Eochy," the little man continued. "Odd name, you're thinking, but not difficult." He made a low bow, sweeping the long fingers of his hand across the floor in a gracious gesture of greeting. "At your service. As for this shop, if you really want to know, it belongs to—"

"Me."

Morgan turned at the sound of this new voice—rich, mellifluous, darkly feminine, inexplicably calming. In the same instant he became aware that the harp music had ceased. Eny's fingers tightened around his arm.

"Excuse me, Falor," the voice continued. "As you can see, I have customers waiting."

The giant grunted and shifted his bulk to one side. In the doorway behind him, poised upon the threshold, stood a tall and stately woman. The yellow light streaming through the screen of beads hung about her shapely form in a gentle aura. Her face was a pale oval, neither very young nor very

37

old. Her eyes were large, green, and almond-shaped. She wore a bell-sleeved, multi-colored satin gown caught at the waist with a scarlet sash, and the golden slippers on her feet curled upward at the toes. From beneath her blue turban flowed an abundance of silky black hair, glossy as a raven's wing. Slowly she began to move toward them, and as she came nearer Morgan could see that her lips were as red as ripe cherries.

"Morgan!" whispered Eny, gripping his arm so tightly now that he could feel her fingernails digging into his flesh. "Let's get out of here!"

"Not yet!" he whispered.

"Welcome," said the woman, smiling broadly and taking him by the hand. "Welcome to Madame Medea's. What can I do for you?"

Morgan swallowed hard and gave Eny a sidewise glance. He could see her blue eye glowing in the dim light, boring into him with a look that burned like cold fire. Turning back to the woman, he cleared his throat and nervously licked his lips.

"My name's Morgan, ma'am," he said, his voice cracking. "Morgan Izaak. I saw the sign outside. *Consultations in the Alchemical Arts.* I've got a lab of my own, and lots of books on alchemy—they used to be my dad's—and I've been trying for a long time to—"

She stopped him with a raised hand—a hand as fair and white as the image on the signboard outside the shop. "With what shall you pay?" she asked.

Morgan felt Eny jabbing him in the ribs, but he chose to ignore her. "I don't have any money," he said, fumbling in the pockets of his corduroys. "We were just on our way home from school when we saw your sign, and—"

Madame Medea reached down and laid an ivory-cool finger upon his lips. She fixed him and held him with her large green eyes. The edges of her mouth curved upward, and her dark eyebrows lifted, unsettling the smooth whiteness of her forehead. Then she laughed, a merry laugh like the chiming of a bell.

"Don't worry," she said. "Madame Medea knows why you have come."

Morgan stared. "She does? I mean—you do?"

"Yes. And I can help you. I have only the greatest concern for you and your pretty little friend." She shifted her gaze from Morgan to Eny. "The girl with the mismatched eyes. The girl with the Second Sight. What is your name, my dear?"

Eny scowled and said nothing.

"Ah!" smiled Madame Medea. "Pretty *and* discreet! But no matter." Still holding Morgan's hand, she rose to her full height and took a step backward. "As I have said, I already know what you want. You have come because you are seeking the Stone."

Morgan turned and gaped at Eny. Eny stared back.

"The Stone of Destiny," the woman continued with a nod. "The Satisfaction of All Desire. In this quest we are one." Her smile faded. "I can help you, but it will not be without cost. Come back to me when you have nowhere else to turn, and I will help you." She lifted his hand to her lips and kissed it softly. "Eochy, please see our young friends to the door. Good-bye, Morgan Izaak. Come back soon. Not without your friend, of course. I look forward to seeing *both* of you again." With that she turned and disappeared behind the screen of rattling beads.

Eochy bowed and offered an arm to Eny. As he escorted the two of them out to the street, Morgan could hear the music of the harp rising again at the back of the shop.

"A word to the wise in parting," said Eochy with a sly look as he led them to the bench where their schoolbooks lay. "After this it might be just as well to be finding another way home from school."

Chapter Four

SIMON BRACH

"Hi, Mom," said Eny as she and Morgan elbowed their way into the crowded little front office of St. Halistan's Church. "Who are all these people?"

Moira Ariello, perched tentatively on a swivel chair behind the receptionist's desk, glanced up over her steel-rimmed spectacles and raised a forefinger. For the moment her auburn hair was restrained by a telephone headset, and it was clear that she was busy with a caller on the other end of the line. Eny would have to wait for an answer to her question. With a shrug, she dropped her books and slumped on a bench just inside the door.

Reluctantly, Morgan sat down beside her. It had been a tense and silent walk from Madame Medea's shop to the church. He knew what Eny was thinking, and he didn't want to talk about it. He was convinced that the woman in the blue turban had the answers he needed, and he was determined to get them from her at any cost. Somehow or other he'd help her find what she was seeking: the Philosophers' Stone, the Stone of Destiny—it really didn't matter what she called it. What mattered was his mother and the hope of the Elixir. Eny didn't have to get involved if she didn't want to.

Brushing the hair from his eyes, he looked up and saw the Reverend Peter Alcuin standing in the corner behind Moira's desk, tight up against the pigeonhole mailboxes above the communion cupboard. Rev. Alcuin's round face was unusually red, and his bald head shone with perspiration. Though his expression remained characteristically placid and congenial, he seemed unable to keep his long, tapered fingers from tugging at his clerical collar as he stared into the eyes of two darkly dressed, clipboard-carrying men. Every so often he responded to their quiet, prodding questions with a brief word or a silent nod. Inspectors, Morgan realized. That couldn't be good.

On the other side of the room, between the water cooler and the oversized closet that served as the church library, George Ariello stood with his shoulder against the wall, intently studying a sheet of blue-green paper and muttering to himself in Spanish as he read. In his left hand he held a red bandanna with which he periodically mopped his brow and shoved stray locks of black hair away from his glistening forehead. Standing next to him was a tall, lanky stranger in a gray coat.

"It's not that I couldn't use you," George said at last, squinting up at the stranger. "You're qualified for the job all right. But I'm not hiring. This is a small church, and we're on a tight budget. My wife and me"—he nodded in Moira's direction—"we can pretty much handle it on our own if we have to."

Moira, whose phone conversation had apparently come to an end, looked up and scowled. Eny shook her head and sighed. Morgan knew how she felt about her parents' long hours at the church.

"I can do floors," said the man in the gray coat. The voice was strong but gravelly, the accent oddly lilting. "I know how to strip and seal and wax, and I'm good with a buffer. Used to have my own carpet-cleaning business back in Kansas City. I do windows, too."

"Windows?" George's tone changed on the instant, as if at the pronouncement of a magic word. Laying the application on the library table, he craned his neck forward and regarded the man closely. "You know, I've been needing a good window man. Someone who knows stained glass."

"A specialty of mine," said the stranger.

"We've got lots of it around here," George went on. "Tricky stuff to clean. All through the sanctuary and up the tower stairs. Come to think of it, there's lots of work to be done up in that tower."

Morgan squirmed. He wasn't sure he wanted anyone snooping around the tower. Most of the men George hired to work at the church were off-season farm workers from the Central Valley or retired longshoremen and cannery hands from the docks. This guy didn't seem to fit into either category. He would have seemed old if it weren't for the sparkle in his eye; tall except for his stooped shoulders; frail but for his large-knuckled fingers. He had an old U.S. Army knapsack on his shoulder, and a big canvas duffel bag lay bulging at his feet. Under his left arm he carried an ancient-looking alligator-skin violin case.

Eny saw the violin case too, of course. Morgan could see her eyeing it, and he knew exactly what she was going to do. Before he could stop her, she was out of her seat, edging her way closer for a better look.

Being in no mood for talking about musical instruments, Morgan closed his eyes and tried to think about *The Ladder of the Wise*. He pictured Madame Medea's face and conjured up a vision of the bright bottles of tinctures and essences lining the shelves of her shop. But no sooner had these images taken shape in his brain than they were shattered and dispersed by the sound of his friend's small voice.

"Do you play, sir?"

Morgan opened his eyes in time to see the stranger smile. By way of answer, the man knelt and laid the violin case on the floor at Eny's feet. He flipped up the latches one by one. Slowly he raised the lid. Inside, nestled in a bed of blue velvet, lay an instrument like no violin Morgan had ever seen. The intricately grained wood was of a dark reddish color; ebony and ivory inlay covered the fingerboard from top to bottom. In place of the traditional scroll, there was a headpiece carved in the shape of a roaring lion. The black tuning pegs were edged with softly reflective mother-of-pearl.

Gently, lovingly, almost reverently, the man in the gray coat lifted the fiddle from its couch. Taking up the bow, he tightened the horsehair and touched it to the strings. A hush fell over the room as a single clear, unwavering note pierced the air. For what seemed a very long time—though it was probably no more than an instant—everyone stood transfixed as if under an enchantment. The spell was only broken when the inspectors, one of them coughing slightly, shuffled awkwardly to the door and exited without a word.

"Where you from, mister?" asked Moira after another brief silence. There was a dreamy sort of look in her hazel-green eyes.

"Oh," said the man with a nonchalant wave of the hand, "all over. Nowhere in particular. Most places at one time or another. Out west. Back east. Up north and down south. Memphis, New Orleans, Quebec, Nova Scotia, Wales, Ireland."

Moira removed her headset and stepped out from behind the desk. "Well!" she said, scrutinizing the craggy face. "You *do* look Irish at that! My mother was a Dehoney from Meath. You are going to hire him, aren't you, George?"

George gave her a wry glance and shoved the red bandanna into the back pocket of his jeans. Then he picked up the blue-green application form and sniffed. "Can you handle the night shift, Mr.——?"

"Brach. Simon Brach," said the stranger. "Of course I can. I've worked plenty of night jobs. Silence and solitude suit me."

"The job is yours, then," said George, standing away from the wall and putting out his hand. "You start tomorrow. Got a place to stay?"

"Good question," said Simon Brach, as he accepted the proffered hand. "An excellent question, seeing as how I just blew into town, so to speak. Any suggestions?"

"There's a furnished room at the foot of the tower. Underneath the stone stairs. My last night man lived there

45

for about six months. It's small and spare, but it'll do. You're welcome to it if you want it."

Simon Brach nodded agreeably. "Kind of you. Very kind. I'll take it, at least for the time being. If only as a place to stow my gear, you know."

"Good. Eny and I will show it to you," said George with a wink at his daughter. "After that, we'll head up to the business office and file your paperwork. Come on, Eny!"

"Ah!" laughed Simon Brach, returning the violin to its case. "Such a lot of stuff I've got to lug around! Perhaps the little lady wouldn't mind carrying this old fiddle for me?"

Eny beamed. Morgan couldn't help but notice how her eyes lit up as she took the instrument from the old man and cradled it in her arms. So that's the way it was, he thought as he watched her follow George and Simon out of the office. Well, she could have her fiddling. He'd other fish to fry.

A hand touched his shoulder. He looked up to see the Reverend Peter Alcuin standing over him with a clouded expression on his face.

"I'm sorry, Morgan," he said. "I didn't mean to startle you. But we need to talk."

Morgan twisted in his seat. "Who were those two men, Reverend Alcuin?"

The Reverend sighed. "City inspectors. Courtesy of Mr. Knowles. Mr. Knowles, it seems, is concerned about St. Halistan's tower. Apparently it's not up to earthquake code. So he turned in a report on us. Part of his civic duty."

"Earthquake code?"

"I'm afraid so. But that's not what I wanted to talk about." Rev. Alcuin sat down beside him on the bench. "Listen. I know all about your mother. I've just been to see her. We had a good heart-to-heart and prayed together for a long time." He smiled a little. "I think it did me more good than her. She's a great lady—a woman of remarkable faith and courage. I just want you to know that I'm going to be stopping in to see the two of you more often. *All* of us here at the church are anxious to help in any way we can."

There was a long, fidgety pause. Morgan could see Moira Ariello peering at him over the top of her desk. He looked down at his shoes and spoke in a small, husky voice.

"Thank you, Reverend," he said. "Thanks very much. That means a lot to me. But you don't have to worry. I think I've got things under control."

The late afternoon sun was shining directly through the stained-glass window at the top of the landing when Morgan slipped in through the double oak doors at the base of the tower stairs. Gems of red, gold, and blue lay scattered all down the steps, and the air was tinged with a dim rosy glow. He paused, staring up through the musty light, while an inexplicable shiver passed over his body—an uncanny sensation that he was looking at the picture in the window for the very first time. Could it actually have changed since he saw it last? That wasn't possible, and yet the angel nearest the bottom of the ladder—had he always been robed in green

47

rather than white? And that figure sleeping on the ground at his feet—had his head always been pillowed on what looked like a great rectangular stone? Morgan wasn't sure.

"Hello there!"

Morgan turned with a start. There stood Simon Brach, just in front of a little green door in the side of the staircase wall.

"Mr. Izaak, isn't it?" said the old man with a grunt, opening the door and dragging his big duffel bag into the tiny cupboardlike apartment under the steps.

"Just Morgan," said Morgan. How did this man know his name?

"Morgan. That's Welsh. I like it. And I can't blame you. I don't hold with being 'mistered' much myself. You can call me Simon. I suppose we'll be seeing a lot of each other?"

"I suppose so."

"You've got plenty of work to do up in the tower, I think?"

"Work?" Morgan swallowed uneasily. Slowly he began to make his way up the stairs. "Oh, sure. Lots of it. You, too, I guess. George can really use the help."

"Yes," said Simon as Morgan drew near the landing. "A good man, George. And I *do* hope to help him all I can. But that's not why I came. I came because *I* need *your* help."

Morgan stopped. As if held to the spot by some invisible force, he turned on the last stone step and gazed down at the gaunt figure below him. There was a soft red light on Simon's upturned face. The last rays of the sun rested like a crown of gold on his sparse silvery hair. Morgan opened his mouth to ask him what he meant, but before he could speak, Simon bent his head and disappeared behind the little green door. The latch clicked. The light in the window died. The air inside the tower faded to gray.

For the briefest moment Morgan stood staring as if spellbound. Then he shook himself and rubbed his eyes. *Crazy old man,* he thought.

Then up the second flight he pounded, taking the stairs two steps at a time, until he reached the door of the tower lab.

Chapter Five

LIA FAIL

It was late when Morgan, having spent a good two hours poring over old copies of *The Sophic Hydrolith,* the *Mutus Liber,* and Fulcanelli's *Mystery of the Cathedrals,* descended the tower stairs. Under his arm he carried a roll of linen, a ball of yarn, and a bundle of short wooden stakes.

On the landing he paused again to gaze at the image of Jacob's Ladder in the darkened stained glass. Odd, he thought, how different things could look in a different light. Without the backing illumination of the sun, the picture was not simply lifeless and dull: It was completely altered. In the enveloping gloom, with nothing but the lofty black stillness of the open stairway all around, the shapes of its flat, colorless leaded panes bore an uncanny resemblance to Madame Medea's *The Ladder of the Wise.*

He smiled at the thought. The steps of *that* ladder were known to him by heart. *Calcination, Dissolution, Separation, Conjunction, Fermentation, Distillation, Coagulation.* The long months of study and experimentation hadn't been for nothing. He was determined to succeed this time. This time he'd confect the Stone by following the prescriptions of what the adepts called the "Wet Path." He'd begin with May-dew,

"gathered on a clear night at the time of the waxing moon."
He gripped his bundle and turned away.

But as he stepped off the landing and down onto the top stone step—the step where Eny always sat to play her fiddle—something caught his eye: a hint of movement in the corner of his peripheral vision; a pulse of light flashing down on him through the window above. When he looked up, the *Ladder of the Wise* had disappeared. Jacob and the angels had returned, their brilliant daylight colors fully restored.

Morgan blinked. Was it his imagination, or had the figures in the picture actually moved? Had that first angel's silvery wing really fluttered as if stirred by a breath of wind? Had the head of the sleeping figure risen, though ever so slightly, from its stony pillow? He leaned forward for a closer look, but in the same instant the vision fled. The darkness closed in, and the window faded to black. *The moon,* he thought. *It must have been the moon.*

There was nothing to see at the bottom of the stairs except a thin line of yellow light underneath the little green door. Tiptoeing softly to the double oak doors, he pushed his way out into the night. But on the sidewalk he again stopped and stared. *There was no moon.* Not even a hint of a moon. Instead, everything—the sky, the top of the church tower, the street, the white stucco duplex on the other side—all were completely obscured in a sea-fog so thick that he could hardly make out the lamp that burned directly over his head. Hardly a "clear night."

His heart sank. *May-dew, collected on a clear night leading up to the full moon.* With a sigh, he glanced down at the bundle under his arm and considered his options. It might not hurt to go ahead with the plan. The fog could always clear out by midnight. Stranger things had been known to happen. He crossed the road and went in at the wicket gate.

Stealing along the side of the house, he came out into the backyard. In the open grassy place between his mother's rose beds and George's vegetable garden he knelt and drew a wooden stake from the bundle. A damp, earthy smell hung in the air; the ground was cold and wet. Producing a small mallet, he pounded the stake into the grass, then got to his feet, paced off a distance of ten steps, knelt down, and drove in another stake. Turning to the right, he repeated the process until he had marked out a space of about fifteen feet by six. Unrolling the linen sheet, he stretched it tightly over the tops of the wooden pegs, tying the corners down with pieces of yarn. *If the cloth sags and touches the earth the etheric forces in the dew will be drained.*

His work complete, Morgan jumped up the back steps and went inside the house. Filaments of fog drifted in around his head and shoulders as the door shut behind him.

"Is that you, honey?"

It was his mother's voice—soft and delicate as usual, but stronger somehow than he'd been used to hearing it over the past few days. There was a light in the kitchen, and a tantalizing fragrance, like frying pork, was streaming down the hallway to greet him. Mom was up and making dinner!

Morgan had been a baby at the time of his father's death, so he had no living memories to teach him how the man of the house ought to behave in a situation like the one he was facing. Of the mysterious, masculine, flesh-and-blood human complexity that was John Izaak, nothing was left to him but books and instruments. But the books gave him hope, and the instruments encouraged him to believe that something could be done to save his mother. Something *would* be done. He would do it himself.

"You're better!" he said as he stepped into the kitchen, his heart full and high and glad. "That's great!"

She was standing at the stove, turning the sputtering chops in the pan, an apron draped loosely over her slight, angular form—the old blue apron that made him think of better days when she used to bake him cookies after school. Her thin, fair hair was done up in a tight circle on the top of her head. She turned at the sound of his voice, and he saw her face, pale but radiant.

"Yes," she said. "I start chemotherapy tomorrow. Dr. Vincent says I'll be out of commission for a bit after that. So I wanted to make us a nice dinner. It'll be our last chance for a while."

"Maybe," he said, his pulse quickening, "but only just a *little* while." Hesitantly he added, "I'm working on a plan."

She smiled at him curiously before turning back to the stove. "I know how hard this must be for you," she said.

"Don't worry about me. I'm doing fine. Can I help? Set the table or something?"

She laughed. "Yes. And use the good china!"

Out in the small dining room, Morgan spread the table with a lace cloth, the one they always saved for Sunday dinners and special occasions. That done, he took two plates from the oak sideboard, two pewter goblets from the cupboard, and a handful of the best silver from a drawer. Hardly had he finished laying the places when his mother came in carrying two steaming dishes. After placing them on the table, she struck a match and lit a white candle in a brass candlestick. Then they sat down to their meal: pork chops, applesauce, steamed broccoli, cooked carrots, and thick slices of buttered white bread.

Not until that moment had Morgan realized how famished he was. Never, it seemed, had he seen such a glorious spread. But he held back, though his stomach growled and his mouth began to water; for as he knew only too well, Mavis Izaak had never in her life eaten a meal without first saying a blessing over the food. He closed his eyes, bowed his head, and waited.

"Lord," he heard her say, "the night is dark. But here inside the house You grant us refuge and warmth and light. Our time in this world is short, but You fill it with all good things. For this we give You thanks."

There was a pause. Morgan glanced up. His mother sat silent before him, her forehead resting on her folded hands, the flickering yellow light shimmering over the smoothness of her fair hair. He could see her lips moving noiselessly. He could hear an unexpected wind stirring in the treetops outside—a wind to sweep the fog away from the face of the moon! Seconds passed, and he shifted in his chair. But just as he was opening his mouth to bring the prayer to an end, Mavis raised her head and said, "Now bless this food of which we are about to partake. In the Savior's name."

"Amen," said Morgan, picking up his fork.

She opened her eyes and smiled at him. As he sat there looking across the table at her, a fleeting image suddenly impressed itself upon his mind: a picture of his mother as an angel—pale, thin, and ethereal, but surrounded by an aura of golden light. He almost thought he could see the oak sideboard through her translucent body. Was it the candle-light? An optical illusion? He peered more closely, a forkful of broccoli halfway to his mouth. But in the next moment the impression was gone.

For a few minutes they ate together in silence. Then Morgan said, "When Dad was here, did *he* say grace?"

Mavis stared up at him, plainly surprised by the question. "No," she answered slowly. "I'm afraid not. It's odd in a way, he and Peter being such good friends. But he never put much stock in prayer and faith. At least not until the end. And by then it was too late."

Morgan swallowed hard. "But it's not too late for *you.*"

She gave him a questioning look.

"I mean, Rev. Alcuin prayed, and now you're better!"

She smiled sadly. "Perhaps it's not as simple as you think."

"But it worked, didn't it? That's all that matters."

"That's probably the part the matters least of all," she said, taking a piece of bread and breaking it. "At any rate, it's early to say yet. And prayer isn't something that 'works' or 'doesn't work.'"

That makes no sense at all, he thought. But to his mother he said, "There are other things that might work too. All kinds of things."

※

When they had finished eating, Morgan scraped his chair back and stood to clear the table. His mother rose to help him.

"Don't you dare!" he said, taking her by the arm. "You've done enough for tonight. Go on out into the living room. Rest on the couch and watch TV or something. I'll take care of the dishes."

She made a feeble show of protest, but he could see the look of gratitude in her tired and watery eyes. He picked up the plates and goblets and carried them to the kitchen as she turned and left the room. But no sooner had he rinsed the dishes and begun to fill the sink than he heard a terrible crash at the other end of the house. He shut off the tap and ran out into the hall.

"Mom!" he cried when he saw her. "What happened?"

She lay with her back to the wall and her legs splayed out across the floor. Her head was bent forward and pressed up against a little mahogany table that stood just outside the living room door. Apparently she'd just missed it in her fall.

"Have you broken anything? Are you bleeding?"

"Just … a little dizzy," she said, opening her eyes and gripping his hand. "It came on me all of a sudden." She raised herself on one elbow and passed a hand over her eyes. "Can you help me to the sofa?"

Grunting with effort, he drew her arm over his shoulders and hauled her up. "Don't worry," he said. "I'll go next door. They'll know what to do."

Once she was settled comfortably, Morgan dashed out into the yard. So loud was the pounding of the blood in his ears, so frantic the whirl of the confused thoughts in his brain, that he barely noticed the clear whiteness of the moonlight streaming in through the widening gaps in the mist and glimmering on the damp surface of the taut linen sheet. He jumped down into the wet grass and crossed to the Ariellos' back door. It was unlocked. He opened it and let himself inside.

All was dark and quiet at that end of the house. For a moment it seemed to him that no one was home. *Working overtime again,* he thought. That wouldn't be unusual on a Friday night. But as his eyes adjusted, he became aware of a faint light glimmering behind a half-closed door at the end of the hall—the door to the Ariellos' living room. Softly he approached. Someone was speaking within:

"So the Danaan folk fled before their enemies. Leaving a decoy beneath the throne of Gathelus, they wrapped *Lia Fail* in a plain woolen cloak and sailed for the legendary isles of Finias, Murias, Gorias, and Falias. But it was not long before they were forced to leave those fabled cities of the sea, sailing over the ocean toward the golden horizon. For their foes had discovered their flight and pursued them."

It was Moira's voice. Morgan remembered now: She and Eny often read together in the evenings. He took a step forward and peered into the room. There on a dingy old sofa sat mother and daughter, their backs to the door, their heads bent close together over a book. The erratic light came from a pair of red candles that were burning on a small end table at Moira's elbow.

"Then westward over the face of the waters they drove their high-prowed ships, ships that were said to have the power to fly through the air. For they had been told that Lia Fail might not rest until it came at last to the extremity of the world, to the land of the sun's going, the place of its final destiny—the Green Island in the West, Hidden Isle of Inisfail:

> *Sweet and pure the air of Inisfail,*
> *Pleasant that land beyond all earthly dreams.*
> *There all the year the fruit swells on the tree,*
> *There month to month the bloom is on the*
> *   flower."*

Moira paused. Thinking that this might be a good place to jump in, Morgan stepped over the threshold and opened his mouth to speak. But just then Eny said:

"Did they ever reach the island?"

"Inisfail?" asked Moira. "Oh my, no! Inisfail lies farther away than tongue can tell. Always just over the horizon. It's the land of the sun's going, the place beyond all places. No, they didn't reach Inisfail. But they did find something nearly as good—Ireland! And that's how it happened that Lia Fail, the Stone of Destiny, the Satisfaction of All Desire, was brought safe to Tara, the seat of ancient kings."

Stone of Destiny? Satisfaction of All Desire? Why hadn't Eny ever told him about this story? Morgan felt his heart skip a beat. He gripped the edge of the door and stood transfixed.

"What exactly *is* Lia Fail?" said Eny.

"Haven't I been telling you? The Stone of Destiny—the Stone of Bethel. It's the Coronation Stone—the fabled 'Stone That Roared.' It was said that whoever possessed it was destined to rule. That's why so many monarchs and emperors and peoples and nations have been so desperate to get their hands on it. Generations of the kings and queens of Tara were crowned upon that Stone. It possessed a peculiar virtue, so that whenever a true king or queen stepped upon it—a genuine son or daughter of the Danaan race—it would acknowledge the royal presence with signs and wonders. Visions and revelations, bolts of light from above, a roaring like the roaring of the sea! Lia Fail conferred the power to command, the power to transform, the power to heal and raise the dead!"

The power to heal. Morgan felt his knees begin to buckle. His mother was waiting. A voice at the back of his mind told him that her situation could be urgent. But he could not move; he had to hear more about Lia Fail. Could this wondrous healing Stone have anything to do with the Philosophers' Stone itself? Was this the thing that Madame Medea wanted him to find?

At that moment the front door opened, and George Ariello walked in, two big bunches of keys jingling at his hip. Jarred out of the trancelike state into which he'd been lulled by Moira's story, Morgan turned and gave him a desperate look.

"George!" he blurted. "It's my mom! She's worse!"

Chapter Six

THERE ARE OTHER STORIES

Morgan sat on a hard plastic chair, chin in hands, staring down at the scuffed and dingy white tile floor. Hours of endless waiting had left him numb; numb to the hum and glare of the fluorescent lights, numb to the smell of alcohol and harsh detergents, numb to the ringing of phones and the periodic coming and going of patients and hospital staff. Though his eyelids sagged and his back bent low, sleep was far from him. The gyroscopic whirrings in his brain kept the tide of drowsiness at bay.

On the dim and hazy edges of his consciousness—that is, in the chair just to the left of his own—a dark-haired, dusky-eyed young woman cradled a flushed and feverish baby in the crook of her bare brown arm. Morgan turned and stared at her vaguely as she whispered to the child in Spanish and stroked its sweaty head with the tips of her slender fingers. Next to her a dirty, greasy, unshaven middle-aged man held a soiled and bloody rag to his ear, moaning and groaning and smelling of fish and beer. Across the room, on a worn leather couch behind a low table strewn with magazines, Eny was sleeping with her head pillowed in George's lap. George himself sat nodding, jerking, and snoring by fitful turns.

Morgan shook himself, rubbed his eyes, and glanced out the window. Beyond the smudged glass a few stars hung like jewels in the spaces between the silvered branches of the trees. Faint and clear they glittered in the cold moonlight. The mist had dispersed entirely. *A clear night leading up to the full moon.*

"I'm sure we'll hear something soon," said Peter Alcuin, who was sitting on Morgan's right.

Morgan yawned and stretched. "It feels like we've been here all night," he said. He didn't know how the Reverend had found out about his mother's sudden distress, but he was glad that he had. There was something reassuring in the man's quiet but persistent presence.

"We have. It's a quarter past five. Why don't you lie down for a while? You look like death warmed over. I'll wake you when there's something to report."

"I can't." He studied the Reverend uncertainly. "Do you think the tower might really have to come down?"

"The tower?" Rev. Alcuin took off his round spectacles and wiped them on the sleeve of his coat. "You're still thinking about the tower? At a time like this?"

"*Especially* at a time like this. I know it doesn't make sense. But there's a connection. Between my mom and the tower, I mean. For reasons I can't explain right now."

The Reverend frowned. "Then I won't ask you to. But to answer your question, yes—there is a very good chance that the tower will have to be demolished."

"Just because of Mr. Knowles? I can't believe he has that much power!"

"Wealth and power have a way of keeping pretty close company. But it's not entirely a question of Knowles's power. It's a bit more complicated than that."

"How do you mean?"

The Reverend passed a hand across his forehead. "I hardly know myself. I just have a sense that we're up against something bigger than the Knowleses. Mr. Knowles isn't alone. There are other people who want the same things he wants. Politics and economics come into it. Besides, he's right about the earthquake regulations. That tower is nearly a hundred years old, Morgan. There were no such regulations when St. Halistan's was built. The next strong shake we get could bring it down. And that would be a disaster."

Morgan tried to imagine a force strong enough to topple the tower. It was hard to picture a soaring, immovable landmark as a pile of shattered rubble on the ground.

"Still," Rev. Alcuin continued, rubbing the morning stubble on his chin, "I can't help feeling that there's something else. The man has some hidden agenda. Some compelling personal interest."

Outside the window the stars were beginning to fade. Morgan squinted and peered out into the predawn darkness.

"Young man—"

He looked up. A young nurse in olive-green scrubs was standing at his elbow. To his great relief, the woman was smiling. "Your mother is resting quietly," she said.

At this, Eny, who had been sound asleep when last he noticed her, sat up straight, brushed a few coppery strands away from her face, and gave Morgan a shy but hopeful smile. George yawned and stretched.

"I know you've been waiting all night to see her," the nurse continued apologetically. "But we'd like to let her sleep for a while. I suggest you all go home and get some rest. You can come back later this afternoon."

"Sounds like an excellent plan," said Rev. Alcuin, laying a hand on Morgan's shoulder and getting to his feet.

Morgan nodded. "Thanks," he said to the nurse. "I think that's just exactly what we'll do."

Shivering in the early-morning chill and damp, Morgan and Eny slid across the cold vinyl seat of George's Ford pickup, their thickly steaming breath fogging the inside of the windshield. The doors rattled shut, George twisted the key in the ignition, and the engine rumbled abruptly into life. Slowly, the truck pulled out of the hospital parking lot and began to move west along Vista Del Mar.

At this hour the streetlights still burned ruddily in the dewy darkness, scattering a bronze glow over the glossy leaves of the curbside elms and ficus trees. Above the housetops the black silhouette of St. Halistan's tower, stark against the dark gray of the early morning sky, stood like a giant sentinel overlooking town and the distant sea. Morgan rubbed his nose and cleared his throat.

"Thanks, George," he said huskily. "I really appreciate all your help. You, too, Eny." He could feel her gazing at him, her blue eye gleaming in the darkness within the cab. But he kept his own eyes fixed on the tower at the top of the hill.

"*La familia primera,*" said George in a matter-of-fact tone. "The Ariellos and the Izaaks—that's family. That's how we feel about you and your mom, Morgan. The Lord knows your dad was like a brother to me. Him and the Reverend."

Morgan slumped back in his seat and closed his eyes. "I'm sorry it had to happen this way. I'm sorry you had to sit up with me all night at the hospital." He opened one eye and gave Eny a furtive sidewise glance. "And I'm sorry about interrupting Moira's story."

"The story?" Eny yawned. "That's the last thing you need to worry about. Mom will get back to it sooner or later. You can bet on that. She loves to tell stories. Especially about the Tuatha De Danann and Lia Fail."

Lia Fail. *The Stone.* The word shot through Morgan's brain like a jolt of electricity. Instantly the memory of the previous night's enchantments flooded in upon him like a spring tide: the spell of the tale, the music of Moira's voice, the gripping images painted by her words. He turned and faced Eny.

"What else do you know about Lia Fail?" he said.

"Not much. About as much as you do, I guess. I'm not sure what you heard."

"But you must know something! Eny, don't you remember?" He leaned closer and lowered his voice. "'You have come because you are seeking the Stone. *The Stone of Destiny.*'"

Eny stared, clearly taken aback. Apparently the connection between her mother's story and the words of Madame Medea hadn't dawned upon her until that moment. But George laughed. "Moira and her stories!" he said. "She hooked you good with that one, I guess! It's not the first time!"

"What about you, George?" Morgan persisted. "Do you know anything about Lia Fail?"

"Lia Fail?" George grunted. "Do I look Irish to you? I know nothing about my wife's stories. Pagan myths and legends. What would the Reverend say?"

"You don't believe them, then?"

"Moira's stories? Those useless fables? Of course not!" He stepped on the brake, coasted to a stop at a traffic light, and turned to look Morgan straight in the eye.

"But there are other stories," he said, a slow, sly grin spreading across his face.

Chapter Seven

La Cueva de los Manos

As soon as George had gone inside, Morgan, though aching with exhaustion, jumped out of the truck and dashed around the side of the duplex into the backyard. Yes, his gathering sheets were still there: taut, wet, and shining. Tired as Morgan was, sleep would have to wait. On this rarest of mornings in Santa Piedra, a morning without overcast or ocean fog, he'd have to work fast if he wanted to collect the May-dew before it had a chance to evaporate.

Bounding into the house, he stumbled across the kitchen floor and found a red plastic dishpan and a brass-lidded Ball jar in the space behind the gingham curtain under the sink. With these he returned to the yard and bent immediately to his task. Cautiously, he undid the bits of yarn, removed the corners of the sheets from the wooden pegs, and wrung the night moisture from the linen fabric into the pan. From the pan he carefully transferred the dew-water to the Ball jar. Capping the jar, he sealed it tightly, carried it into his bedroom, and stashed it in a dark corner of his closet. When all was complete, he kicked off his shoes, tore back the covers, and jumped into bed.

Morgan was still asleep when Eny, having napped soundly for two or three hours, rose about nine o'clock, dressed quickly, took her fiddle from the corner, and slipped out the front door.

It was a fine, fresh morning. A steady breeze, heavy with the scent of salt from the Inlet and resinous pine from the Point, caressed her cheek and sent her hair streaming back over her shoulders. The cars on Alta Drive were few and far between at this hour on a Saturday, and she exulted in the delicious feeling of being alone in the middle of the sleepy town. Down the hill she went, covering the three blocks between St. Halistan's and Front Street rapidly, walking, trotting, sometimes even breaking into a run. From there she took Front Street southward along the beach, stopping only once to laugh at her ruffled reflection in one of the shop front windows.

At the end of Front Street, where the old wooden footbridge arched over the chattering waters of Pillar Creek, she stood still for a moment, her eyes closed, her head thrown back, a sense of secrecy, freedom, and quiet joy rising from the pit of her stomach to the top of her head. She sniffed the pungent air and smiled. Then, pounding across the thrumming bridge with the fiddle swinging at her side, she stepped out into the wondrous world of La Punta Lira, the Harp-shaped Point.

Straight ahead the rough terrain swept steeply upward, quickly becoming a pine-clad slope. So thick was the growth of tall, thin-stemmed evergreens that a traveler would have been hard-pressed to find a way between their rough and slender trunks. Here again Eny paused to listen, for the air was filled with a cheerful cacophony of morning birdsong. Sparrows darted from treetop to treetop. Finches, nuthatches, chickadees, and greedy jays chorused in the branches. Here and there an invisible mourning dove cooed plaintively in some hidden refuge among the forest shadows, and the clear liquid note of the red-winged blackbird dropped from the hidden heights of the canopy into the needle-strewn floor of the forest. Further off, the harsh and lonely cries of the gulls came echoing off the water. The deer that inhabited the Point were nowhere to be seen.

To the right a gravel trail left the bridge and skirted the hillside, following the winding contours of the slope north along the creek. Eny set off in this direction, whistling to herself in the soft sunlight as she hefted her violin case and went crunching up the path. The trail began amid low-growing sage, wood mint, and prickly wild blackberry, but rapidly ascended a ridge where dark green coastal scrub, beach grass, and live oak grew in rich profusion. Every so often she was obliged to brush aside a tangled shroud of gray lace lichen that hung over the path from the branches of a solitary pine. At the top of the rise grew a windblown cypress, a majestic old tree that seemed to bow before her and stretch out its arms in greeting as she approached. Here she halted again to catch her breath.

It never ceased to amaze her—the beauty that burst upon the eye at this particular turn of the path. Here, at a point some fifty feet above the creek bed, the track leaped out onto a narrow ledge that traversed and descended the face of a yellow sandstone cliff in a long and gentle incline. Below and to the right, where Pillar Creek widened out to join the Inlet, sparkled the emerald-green waters of Laguna Verde. Even at this hour there were spotted sea lions and jet-black seals sunbathing on the gray-green rocks of the lagoon. Beyond the mouth of this enchanted cove, seen partly through a natural archway in the protruding cliff wall, heaved the deeper blue of La Coruna Inlet itself, its broad face rippling with landward sweeping swells. To the north, at the far end of the scimitar-like curve of the beach, where the foamy breakers crashed in endless succession, she could just make out Fisherman's Wharf and the top of the Fun Zone Ferris wheel.

She followed this path down and around the north end of the Point until she stood at the base of the sea-cliff. Here the waves broke thunderously around the mussel-encrusted rocks and the salt spray hung in a perennial mist. Straight over her head towered the black bulk of the Rock itself, *La Piedra,* the famous stone formation from which the town supposedly took its name. It was said that both Drake and Vizcaino had come ashore at this spot. Though she couldn't see it from here, she knew that above and beyond the Rock, among the pines covering the western corner of the Point, stood the dilapidated ruin of an old abandoned hotel.

But Eny hadn't come to see the Rock or to explore the hotel. Not this time. Much as she loved the jade waters of the lagoon, the sporting of the sea otters, and the ceaseless pounding of the waves, it was something else that had drawn her to this spot on this sunny May morning. She had come to be alone: to fiddle, to think, to pray, to soak herself in the silence and solitude of the sea and the cliffs and the caves of La Punta Lira.

Though by no means a secret, these caves were seldom frequented by visitors or tourists. They were too inconvenient and too far out of the way. To reach the place, one had to wade out into the boiling surf, pass beneath a sandstone archway, and then clamber up a stair-like series of rock pools to a small cove at the base of the Rock—a thing that could only be accomplished at low tide.

Holding her violin above her head with both hands, Eny plunged into the water and splashed her way under the arch. Once through, she turned and sloshed up the steep pebbly shore until she stood on a short stretch of sparkling white sand. Here the face of the cliff was honeycombed with a series of caverns and holes. Some of these cavities stood at ground level, others at various heights above the beach. Tucking the fiddle under her arm, she ducked into the largest of them, a sizable grotto that opened directly onto the sand.

Through this doorway the air was cool and damp and smelled of sand and sea. Once inside, she laid her violin case on the dry sandy floor then straightened up. Behind her and to the left the spacious inner reaches of the cavern wound away into the cliff side, disappearing at last in an all-engulfing darkness. But to her right the morning light poured in through the entrance and struck the wall, clearly illuminating the most remarkable feature of the cavern: the painting of the hands.

There were hundreds of them: rust-red handprints, splayed all across and up and down the wall; a vertical cloud of upward-reaching palms, each of them with long, flamelike fingers ceaselessly stretching toward the shadowy dripping ceiling. The brochures at the tourist information center said they had been there for more than four thousand years, traced upon the rock by the most ancient inhabitants of the Point. For this was the famous Cave of the Hands, *La Cueva de los Manos,* a Santa Piedra historical landmark and one of Eny's favorite haunts.

For a moment she stood gazing up at them. Four thousand years, she thought, is a long time to be reaching upward into the darkness. She wasn't sure what those ancient people were thinking when they dipped their fingers into a mixture of ochre and lime and pressed them to the rock. But she had a pretty good idea. She suspected they were feeling weakness, inadequacy; they were looking for help from above. They were straining to lay hold of something, a thing so close they could almost taste it but always just an inch or two beyond their grasp. It reminded her of one of Rev. Alcuin's sermons—a message about people who "grope" for God without realizing what they're doing.

Eny understood that helpless feeling. It was especially strong with her this morning, after her long night with Morgan in the hospital emergency room. Leaning against the wall of the cavern, she laid her palm and fingers flat against the palm and fingers of one of the red hands. She closed her eyes and whispered into the silence. "Remember Mavis Izaak, God," she said. "And please—help Morgan find what he's looking for."

Turning away from the wall, she sat down on the cool sand and undid the brass clasps of the violin case. Then she raised the lid, lifted the instrument from the case, and attached the chin rest. Next she took out the bow, tightened the horsehairs, and rubbed them up with a small block of rosin. Placing the fiddle under her chin, she paused to savor the heady scent of wood and glue that wafted to her nostrils from the delicately carved f-holes. Then she touched the bow to the strings; two high, sweet notes burst forth and flew upward into the cavern. Like a pair of bright birds they chased one another from wall to ceiling and ceiling to wall, from alcove to grotto and back into the silences at the very heart of the cliff. Eny twisted the wooden pegs with one hand, bowing slowly all the while, until all four strings were tuned to her satisfaction. Then she sat back and began to play.

She played "The Dawning of the Day" and "The Lark in the Morning." She played "Out on the Ocean" and "The Turn of the Tide." She struck up reel after reel after reel: "The Star of Munster," "The Gravel Walk," "The Salamanca," "The Banshee," "The Sailor's Bonnet." She followed these with two sad airs, "The Dark Woman of the Glen" and "Auld Swarra." After that she moved on to "The May Morning Dew." She fiddled long into the afternoon until at last her eyes grew dim and she felt she could play no more. Then she dropped the bow on the sand and laid the fiddle in her lap.

That's when she heard it: a rasping, grating sound that echoed brashly off the cavern walls, loud enough to drown out the crashing of the sea waves and so harsh that it made her jump with surprise. She set the fiddle aside and got to her feet.

That's when she saw it: a huge black crow with large red eyes and a gleaming yellow beak, bobbing its head up and down and dancing from side to side in the darkness at the further end of the cave. Furiously it cawed and croaked, ruffling its feathers and flapping its glossy wings. Eny smiled with relief. She bent down and tucked a strand of hair behind her ear.

"How did you get in here?" she said soothingly, slowly approaching the crow. "Can't you find your way out? Come on," she coaxed, holding out her hand. "I won't hurt you."

But the bird, clacking its beak viciously, hopped round and charged her from behind, as if trying to drive her further into the cavern. Eny twisted and turned and flung out a hand. The crow jumped up and bit her on the finger. She cried out and fell forward on one knee.

"What did you do that for?" she shouted. She had some acquaintance with crows and knew they could be feisty, but never before had she run across a crow as vicious as this. Scowling, she jammed her finger into her mouth. It tasted of blood.

Then she heard another sound: the sound of voices. Not voices from the beach outside, but voices from somewhere within the chamber. She bent her head to listen. There was no mistake about it. *They were coming from the shadows at the back of the cave.* And they were getting closer.

Eny made a bold leap for her fiddle. The crow, apparently taken off guard, gave one last raucous caw, hopped to the entrance of the cave, and flew out. Seizing fiddle and bow, she shut them in the case and snapped the clasps. Then, violin in hand, she ducked through the doorway and dashed out into the open air.

"A good day to you, my dear. Isn't it a lovely morning?"

She stopped. Not ten feet in front of her, at the edge of one of the pebbly tide pools, stood a crooked old woman in a tattered blue shawl and a dripping gingham dress. She had a big wicker basket on her back and a pile of wet rags at her feet, and she appeared, of all things, to be washing her clothes in the surf.

"You're just in time, love," she croaked, stretching out a withered hand. "Granny's been waiting for you. Come along, now. I've something to show you. That's a good girl."

Eny felt the hair rising at the back of her neck. There was no time to think, no time to ask herself why she was afraid or what it was that she feared. Lifting her fiddle above her head, she picked up her feet and ran, crunching and clattering down through the rocky pools and into the churning foam, making straight for the yellow arch in the extension of the cliff.

When she was near the top of the narrow climbing path, she turned and looked back. Though there had been no sign of it just a few minutes earlier, a thick white fog was creeping in off the ocean and rapidly covering the face of the Inlet. So striking was the sight that she drew in a sharp and sudden breath. When the fog came—which it did more often than not—it usually rolled in toward the end of the day, lingered through the night, and vanished in the morning. There were exceptions, of course, but this sudden and rapid early-afternoon onslaught from the sea was something more than an exception. It was uncanny and unnatural; somehow Eny knew it to be so.

As she watched, a dark silhouette rose out of the swirling whiteness beneath the stone arch. From where she stood it looked like the shape of a man: a gigantic man, more than eight or nine feet tall. Rubbing her eyes, she bent forward and peered again into the gathering gloom, but in the next instant the mist poured over the arch and into the lagoon, and the figure was lost to view.

Then came a rush of wings and a breath of air against her cheek. Eny lunged to one side and looked up in time see a huge black crow swooping down over her head, cawing loudly as it passed.

She gripped her fiddle under her arm and ran the rest of the way up the trail.

Chapter Eight

Mist and Shadows

The cleansing fire is merciless, but only falseness dies.

Morgan was sitting at his cluttered workbench, his eyes glued to the first page of the Third Treatise of the Second Book of *The Philosophy of Theophrastus,* his hands busy with an old stone pestle and mortar. Since rising at about ten and gulping down a hasty breakfast of corn flakes and toast, he had been hard at work in the tower, grinding the scorched remains of a mixture of seaweed and beach grass into a fine gray powder.

Calcination. Dissolution. Separation.
Conjunction. Fermentation. Distillation.
Coagulation.

Slowly he rehearsed the seven steps in his mind. All the books agreed that the first stage of the process—the heat and flame of the fire—had a purifying effect on the subject of the experiment. Too bad it didn't do the same thing for the air inside the lab. This particular mass of charred vegetable matter had been seared and cooked five times over until it left the whole place smelling of smoke and sulphur and burnt kelp. Morgan coughed and wrinkled up his nose—at times like this he felt grateful for the open-air ventilation of the old church tower.

> *Every body or tangible substance is nothing else but coagulated mist or smoke.... All colors and all elements are present in everything.... Nature lies invisibly in bodies and substances.... The first matter of minerals consists of water, and it comprises only sulphur, salt, and mercury....*

According to Paracelsus, there was but a single substance in all the universe: the *materia prima*. The four elements of earth, air, fire, and water were but varying manifestations of this One Ubiquitous Thing. Hidden at the heart of the *materia prima* lay the Philosophers' Stone: a universal healing agent, a panacea capable of curing any disease, the Elixir of Life itself. It was this that Morgan was hoping to extract from his lump of purified and calcinated ash. He raised his elbow for leverage and leaned into the work, churning, crushing, and pounding, biting his tongue in the effort.

> *Dew, the distilled essence of heaven above and earth below, is a condensation of the Universal Spirit or Secret Fire.*

Once the stuff was completely pulverized, he'd dissolve it in the May-dew he'd collected with his gathering sheet. Then he'd purify it again by slowly heating and distilling the mixture in an alembic. After that it was a matter of recombining, reheating, and repeating the pattern as often as necessary until the proper succession of colors began to emerge. It was a long, laborious path. But he was confident it would eventually yield success.

> *The processes to which the matter is subjected in the course of the Great Work are often likened to a ladder or steps leading to a Temple. Like Jacob's Ladder, this connects the above with the below. In this way the mighty gifts are learnt, just as …*

There was a knock below. Morgan looked up from his book. Someone was pounding on the door and calling his name. Setting mortar and pestle aside, he got up and scrambled down the ladder.

"Thank goodness!" said Eny breathlessly as soon as he managed to get the door open. "When I couldn't find you at home I came straight here." She was standing in a puddle on the landing, fiddle in hand, dark water dripping from her jeans. Her hair was disheveled and her one blue eye shone bright in the dimness of the stairway.

"What for?" Try as he might, Morgan couldn't prevent a slight hint of irritation from creeping into his voice.

"I'm afraid you won't believe me when I tell you!" She gripped him by the arm and pushed her way inside. "I just came from the Point. From the Cave of the Hands!"

"So what? You're always hanging around out there."

"Yes, but somebody else was there this time. And they were *after* me!"

"*After* you?" He pulled away and eyed her doubtfully.

"I know it sounds crazy. But it's true! There were voices in the cave. And a big crow. And an old lady by the tide pools. And a strange fog and a giant man out in the surf. He was just like that huge person we saw at Madame Medea's—only bigger!"

Morgan knew Eny too well to doubt her earnestness. She had a fertile imagination, it was true, but he had never known her to be a liar. She hadn't even inherited her parents' talent for telling tales. There was something in her manner, something about the light in her eye, that made him tremble. He wanted to scoff. He wanted to laugh the whole thing off. But somehow he didn't dare.

"It was probably just … tourists," he said. "Why don't we go home and tell your mom and dad?"

"No! It would only frighten them. It wasn't *tourists,* Morgan! I think it had something to do with that *woman!*"

Morgan looked away. A white mist was oozing in through the slatted windows and it seemed unusually dark outside. He checked his watch: It was nearly half past four. So engrossed had he been in his work that he had lost all track of time. Without waiting to hear more, he took her by the hand and drew her out to the landing.

"I don't know what you mean," he said. "You can do what you like. I have to go home anyway. I've got to get to the hospital." With that he locked the door and headed downstairs with Eny close behind.

Simon Brach was waiting for them when they got to the bottom of the staircase. They found him standing just inside the double oak doors, his violin under his arm and a wide smile on his craggy face. He lifted the instrument in greeting when he saw them and gave Eny an exaggerated wink.

"The little lady with the fiddle!" he said, bowing slightly in her direction. "The very person! I was thinking that a session on the stairs might be just the thing before getting down to work. Would you like to sit down and scrape out a few tunes with me?"

Eny turned and looked at Morgan. The shadows of fear and alarm had completely vanished from her expression, and once again he saw an inexplicable light rising in her face, the same light he had seen there the previous afternoon at their first meeting with Simon Brach. Her brow was smooth, her cheeks flushed with pleasure. The piercing brightness of her eye had mellowed to a warm glow.

"You go ahead," she said. "I think I'll stay and play with Mr. Brach for a while."

Morgan put his shoulder to the door and shoved it open. "Whatever," he said. *If that's what really matters to you,* he thought to himself.

He could hear the two of them tuning up on the stairway as the great door swung shut behind him, its boom muffled by the enveloping mist that had now covered the town and blocked out the afternoon sky. No sooner had he stepped out on the sidewalk than an even more irritating sound reached his ears: a cacophony of shouts and a hail of rude laughter rising out of the swirling vapors, bouncing off the walls of St. Halistan's, and falling dead into the thick blanket of whiteness that surrounded the church buildings like a sullen tide.

"Look who it is!"

"The Dreamer in the Outfield!"

"The Sorcerer's Apprentice!"

"Robot Mouth!"

Morgan groaned. He could feel the blood rising up the back of his neck. His ears grew hot. His cheeks burned and the muscles in his arms and legs tightened like steel bands. He licked his lips and ran the tip of his tongue over the metallic sharpness of his braces.

"My dad was no sorcerer!" he shouted at the passing cyclists—Baxter Knowles and a couple of his cronies. "He was a scientist! And a philosopher!" He hesitated a moment, then picked up a rock from the gutter and hurled it after them.

It was a rash thing to do, and he regretted it immediately. The bicycles slowed and circled. Morgan's throat contracted, and his heart began to pound as the three riders swung around and headed back toward him through the haze. Baxter skidded to a stop at the edge of the curb.

"Scientist! I suppose that's what *you* are? What you've been up to in your magician's tower?"

"What do you know about it?"

"Everything I need to know. What you need to know is that this rock pile is coming down. Soon."

Morgan fumed. "You can't say that!"

Baxter grabbed him by the collar. "Shut up, Izaak—you ugly-looking girl." His gray eyes were small and steely, his voice low and threatening. "I'd hate to have to ruin your *other* shirt. My dad knows what's best for this town, and he's got plans for this hilltop. Big plans. The future of Santa Piedra is in the tourist trade. Nobody ever comes to this old church anyway."

"Some do," said a voice out of the fog.

Baxter released his grip and glanced up. Morgan turned and followed his persecutor's gaze. There on the tower doorstep, a tall shadow in the mist, stood Simon Brach.

"Who's this?" said Baxter with a sneer. "The Hunchback of St. Halistan's?"

Simon said nothing. Descending the steps, he reached the curb in three long strides. There was a stern look in his eyes, a kind of pure and searing light that Morgan hadn't noticed there before. The old man seemed to grow in stature as he loomed above them in the fog.

Baxter blinked. A sudden look of panic besmirched his stupid good looks. He pulled back on his handlebars, spun the bike on its back wheel, and sped away, his two followers pedaling after him with all their might. Bewildered, Morgan stood watching them as they disappeared into the gloom.

"You'd better get a move on," said Simon when they had gone. "It won't do to keep your mother waiting."

※

Within the hour Morgan was pacing the floor of the hospital waiting room, a cold and curious leaden lump in the pit of his stomach. A voice at the back of his mind kept telling him that it was all *his* fault. Somehow or other, *he* was to blame for his mother's illness. He had failed her as a son. He had taken her for granted. He had lived as if her soft-spoken gentleness and constant watch-care were guarantees of nature, inexhaustible as earth, air, fire, and water.

A doctor and a nurse stood conversing quietly just outside the door of his mother's room. He knew he wasn't supposed to overhear, but when they weren't looking he managed to get close enough to catch a few disjointed words and phrases: metastasized … rapidly growing … in the lung.

He glanced out the fourth-floor window. Below lay the town of Santa Piedra, a collection of shapeless shadows beneath a veil of obscuring mist. He leaned against the wall and kicked at the black rubber baseboard. How could he possibly repay his mother for everything she'd done? The meals she'd cooked, the clothes she'd washed, the hundreds of hours she'd spent working at La Coruna Gifts and Cards just to make ends meet? Even if she didn't die, how would he ever make it up to her? Maybe he couldn't. Maybe there was nothing he could do to atone for his own carelessness and negligence.

But if he worked hard enough, he might be able to save her life. If he was responsible for this mess, then he would have to fix it.

One primal element … Elixir of Life … in it all the power of the stars …

"You can come in now, young man."

Morgan looked up and straightened himself. He combed his fingers through his ruffled yellow hair, tucked his shirt into his jeans, and, with a fluttering feeling in his chest, approached the door to Room 247. The nurse moved aside and let him enter.

Two steps into the room he had to stop and stare. Never in his life had he seen his mother looking quite like this: frail and weak, almost on the point of fading away, yet somehow inexpressibly lovely. She was sitting up in bed, her ivory hands folded in her lap, her fine angel hair pulled back at the nape of her neck. Though her cheeks were wan and hollow, her eyes were wide and radiant. Her face was like the face of the moon: pale but luminous with a light not its own. She beamed at him as he came forward and sat on the edge of a chair beside the bed.

"I'm sorry, Mom," he said, bending forward and laying his head in her lap.

She took his face between her two hands and lifted it. "Sorry for what?"

"I was scared. Twisted up with fear all night long. Wondering what was going to happen to you. But I won't be scared anymore. I promise. I'm going to *do* something to help."

She smiled. "You sound like your father. Listen to me, Morgan. You have nothing to worry about. You've *always* been a great help to me. Besides, it's not wrong to be afraid. I'm afraid too. That's only natural. But the doctor knows what he's doing. And the Lord has us in His hands."

Morgan disengaged himself and sat up straight. "That's what you said last night. And now you—well, what I mean is … what good have all the prayers done?"

"I told you, Morgan. Prayer isn't about getting results. It's about knowing Someone. It's about trust."

"But you don't want to die, do you?"

She took him by the hand. "I think I'd go on living forever if only it meant being your mother. Packing your lunch, washing your shirts, getting your dinner—what could be better? Life is so short."

"Don't say that!" Morgan said. There was a distant sound in her voice that frightened him. "You're going to live for a long time. I know it."

She looked at him out of watery, shining eyes. "None of us lives forever. I don't know what's going to happen tomorrow, Morgan, but I'm hopeful. For both of us. Have you ever watched the sunset on the ocean? I mean really *watched* it, until it faded away into nothing but a golden thread on the farthest horizon? There's a part of me that has always wanted to follow that rippling thread right down over the edge of the world."

"You listen to me, Mom! You're not going anywhere. I've got Dad's books and instruments!"

"I don't want you—" she began, but just then she began to cough; for several minutes the fit racked and shook her delicate body, her chest heaving, her eyes streaming. It seemed to him that she would cough herself to pieces. He sat with her on the edge of the bed, trembling and holding her hand until the hacking and wheezing subsided.

When she had been quiet for a long time Morgan asked:

"Mom—what really happened to my dad? I mean, exactly how did he die?"

She took a clean handkerchief from the table at the bedside and blew her nose. Then she turned and regarded him intently. Her eyes, red and teary, searched his. It was as if she were probing his mind, testing the waters, gauging the level of his mental readiness to receive what she had to say. Finally she spoke.

"He didn't."

"Didn't?" The words hit him like a lightning bolt out of a blue sky. For a moment he was speechless. "What do you mean?" he managed to stammer at last. "If he didn't die, where is he? Why don't I know him?"

"He was *taken.*"

"Taken?" Morgan stood up. His legs were stiff and numb as two pillars of stone, his mind was a white-hot blank. *If this is true,* he thought, *it changes everything.*

"Yes," his mother said. "I don't understand how or why or where. I don't even know how I know it. I just *do.* There was a letter. It made no sense to me. But of one thing I feel certain: Those books and tools he left behind had something to do with it." She looked up at him. "I don't want you to have anything to do with them."

He gazed at her, uncomprehending.

"Your father," she went on, "believed he could gain the power to control our destiny—mine and his. He had his reasons for trying. Troubles and debts had made him a very different person from the man I married. Depressed and desperate. It overwhelmed him in the end. I'm not sure how. All I know is that he was caught up, swept away. *Taken.*"

Morgan stood there, paralyzed. His brain seemed to have short-circuited. For a long time he couldn't speak. At last he said, "You don't know what you're asking! I can't give up now! If I do—"

Again his speech was cut short by one of her coughing spells. He dropped beside her on the bed, holding her close, squeezing his eyes tight and burying his face against her shoulder.

"I'm sorry," said the nurse, softly entering and drawing him from the bedside. "She needs to rest. Visiting hours are nearly over anyway."

As he pedaled his bike furiously back up the hill, Morgan could see the tower of St. Halistan's heaving its dark bulk up into the overarching gloom. A stiff breeze had lifted the fog from the face of the earth, transfiguring it into a low and eerily lit ceiling of patchy cloud. Somewhere over the western ocean the sun had gone down at the edge of the world. In the gathering dusk a yellow moon shone sporadically through the breaches in the racing clouds.

Morgan rattled up to the duplex and dropped his bike beside the front porch. He began fishing in his pocket as a gleam of moonlight flashed out across the rough gray stones of the tower's four stone pinnacles. Then, as the mists closed in again above St. Halistan's, he pulled out his key, opened the door, and stumbled into the house.

In his weariness, haste, and confusion he failed to notice the great shadow looming over the tower: a gigantic man-shape, tall as a mountain and black as midnight, lumbering down the hill toward the sea.

Chapter Nine

TREMORS

In the days that followed, Morgan's life fell into a grueling routine.

When he wasn't at school he was in the tower lab, sweating over his workbench, grinding, boiling, mixing, stirring, distilling. When he wasn't in the lab he was lying in his bed, drowsing fitfully or staring into the silent and empty darkness. When he wasn't doing any of these things, he was taking his meals with the Ariellos and Peter Alcuin. The Reverend quickly discovered that dinnertime was the only time he could hope to catch up with the boy.

When Moira asked Morgan what he was doing night after night in the church tower, his answer was always the same: "Homework." This always drew an accusatory look from Eny, but he ignored her disapproving scowls and frowns. "It's too lonely in the house," he'd say. "I'd rather study in the tower until my mom comes home."

But Mavis didn't come home. A week went by, and still she remained in the hospital, her condition gradually worsening. Morgan saw little of her during this time. He knew he ought to visit more often, but the sight of her thinning hair and hollow eyes pained him. He was keenly aware, too, that he was disobeying her wishes by proceeding with his alchemical experiments, and he couldn't bear to face her with this offense on his conscience. But neither could he afford to stop what he was doing. He was convinced that her life depended on it.

On Sunday morning, long before the first worshippers began to arrive at St. Halistan's for the nine o'clock service, Morgan jumped out of bed, threw on some clothes, and dashed across the street to the tower. Jacob's Ladder was gray and lifeless as he passed it on his way up the stairs. Gray, too, were the pale shafts piercing the dusky emptiness of the lab as he poked his head up through the trap door—the strange fog had not yet released its grip on the town of Santa Piedra. But though the world seemed dull and dim on this silent and solemn morning, Morgan's heart beat high with a rising hope. He trembled with anticipation as he surveyed his litter-strewn workbench. *Today*, he told himself, *is the day.*

Reaching under the table, he drew out the sealed jar containing his precious solution and held it up to the light. It, too, was of a flat gray hue—just what all the books had taught him to expect. The succession of colors had unfolded according to the specifications of the adepts: black to yellow, yellow to pink, pink to rainbow, rainbow to green. The last transformation had been from green to gray. Only the final step remained. Following the instructions set forth in Edward Kelly's translation of the *Hermetica,* he poured six ounces of the mixture into a glass alembic. Placing the alembic over the Bunsen burner, he lit the flame and slowly turned up the heat.

Eny, too, had risen early that morning. Next to fiddling on the tower stairs or down in the Cave of the Hands, she liked best to sit thinking at dawn in the sanctuary of St. Halistan's Church, watching the stately figures in the tall stained glass windows emerge from the darkness and quicken to life by slow, imperceptible stages. She loved to see them flame with cherry-reds, flash with cobalt blues, and glitter with sparks of gold in the rising sun. Even on a morning like this, when the light outside was dull, there was something reassuring in the solemnity of their muted colors and the firmness of their solid black outlines. They were like old friends: the fisherman with his dragnet, the sower with his grain bag, the woman seeking her lost coin, the father embracing his prodigal son.

On this particular Sunday she had been at it since the first birds began piping in the tops of the trees. She was thinking hard about the things she'd seen out on La Punta Lira: the crow, the old woman, the ominous figure in the mist. All week long she had pondered these mysteries and tried to grasp their meaning. Now, ensconced in a corner of one of the long polished pews, she was attempting to banish them from her thoughts by fixing her mind upon the familiar images in the windows. But it was no use. Despite her best efforts, the portents she had witnessed continued to hang over her head like a dark cloud.

She was thinking, too, about Simon Brach. Eny had been thoroughly taken with the man since their first meeting. It was partly the music, of course: Never before had she heard fiddling like Simon's. But it was more than that. There was something *different* about the new church custodian, something that warmed her on the inside and encouraged her to trust. Morgan might be skeptical, she thought, but Simon would understand. Simon would listen if she told him what she had seen. Maybe she *would* tell him—when the time was right.

Her thoughts were interrupted by a sudden shock. It rattled the windows and set the great arched rafters groaning above her head. She looked up to see the big chandeliers swaying slightly in the darkness. A door opened at one side of the sanctuary, and her father came in, keys jangling, to switch on the lights and open the sanctuary for the morning service.

He grinned when he saw her sitting there. "Nothing to worry about. It was only a tremor."

Morgan felt it too. Just as the pallid gray mixture was beginning to bubble and seethe inside the glass globe, a ripple of clinks and chinks went shuddering down the ranks of pots and jars ranged along his workbench. The creak of wooden beams drew his attention up into the shadows near the ceiling. Then the walls of the tower shook and the workbench lurched. The alembic tipped, fell, and shattered. Morgan held his breath and braced himself for another jolt. But it never came. Just a tremor, he thought. Gingerly he took a new alembic from a box on the floor and filled it with another six ounces of the solution.

Eny was still studying the pictures in the windows when the final notes of the opening hymn had faded into silence. She maintained her concentration as the people around her rustled and rumbled back into their seats. Not until Rev. Alcuin was mounting the pulpit did she direct her attention to the chancel, watching with grave expectancy as the minister climbed the steps, adjusted his glasses, and opened the great leather-bound Bible. A hush fell over the congregation as he began to read:

> My father was a wandering Aramaean, and
> he went down to Egypt and sojourned there,
> few in number.

"Wandering," the Reverend repeated, looking out at the people over the rims of his silver-framed spectacles. "*Went down. Sojourned. Few in number.* These are the elements of ancient Israel's earliest confession of faith. We should pay close attention to them. For we are *all* wandering sojourners. We are *all* small and few in number."

> He went down into Egypt and sojourned
> there, few in number; and there he became a
> nation, great, mighty, and populous.

"You've heard it said," Rev. Alcuin went on, "that what goes up must come down. This passage turns that old saw on its head. It suggests that what goes down will come up. It declares that the last must be first. It tells us that weakness is a kind of strength. It explains how a boy like David could bring down a giant with nothing but a sling and a stone."

He paused and took off his glasses. "I've seen this principle put to the proof this week, my friends. I've seen it in the face of a woman—a longtime member of this church—who at this very moment lies stricken in a hospital bed. As her strength ebbs, her spirit grows. Her frailty is the measure of her faith. The more she's shaken, the firmer her foundation becomes. You have only to look at her to know it."

As Rev. Alcuin spoke, Eny's eyes strayed again to the pictures in the windows. *I wish Morgan was here to hear this,* she thought.

Morgan was up in his lab, far above the heads of the people in the church, reaching out into the vast unknown, seeking to lay hold of the healing power that lay hidden within the elements and behind the stars. With unwavering eye he monitored the guttering flame as it sparked and flared beneath the Bunsen burner. With bated breath he watched the boiling liquid inside the alembic become a tiny tempest of swirling steam. With pounding pulse he saw its gray color grow lighter and whiter by the minute. He bit his lip and adjusted the heating element. A fire of very low temperature.

Eny was the last to leave the church at the end of the service. Simon Brach was waiting for her at the door under the tower stairs.

"Well now, missy," he said, "it looks like I've got the afternoon off. What do you say to a bit of music?"

For a moment she stood staring up into his face, her heart thumping like a drum. *Should I tell him?* she wondered. *How do you tell a person you barely know that you've seen a giant?* The blood rushed into her cheeks. Her hands went numb, and she felt as if she were choking. But then Simon smiled, and at the sight of his bent nose and sparkling eyes her heart was suddenly filled with an inexplicable lightness. Fear and apprehension vanished like morning mist.

"I'll get my violin," she said. "It won't take a minute!"

Before long the two of them were seated together high on the stone steps, just below the landing under the stained-glass window. As they opened their cases and rosined their bows, the sun broke briefly through the clouds and Jacob's Ladder flashed with fleeting color. Then, as the brightness faded, Simon took up his fiddle and glanced at Eny out of one eye.

"Do you know 'The Silver Spire'?" he said.

Without waiting for an answer, he touched bow to string and launched straight into the tune. She tried to follow, but so frantic was the pace he set that it was all she could do to keep up. Sparks of light seemed to fly from his bow as it lashed the air. The clear, sweet tones pouring from his instrument leaped and danced in the open spaces above their heads.

"Usually," he shouted above the melody's stream, "I take this one straight into 'Rakish Paddy.'"

And with that he jumped from one tune to the next without a hitch or pause. He closed his eyes, and his foot began to tap. The thin gray wisps atop his balding head swayed in time with the strands of horsehair streaming from the tip of his bow. There was a light on the stairway and a strangely pleasant fragrance in the air as the wheels of the music rolled on and on, expanding outward like ripples on a pond, gaining momentum at every turn. Never in her life had Eny heard such playing.

Morgan heard it too. Up in his laboratory he removed the alembic from the flame and paused to listen. From far below the fierce and frantic melody ascended the stairs, penetrated the walls, and burst upon his ear. It pounded at the door of his brain and sought admittance to the innermost chamber of his heart. It seemed to be singing two words over and over again: *Let go.*

Let go of what? thought Morgan, and even as the words passed through his mind he felt his fingers losing their grip upon the alembic, allowing it to slip from his hand. He caught himself just in time to save it from falling. That's when he looked down and realized for the first time what his experiment had produced.

A powder. A thin layer of fine, white powder that lined the narrow connecting tube and coated the globular walls of the alembic's secondary chamber. *A fine white substance of a powdery yet waxy consistency, displaying a markedly crystalline quality.*

He peered at the glass. He turned it this way and that in the dim and dubious light. Was this success? Was this the long-sought Philosophers' Stone? The *Elixir Vitae,* the Salt of Life, the universal healing agent—*in it all the power of the stars?* The thought made him quiver with excitement. He had done everything by the book, and everything had gone according to plan. But now he had reached an impasse. On his own he could go no further. He lacked the necessary equipment to verify the results. Without athanor or crucible he could not test the powder's virtues. There was only one thing he *could* do. There was only one person who could give him the answers he needed. He had nowhere else to turn. *Madame Medea.*

By the time he reached the landing at the top of the stone stairs, Simon and Eny were playing an entirely different sort of music: a slow and solemn air in a minor key. Morgan stopped and stood watching them, sweating and shaking, both hands clasped tightly around the smooth and glassy surface of the alembic. It seemed to him that an unearthly light hovered over the heads of the musicians as their bows swept in unison over the singing strings. He wanted to speak. He wanted to shout *Eureka!* He wanted to tell someone what he'd done. But as the music slowed and the light fell upon Eny's face, a different sort of thought occurred to him. *She doesn't care. She won't understand.*

Then Eny struck up another tune. It was a melody Morgan had heard before: "The May Morning Dew." She played it through once; she played it again; and then Simon, in a haunting tenor voice, began to sing:

> *The house I once lived in,*
> *There's not a stone upon stone,*
> *And all round the garden*
> *The weeds, they have grown;*
> *And all the kind neighbors*
> *That ever I knew,*
> *With the red rose they've withered*
> *In the May Morning Dew.*

The old man's voice drifted up the stairway until it passed into darkness and silence. Then the music ceased. In the stillness a spark of light flitted past the window, causing Jacob's ladder to flash like a chain of gold. Then Morgan, like one waking from a dream, roused himself, thrust the alembic into his shirt, and dashed down the stairs past the two startled fiddlers.

The stairwell shuddered as the street door closed behind him. The window frame shivered and shook. Outside the window the brief spark died. And a shadow, like that of a huge hand, fell over the stairs.

Simon looked at Eny and shook his head. "Giants in the land," he said.

Part 2

Chapter Ten

THE GREEN ISLAND

It was Monday, a close and heavy afternoon. School was out, and the day was drawing almost imperceptibly to its cold, gray conclusion. Eny sat on an outcropping of rock high above the waters of Laguna Verde, staring out into the folds of dark and light within the mantle of fog that lay upon the inlet. She was pondering the words of Simon Brach—the last words he had spoken to her on that never-to-be-forgotten Sunday of fiddling on the stairs: *Giants in the land.*

Never once during that sublime session had she stopped to tell the old man about her fears and apprehensions. She'd never had the chance: There hadn't been a minute for anything but the music. At the time she might have regarded that as a cause for irritation—if she'd had the presence of mind to think about it. But today it didn't matter. For one thing, the music itself had been more than enough for her, filled as it was with exhortations and encouragements and illuminations all its own. For another thing, it was clear now that she didn't need to tell Simon anything. Simon *already knew* about the giants in the land.

That's why she was here, sitting on this rock, straining her eyes into the heart of the shifting haze over the ocean. Simon's words and Simon's tunes had convinced her that there was only one way to learn what she needed to know. Somehow she had to find the courage to face her fears. She had to return to La Punta Lira and seek the answers for herself.

Turning away from the sea, she reached into the pocket of her hooded sweatshirt and pulled out her newest plaything. It was a sling for throwing stones: She had made it herself the previous night under the inspiration of Rev. Alcuin's reminder of the story of David and Goliath.

Scanning the ground at her feet, she bent and picked up a smooth, round pebble. For a few seconds she sat hefting it in the palm of her hand; then, satisfied with its shape, size, and weight, she folded it carefully into the sling's leather patch. Gathering the two straps into the palm of her left hand, she reached up and began swinging the sling over her head. Three times she swung it; four, five, six. At the right moment she released one of the straps and let the stone fly. Far out over the ocean it soared in a gentle arch, graceful as a bird in flight.

Out where the gulls swoop and the fish leap it dropped with a tiny splash into the face of a sloping green wave. Eny saw it fall.

But then she saw something else as well. Just above the place where it entered the water, at the level of the hidden horizon, she caught a glimpse of a spot of coppery light, like the flame of a candle in a clouded mirror. Sunset, she knew, was at least an hour off, and yet this light had all the ruddy hues of the sinking sun.

As she watched, the light flashed brightly, then drew in upon itself and changed color. In the next instant it had become a tiny pulsing point of intense whiteness. The fog thinned, shredded, and tore apart, opening a small but clear window upon the ocean and the sky beyond the edge of the world—the first patch of blue sky she had seen in over a week.

In that window, hovering over the horizon, the point of white light hung small and serene in the blue of space, like the morning star, casting down its radiance upon the surface of the sea in a gentle silver shower. And just below it, green as an emerald, green as hills under rain in the grass-clad spring, shimmered something like a mountain in the midst of the ocean, a bit of distant verdure floating on the face of the deep.

Eny jumped up and rubbed her eyes. "The Green Island in the West!" she whispered.

Without thinking, she took to the trail, ran down the cliff-side, and plunged, jeans, sneakers, and all, into the gently breaking waves, seeking a clearer view of the shining object floating on the line between earth and sky. But in the next moment the hole in the gray curtain sucked itself shut again. The light behind the veil trembled and wavered. Then it went out altogether.

How long she stood there in the bubbling surf, gazing out to sea, Eny couldn't have said. But when at last she came to herself, it was with an odd feeling of having reached an unsought and unforeseen conclusion. It seemed to her that she had seen the Hidden Isle of Inisfail: the land of the sun's

107

going, the destined resting place of the Stone called Lia Fail. It was a vision, according to her mother's stories, that comes only to the few, and no more than once in a lifetime. But why had it chosen to reveal itself to her? And what did it mean?

The answer was not long in coming. Somehow, she thought, the music had something to do with it. In some unexplained way, the two must be connected. Even now she could hear the ascending melody of "The May Morning Dew" rising up from the deepest recesses of her mind. Or was it echoing off the rocky face of the cliff behind her?

Yes!

She was sure of it now. The tune was actually ringing in her ears, not merely in her imagination. Only on this occasion it was not the plaintive strains of the violin she heard, but rather the gently dropping notes of the wire-strung harp. She turned and looked up the beach in the direction of the Cave of the Hands.

Eny followed the music, shoes squishing and clothes dripping, through the shallows, under the arch, up the slope, and straight on toward the cavern's black mouth. At every step the tune altered slightly until at last it had become a melody she had never heard before, haunting, sensuous, and otherworldly. Slowly, imperceptibly, it wove its strange spell around her, drawing her onward and upward, until she stood panting and blinking into the dim spaces in the opening in the cliff.

There she paused and sniffed. From the entrance to the cavern, mingled somehow with the music and the cool, damp air that flowed out of the darkness, wafted a fragrance like a mixture of orange blossoms, jasmine, and honeysuckle. Eny checked herself, tilted her head slightly, and took another breath, drinking deeply of the earth's sweet exhalations. Then she took a tentative step forward into the cave.

Though gray and fading, the light from the sea was still sufficient to illuminate the copper-colored hands ascending the wall of the cavern. Eny stopped just long enough to touch them with her fingertips. She would have lingered in that familiar spot, but the notes of the harp and the strangely attractive aroma would not permit her to stay. Without growing the least bit louder—indeed, if anything, it seemed to be diminishing in volume—the melody somehow became more aggressive and insistent, penetrating her brain, calling her deeper into the cave. Persistently it wormed its way into the center of her consciousness, thrumming as if it were the pounding of her own heart within her chest or the pulse of her bloodstream behind her ear. Or was it rather the beat of a drum that she was hearing? Eny followed the relentless sound forward, noticing for the first time that a faint light was illuminating the rear of the cave, quite near to the spot where she had seen the crow. Again she halted and cast her eyes around the cavern's damp and dimly lit walls.

"Oh!" cried Eny in spite of herself, the sound of her voice setting off a series of unexpected reverberations. She clapped a hand over her mouth and took a step back.

At her feet, just at the place where sand and bare rock yielded to wet, impressionable earth, she could see footprints coming and going across the floor of the cave. There were two distinct sets, and they had obviously been made by two very different kinds of people. The first were quite small: possibly the tracks of a child. By contrast, the prints in the second set were extremely large—even unnaturally large. Eny felt as if she were looking at the footprints of a giant.

All this while the beating of the drum had become more pronounced, almost drowning out the strains of the harp altogether. At the same time, the flowery fragrance was growing stronger and more enticing. The air felt warmer and lighter now than when she had first come into the Cave of the Hands. Her heart was pounding as loudly and persistently as the drum itself.

Eny bent forward, squinting and straining her eyes in an attempt to discover the source of the illumination at the back of the cavern. To her great surprise, she found that it flowed from a passage that opened between two squat boulders that stood in a corner where the dripping ceiling sloped down to meet the floor. She closed her eyes and drew in a chest-deep draft of the sweet fragrance that came drifting from that quarter of the chamber.

At that moment the music took an upward turn, then suddenly faded and ceased. Eny let out all her breath in a long, shaky sigh. Then she squared her shoulders, walked to the rear of the cave, ducked between the boulders, and stepped into the light of the narrow passage.

Chapter Eleven

THE TUNNEL OF LIGHT

Light. But not as she'd been accustomed to think of it. Swirling, churning, eddying in little whorls and back-currents and dust-devils of luminosity and brightness. Bubbling and boiling, flowing and skimming over the stumps and bumps and outcroppings of rock in the floor and walls and ceiling. Light that reminded her sometimes of water, sometimes of glowing clouds of mist. Light like some kind of tangible, workable, malleable stuff. Fine threads or fibers of light that spun themselves out interminably in all directions like sparkling cotton candy or glittering spider webs. Clinging strands of light that wrapped themselves around you and got tangled in your hair. Light bodied forth in the form of reaching hands and grasping fingers. Winding and binding strings of light, an inescapable shining net of light, leading you on, drawing you down, overpowering you, forever eluding your grasp. Light that passed straight through

*you like shafts of pure energy, and then
went whirling and spiraling away into the
surrounding emptiness. Light like none she
had ever seen before....*

Beyond the two boulders at the rear of the cave Eny found herself in a brightly illuminated tunnel. On either side its walls flickered and shimmered, like the walls of a pool or an aquarium, under the liquid waves of the mysterious phosphorescence. She put up a hand and touched the damp, shining surface of the cold, rough rock. Then, feeling her way along with her fingertips, she began to move forward, down into the heart of the sea-cliff.

How had this tunnel come to be here? How, in all of her many visits to *La Cueva de los Manos*, had she failed to notice it? That was a mystery she'd have to plumb some other day. For the moment, every particle of her mental and physical being, every taut nerve and sharpened sense, was intent upon one thing: the downwardly sloping course of the narrow corridor that stretched away in front of her. A quest had been laid upon her. Her purpose was clear. She had to discover the source of this strange luminescence. She had to find the incandescent subterranean well from which these waves of light came sweeping irresistibly up the descending passageway.

It was neither a natural nor an earthly light. Of this Eny was certain. Her first thought was that it was like the light she had seen surrounding her vision of the Green Island in the

West. The similarity between them wasn't limited to color: a soft silvery whiteness tinged with green and gold, hinting of sunlight on grass. In both cases the most striking thing about the light was its otherworldly quality, and something else that she could only conceive as a kind of bodily intensity. This light seemed to be a thing possessing substance and form. It flowed across the floor and up the sides of the tunnel in ever-shifting, shimmering, vacillating strands. When she stretched out a finger to touch them, these strands clung to her hands and arms like hairs or statically charged fibers. They wrapped themselves around her in bright rippling circles. They pulled at her and drew her gently along. Yet she could never be absolutely certain that she actually *felt* them.

The passage plunged forward, proceeding through a series of winding curves and sharply angled turns: first left, then right, then left again. Never did it keep to a straight course for more than four or five paces together. On and on it went, delving deeper and deeper into the earth, until at last Eny lost all sense of location, direction, and time. She felt as if she had been walking forever, down, down, down into the center of all things seen and unseen. And always, spilling and curling around each successive bend in the path, growing progressively brighter at every turn, the strings of light reached out to her from the invisible place of their origin, grasping her, enfolding her, leading her further into the rock.

At last she reached a spot where the passage widened out into a broad colonnade of gleaming stalagmites and stalactites. Eny put up a hand, shading her eyes against the light, leaning into the strangely elastic stuff of which it was made. Slowly and tentatively she made her way forward, the ceiling of the cave rising to loftier heights above her head at every step. At length the pillared grotto became a vast, dripping, echoing hall of flashing crystals and smoothly fluted columns. Every facet of every jewel danced with light. Every formation, every inch of wall and floor, glittered with bright festoons and frills of illumination.

By this time the light was so strong that Eny felt she could no longer make any headway against it. So thoroughly had its threads and strings and cords wrapped themselves about her and tangled themselves in her clothing and hair that she was finding it difficult to move or breathe. Her steps grew slow and heavy. Her thoughts became sluggish and confused.

She stopped and gazed around, squinting into the intense brightness, and found that she was standing in a broad open space where the stony floor once again gave way to moist, soft sand. Impressed upon this sand were the same footprints she had seen in the Cave of the Hands. Clearly, the creatures or people who had left *those* tracks had also made these. They too must know about the strange light and the tunnel below the cliff.

Through the thinning forests of stalactites and stalagmites to her right and left, at a distance of about fifty feet on either hand, she could see rising walls, as straight and smooth as if they had been the work of skilled masons. At intervals these walls were marked by even smoother spaces—blank, polished, and rectangular—that looked oddly like doors except that there were no seams or breaks of any kind to set them apart from the surrounding rock.

Directly ahead the columns of stone ceased altogether. The ceiling of the cavern lifted higher and ever higher until it was completely lost to sight. In that vast and empty space the threads and strands of light swirled and pooled and spiraled together, like the swift currents of a stream trapped in a churning backwater. At a great distance above her head they stalled and spun and congealed, forming knots and balls and pinwheels of stunning splendor like stars in an underground firmament. Far below them, at the bottom of a gentle sandy slope, heaved the sparkling swells of what appeared to be a limitless underground sea.

Down to that sea went Eny, weary, weak, and irresistibly drawn by the cords of light that bound her hands and head and feet. Helpless she plunged forward into the foaming breakers, head over heels and heels over head, rolling, floundering, spinning, and sinking until she no longer had any sense of up or down. *I'll drown*, she thought vaguely; but it wasn't so. For the water in which she was tossed and flung from side to side had no wetness about it at all. It was warm and airy and downy. It, too, seemed to be fabricated of the bright and sinuous fibers of never-resting light. With something like a satisfied sigh, she rolled herself into a ball and gave herself up to be tumbled along by the silky undulations of the fragrant glowing billows.

And now began a long and dreamlike journey in which the beating of her heart merged with the rhythm of the unceasing drum and the gently floating music of the harp. Consciousness slipped away like a little boat loosed from its moorings. She was unaware of breathing, moving, waking or sleeping. She did not know whether she was blind or seeing, whether her eyes were open or shut. And yet she felt, perceived, and envisioned many things.

Flocks of seabirds with broad iridescent wings. Geese and swans in arching skyward flight. Fleets of pigeons and squadrons of doves, bursting up from behind the sun, scattering storms of pearly feathers, dipping and rising and disappearing beyond the watery blue zenith.

White-sailed ships upon the water. Winged vessels soaring through cream-colored clouds. Sun, moon, and stars in a dimpled pool, green cataracts thundering over the edge of the world, fountains of silver foam and coppery sparks. Glittering green coils and writhing, red-mouthed serpents.

White wings and white feathers. Black wings like long-fingered hands. Bubbles and brine and dark headlands in the sea. Hulking shapes stalking across barren fields. The moon behind a veil of rain, the moon through parting clouds. A face—a pale but luminous face: oval-shaped, green-eyed, smiling, always smiling.

Eny opened her eyes. Sunlight was filtering down through a lacy canopy of delicate branches and young green leaves. Groggy with sleep, she squeezed her eyes tightly shut, rubbed them with her knuckles, then opened them again and blinked. Raising herself on one elbow, she yawned, stretched luxuriously, and looked around.

She was lying under a slender beech tree atop a small round hill of glittering white sand. At the foot of the hill a green ocean flashed in the sun beneath a clear and cloudless blue sky. Beyond the breakers, halfway between the shore and the horizon, a humpbacked island raised its bulk above the tossing white wave-caps.

She got to her knees and shaded her eyes. Was it possible? Could this be the island she had seen through the mist off La Punta Lira? Heart pounding, she staggered to her feet and took a few uncertain steps down the hill, craning her neck for a better view, lifting a hand against the glare. But in the next instant her hopes were snuffed like a candle. For this island was not lush and green like the one she remembered. It was dark and rough and bare in the open sunshine. Its cliffs were of stark red rock, and from its highest point a spike of smooth black stone shot skyward like a forbidding finger. Gray and pebble-strewn its steep flanks rose dripping from the sea, and from its rocky shores—

Eny stopped dead still, her heart in her mouth. Out past the churning surf, between the dark island and the white sands at her feet, something was coming toward her over the restless sea: not one, not two, but *three* gigantic man-shapes. *Three* lumbering giants like the one she had seen below the arch outside the Cave of the Hands: black silhouettes against the sky, huge-limbed, round-skulled, heavy-faced, moving mountains amid the waves. Slowly, steadily, laboriously they came wading through the billows, making directly for the spot where she stood.

Cold from head to toe with sudden dread, she let out an involuntary gasp and took a step backward. Something struck her on the head—something soft and feathery, like a puff of air or a brush of wings. Startled by the wild fluttering sounds that accompanied the blow, she cried out and dropped to one knee, flailing her arms frantically above her head as a great black crow swept past her ear and went winging out over the deep.

"Don't stand there gawping like a lummox!" shouted an oddly familiar voice in her other ear. "Can't you see it's after *you* they're coming? Up with you and away!"

A pair of hands, small but strong as a vise, grasped her by the arm and jerked her to her feet. Blindly she turned and stumbled forward, her brain spinning, her arm throbbing under the unrelenting grip of hard, bony fingers. Her companion—or assailant—dragged her up the sandy heap and past the drooping beech to a place where the ground become more solid and the sand yielded to smooth and clumps of fragile white flowers. Then the two of them began to run in earnest, chests heaving and feet pounding, straight for a grove of tall trees at the top of a gentle rise.

Glancing to one side, Eny discovered that she was running alongside a wiry little man with a wizened, walnutlike face, wild, woolly eyebrows, and a bulbous nose that showed signs of having been broken in several places. Even in the act of lunging desperately up the hill, gasping for breath at every step, she found herself gaping in disbelief at this odd little man. He was strikingly similar in appearance to Eochy, the strange, diminutive person she and Morgan had met in Madame Medea's shop. As a matter of fact, he might have been Eochy's brother. But he was leaner and hungrier-looking, and his clothes were much shabbier and dirtier. Instead of shoes he had filthy rags bound upon his feet. In place of a cap he wore a faded red cloth wrapped about his head. As he ran, a lumpy leather bag or satchel swung madly from his frayed rope belt, bouncing like a cow's udder just below his belly.

"Go on with you!" he shouted to several others of his kind who stood cowering under the eaves of the forest. "Follow Sengann to the village! Get weapons and supplies! I'm taking the girl to the wood above the dun!"

Soundlessly the little band disappeared into the shadows within the grove. An instant later Eny and her escort reached the top of the ridge and plunged in after them.

"Wait!" screamed Eny, collapsing in terror and exhaustion the moment they were under the shelter of the trees.

"Can't you wait a minute?" With one last desperate burst of energy she jumped up, freed herself from the little man's grasp, and flung herself against the trunk of a towering oak. "What is this place? Who are you? And where are you taking me?"

With a grim look, he seized her by the wrist and drew her face down to his.

"It's in the Sidhe you are, where Overlanders like yourself come rarely. Rury of the Road am I. And it's over Mag Adair and past Beinn Meallain we be bound—as far from *her* and Tory Island as we can go!"

Chapter Twelve

PURSUED

The slope grew steeper as Eny, sweating and panting, stumbled up the thickly wooded hillside behind her solemn and silent guide. It was amazing how quickly the bent and stooping little man could go. Deftly he threaded his way between the thick-boled trees, around lichen-covered boulders, and over broad patches of pale red-speckled mushrooms, his nose thrust forward like the snout of a dog, his skinny arms akimbo, his bandy legs churning up the leaf-strewn forest floor like a whirlwind. Eny was barely able to keep up with him. It was not a time for questions, and so with every step her distress grew more profound. *What am I doing here?* she wondered. *How did this happen to me? And how will I ever find my way home?* But there were no answers for the present. Never once did Rury stop or speak or turn around as the trees and shadows flew past on either side.

After half an hour or so of this desperate, breathless flight they came out from under the spreading oaks and broad-leafed elms into a lighter and airier stand of tall, straight pines at the top of a rocky ridge. Between the stems Eny could see the flash of the sea and a ribbon of bright sand along the shore. Not far from the silvery beach stood a huddle of wretched-looking thatched huts from which a gravel track wound its way up the green slopes below the wooded ridge. Along this narrow path seven small and heavily burdened figures were making their way laboriously up the hill and toward the grove of pines.

Rury stepped out into the open and waved a hand at them. "This way!" he shouted. "Isn't it any faster you can go?"

The leader, a narrow-faced fellow with a wispy red beard, wiped his brow and spit as the group drew near. "We're coming as fast as fast may be, carrying such a load. Is it miracles you want?"

"Not miracles, Sengann," answered Rury as the rest of the group came trooping in under the branches, "but something like. For here's a miracle in our midst to be sure—a visitor from the world above!—and a storm following after. No rest for us when Fomorians pursue. It's forward we must, and no delay."

He turned to Eny with a slight bow. "Little's the leisure we have for introductions. But you must know that we are the *Fir Bolg*—People of the Bags. Here is Sengann, my right hand, and Slanga his brother, and Crimthann carrying the bundle of spears. There's Liber, my wife, and Genann with his woman, Crucha, and Anust the daughter of Dela. Silly geese, you may be thinking, and right enough from a certain point of view. But tough they are, and good-hearted, and enemies to her until death!"

Eny cast a glance around the circle. Not man or woman in it stood above five feet in height. Like Rury and Eochy, all

122

were long-armed, bow-legged, brown-faced, and wrinkled. The men had beards and were dressed in rags. The women wore plaid shawls over long skirts of gray or tow-colored linen, frayed and liberally patched. Rury was bony and grizzled, Liber gray-headed and stout, Genann and Crucha white with age. Anust, small and round-faced, smiled pleasantly as she bound up her long red hair in a tattered blue cloth. Slanga, dark and thin, leaned on his staff and inclined his head in greeting. Crimthann, yellow-haired and taller than the rest by a good three inches, grinned and winked. Sengann muttered and scowled. Besides the heavy packs on their backs, each had a bulging leather bag or pouch dangling from a rope or a leather strap about the waist.

At sight of them a host of questions crowded Eny's mind and danced on the tip of her tongue. But there was no time to satisfy her curiosity. No sooner had Crimthann handed out the weapons—spears with short oaken shafts and dull stone tips—but they hefted their baggage and set out. Sengann led the way, his unruly red head bobbing from side to side at the end of his sinewy neck. Rury trotted in the rear, keeping watch like a wary gray wolf. Crucha marched with Eny directly in the center of the line, holding her firmly but gently by the hand.

They moved at an incredible pace, running whenever possible, leaping over fallen logs, ducking under dangling branches, skirting around patches of marshy ground. The deeper they penetrated into the forest, the stranger and more marvelous grew their surroundings. Soon they were among trees and plants like none Eny had ever seen before. Ivory-white trunks like pillars of marble soared into a lofty canopy of green-gold leaves. Smaller trees, their twisted and blackened boughs heavy with reddish-purple fruit, took shelter in the shaded avenues. Around the travelers' knees nodded ferns and flowering shrubs, their fronds and branches quivering softly in the liquid play of dappled sunlight, every leaf and blossom glistening with rainbow-refracting dewdrops. Moisture from the sea dripped in a soft but relentless rain from the interlacing branches. Delicate gold-winged seedpods and wisps of gossamer spiraled down through the mote-spangled air. Ropes of budding vines and nets of curling tendrils hung in loops above their heads. Birds, broad-winged and multicolored, darted from bough to bough, and gigantic yellow butterflies and big orange bees buzzed and fluttered past their ears. On all sides the green thickets rustled and shook with the movements of tiny hidden creatures.

They trekked for several miles before emerging from the wood onto the rounded brow of a treeless hill. Here, behind a screen of low-growing gorse and purple lilacs, Sengann halted and signaled a short rest. As soon as the order was given, Crucha, releasing Eny's hand, dropped her pack and plumped down on the ground where she was. The others followed her example—all except Rury, who skipped to the edge of the height and stood gazing out over a broad grassy plain, divided by a meandering silver stream, to a heap of velvety green hills in the blue distance. Eny, shaken and exhausted, came up and crouched beside him.

"That's our road," said Rury. "Through the pass of Beinn Meallain. Beyond the settlements of the Tuatha De Danann, on the south side of Mag Adair, lies the dun of my brother Semeon. There we'll get shelter."

Eny nodded. But she wasn't really listening. Her mind's eye was filled with dreadful shapes and horrid apparitions. Her mouth was dry, her hands cold, her head drenched with sweat. She stood up and bent close to the little man.

"Who are the Fomorians?" she whispered, somehow fearing to speak the name aloud. "Why are they chasing me?"

Rury turned and cocked an eyebrow at her. "Are you not knowing?"

"Me?"

"And why not? Plain it is those lumbering apes have taken a keen interest in you. Not twice in a hundred of your years do we see an Overlander in the Sidhe! And you not to be knowing why!"

"But if *you* don't know, why are you helping me?"

"The Fomorians themselves are reason enough."

Eny groaned. "But this is crazy! How am I supposed to know what's going on? I'm not even sure what the *Sidhe* is! Is that my mother's Irish fairyland?"

"Faery it is, whatever your mother may say. What is it brought you here?"

Eny shut her eyes and pressed the palms of her hands against her temples. Her brain was reeling, and her head felt dizzy. "I'm not sure. It's all so confusing! I saw a green island. And a crow, and an old woman. There was a strange light, and harp music. I heard a lot of talk about a Stone. I sank in deep water and fell into a dream. I—"

Rury gripped her by the arm. "*Stone* did you say?" His eyes were round and filled with fire. He stepped back and examined her at arm's length. "That face!" he exclaimed. "Those eyes! Is it possible—?"

But his words were cut short by a terrible din. From the forest behind them came sounds of shattering wood and crashing timber. The earth quaked, and the trees flailed from side to side as if bent by a violent wind. Rury leaped down from the rock, peering back in the direction of the wood. Already Sengann and the others were on their feet.

"Dark shapes coming after us!" Sengann cried. "Like hounds after the hare!"

"Follow me, you flat-footed clumps!" shouted Rury as they quickly shouldered their burdens. "Across the meadow and over the water! They'll find it harder to catch us among the folds of the hills!"

They were off at once. Down the slope they dashed, out across the plain, their packs rattling on their backs, their leather bags bouncing at their waists. Eny kept pace as best she could, jumping over little hillocks of grass, stubbing her toes on outcroppings of rock, scraping her shins against dead tree branches that lay hidden in the tall grass. Her legs felt like rubber, her lungs burned for want of air. But she pushed on, running as she'd never run before. They were nearly at the stream when her foot broke through the crumbling earth at the edge of a rabbit hole and she fell sprawling on her face.

When she looked up the others were already plunging into the shallow rivulet. Groaning, she scrambled to her knees. She opened her mouth to cry out, but her voice stuck in her throat. She tried to get up, but her legs and arms wouldn't move.

In that instant everything changed. Sound and motion ceased. Time seemed to stand still. A veil descended over the scene, a hazy indistinctness clouded everything within her field of vision—everything, that is, except the jewel-like pebbles that lay shining beneath the bright water in the shallows of the stream.

Suddenly a figure appeared among those sparkling stones: a woman in a blue shawl standing ankle-deep in the water and washing a pile of old clothes. She looked up from her work and fixed Eny with her large green eyes. Her face was pale and oval-shaped beneath the shadow of her broad-brimmed hat. She smiled and reached out her hand. With a painful effort, Eny struggled to her feet and took a single step forward. But then someone laid hold of her arm.

"After me, now!" said an urgent voice at her ear. "Across the stream! Already they're upon us!"

She looked. Rury stood at her side. The strange vision had passed; the washer at the ford was gone. Glancing back over her shoulder, she caught sight of three gigantic men, tall as trees, thundering down the side of the valley and into the plain, pounding over the ground with heavy, booted feet, waving their ham-fisted hands above their boulder-shaped heads, filling the air with their deep-throated curses and shouts. Something like a bolt of electricity shot through her brain, and she turned and fled with Rury over the brook.

"It's stand and fight we must!" shouted Sengann as they came splashing up on the other side. "All other hope is past!"

And then arose a tumult so great that Eny could hardly hear own thoughts. Genann and Crimthann came clattering down to the stream and stood beside them, their short spears at the ready, their heads thrown back, their voices raised in a shrill battle cry. On the bank behind them stood the women, screaming and wailing, tearing at their shawls and skirts, ripping up clods of grass and dirt and tossing them into the air. In front of them the three giants came on, their big round heads lowered like the heads of charging bulls, their great boots plowing up the earth, their massive legs devouring fifteen feet of ground at a single stride.

"Now!" shouted Rury as the first of the Fomorians drew near enough for the ugly, bulbous features of his misshapen face to be clearly discerned. "Now or never! Cast and thrust! For Semeon and Erc!"

And with that the Fir Bolg heaved their awkward little spears straight at the advancing giant. Sengann's cast was most successful: the stone tip of his spear struck the steel toe of the giant's heavy leather boot and glanced aside. The other three weapons fell short and bounced crazily end over end through the grass, their pointed ends too blunt to stick firm in the earth. With shrill cries of dismay, Genann and Crimthann picked up their feet and retreated to a position just in front of the women. But Rury seized Eny by the elbow and urged her to run.

"Split up!" he shouted to the others as the huge shapes descended upon them. "Liber with me and the girl! To the hills we'll go! You others run south along the water! It may confuse them," he added as he helped Eny up the bank. "It's none too smart they are."

At that moment Eny knew what she had to do. In two more strides the first Fomorian would be at the water's edge. In three he would have them in the iron grip of his massive paw. With a sudden, violent motion she twisted aside and freed herself from Rury's grasp. Then she reached into her pocket and drew out her little leather sling. Stooping down, she scooped up a smooth round stone from the bed of the stream. Quickly and deftly, for there was not a second to be wasted, she folded it into the sling's pouch. Then she straightened up, faced her enemy, whirled the sling above her head, and let it go.

Crack! A sound like a baseball coming off a bat split the air. In the brief silence that followed Eny saw the Fomorian stop dead in his tracks. His hand shot upward to his eye. A look of pain and confusion crossed his dull features, like a flash of lightning rippling over the underside of a thick gray cloud. Then he tilted his face up to the sky and let out a wail that shook the earth and raised the hair on the back of Eny's neck.

Rury ran up beside her and pointed at the other two giants. "Look!" he said. "It's running away they are!"

He was right. In complete dismay at the sight of their leader's discomfiture, the companions of the wounded Fomorian were turning around and stumping back toward the forest. It was obvious they hadn't expected to encounter resistance—at least not resistance of such a sharp and stunning kind. In the next moment the injured giant was stumbling after his fleeing comrades, screaming and cursing furiously, his hand still clamped tightly over his bleeding eye.

A cheer went up from the Fir Bolg. Eny looked back at them and grinned, a hot flush spreading over her cheeks and up behind her ears.

"On to Beinn Meallain!" ordered Rury, seizing her by the arm and dragging her up the rocky scree on the far side of the brook. "We haven't a moment to lose! Take this chance and make it good, and it's clean away we may be before they come back!"

Together, Eny and the Fir Bolg set off at a run toward the soft green hills at the eastern edge of the plain.

Chapter Thirteen

THE SONG OF THE STONE

Once among the wooded glens and dales of the mountains the little troop slackened its pace and slipped beneath the shadows of a dense growth of aspens. Here they fell immediately into single file and, after a brief moment's rest, addressed themselves to the ascent of the steep-sided slopes. As earlier in the day, Eny marched at the center of the line, just behind Crucha, who, in spite of her white hair, pressed forward at a rate sufficient to stretch the young girl's endurance to the limit. By the angle of the intermittent light in the forest Eny could tell that the path was climbing southward. Between the slender black-and-white stems of the trees, she sometimes caught glimpses of lush green hillsides, lavishly starred with tiny white flowers, steadily rising toward a yoke or saddle between two sharp peaks at the top of a rocky ridge.

"Where are we going?" She wheezed. "Is it far?"

"Above us stands the Pass of Beinn Meallain," answered the old Fir Bolg woman. "The only road over these mountains it is. The two hills on either side we call *Na Cupla*, the Twins. Beyond them, in a sheltered vale, lies Baile Daoine Sidhe, the fortress town of the Tuatha De Danann."

The Tuatha De Danann! Eny's mother had told her stories of the Tuatha De Danann. A tingle of excitement ran down her spine. "Is that where we're stopping for the night?"

"Stopping!" roared Rury from the rear. "There'll be no stopping, by the beard of Erc! It's straight on to the coast we're bound. The Baile might be safe enough at a pinch, but *she* knows the place, though it be so tight and well defended. Besides, Bag People aren't always welcome there. We're for Semeon's Dun!"

So sharp was the little man's tone that Eny blushed with shame. She fell silent at once and made up her mind to keep her mouth closed for the rest of the journey, a resolution she knew she could keep since she had so little breath to spare in any case. Grim and mute, then, she trudged up the relentless incline after Crucha, cracking the dry twigs beneath her feet, stumbling over hidden roots, wading through pungent heaps of moldering leaves. But the further she went and the higher she climbed, the deeper her sense of disappointment grew.

Now that she had accepted the notion of being in the Sidhe at all—now that the perils of the way had made the Otherworld undeniably and terrifyingly real to her—Eny wanted to lay eyes on the Danaan people of her mother's stories. So strong was this desire that she could almost taste it; but, chastened by Rury's rebuke, she determined to speak of it no more. It would be wrong, she realized, to jeopardize the Fir Bolgs' lives any further when they had already risked so much for her sake. It would be selfish to expect them to stop just to satisfy her longings. Nevertheless, a hope deferred often makes the heart grow sick, especially when it's a hope spawned in fairyland. As the trek dragged on, Eny's heartsickness increased and spread until it engulfed not only her heart but her head and hands and feet. Before long she was sweating great drops and trembling with pain and exhaustion. But she said nothing about it. Instead, she bit her lip and plunged on after Crucha, step after tortured step.

As they mounted upward the aspens gave way to a stand of lordly redwoods and the bed of leafy mulch beneath their feet became a cushion of dry needles. At every step, it seemed, the great trees rose higher and higher above their heads. Soon the giant trunks were so broad at the base that three men joining hands could not have compassed them about—then six men, then eight. At length the boles were as wide as small houses, some of them pierced by cracks and fire-charred crevices that looked like the dark doors of elvish or gnomish dwellings. In the spaces between the gigantic trees grew smaller pines and firs, interspersed with feathery ferns and banks of flowers—purple asters and violet rhododendrons and pink and yellow columbines.

Eny saw all this as one beholds vague colored shapes through a pane of rippled glass or a watery lens. Her sickness had now become so desperate and gripping that she hardly knew who she was or where she was going. Her head spun. Her mouth went dry. Her eyes felt hot and swollen. Mechanically she placed one foot in front of the other, shaking and shuddering as her body passed from chills into fever and back to chills again.

Somewhere among the convoluted gyrations of her thoughts it occurred to her that this condition was but the flowering of a seed that had dropped into her brain at the ford of the stream, where she saw the strange woman washing clothes among the jewel-like pebbles. As she plodded onward, her forehead burning and her throat tightening, she seemed to see again the pale oval face beneath the broad-brimmed hat. Once more she trembled in the cold glow of the intense green eyes. She cried out, stumbled, and fell. Crucha, seeing her distress, stopped and lifted her. And then something happened that altered Rury's plans and changed the course and destination of their expedition.

They were at the edge of the woods and on the point of stepping into the rocky path that led upward to the pass. Suddenly, from a brake of tall, slender flowering reeds, a small herd of deer burst out across their line of march. So unexpected was the apparition and so thunderous the pounding of the animals' hooves that the Fir Bolg fell back and fanned out across the trail in a wide semicircle. At the head of the herd stood a huge six-pointed buck with a white mark in the middle of his forehead in the shape of a great staring eye. All the deer had red ears and flaming red eyes—all except one tawny doe, whose eyes, as Eny stared at them, seemed to glitter a cold green.

With a great shout, Rury, Slanga, and Sengann lowered their blunt spears and charged, sending the herd clattering away into the forest. But as the deer fled, the green-eyed doe turned and darted a piercing glance in Eny's direction. At the same instant a great black bird swept over Eny's head and flew away into the high, creaking branches of the upper forest canopy. Eny's eyes went dark and she fell heavily on her side.

"The girl!" she heard Crucha call as her head sunk into a cushion of soft needles. "Don't you see, Rury? She's done! She can no further go!"

Eny felt a cool hand laid across her forehead. "Och!" said the gentle voice of Liber. "It's burning up she is!"

"Like an oven!" whispered Anust.

Rury was the next to speak. "Let me take your pack, Sengann. You will have to carry the girl. To the Baile we'll go and throw ourselves on the mercy of the Daoine Sidhe. We have no other choice."

The voices faded from her ears, and she knew no more.

"Here. You may lay her down on this mat."

Eny opened her eyes as these words, spoken slowly and distinctly in a deep, melodious voice, broke in upon her consciousness. As her vision cleared, she saw a man's face bending over her. It was a kind face, framed by dark red hair, with a long chin, a straight nose, a firm mouth, and a pair of blazing blue eyes. A golden brooch set with red rubies flashed at the man's shoulder, and he wore a dark green cloak of some heavy material over a fine white silk shirt fastened with small silver buttons. He was kneeling beside her, supporting himself on the shaft of a long red spear set with tiny golden brads. Behind him and around him were ranged the frowning and worried faces of the Fir Bolg.

"She wakes!" said Crucha. "See—her eyes!"

A solemn expression came over the man's face. "You spoke true," he said, turning to Rury. "They are the eyes of Eithne."

Eny tried to raise her head but immediately fell back against the straw mattress on which she was lying. She opened her mouth, but her throat and palate were too dry to speak.

"Give her water," said the Danaan man—for that, Eny realized with wonder, was exactly what he was. "I doubt not she'll be better in a day or two, but now she needs her rest." He laid a hand on her forehead and stroked her hair. "Meanwhile, let you others come with me and take some refreshment."

He rose and turned away. One by one, the Fir Bolg followed.

Liber leaned down and touched her hand. "Try to sleep," she said. "We will return quickly."

As the old woman moved off, Eny turned her head and tried to take in her surroundings. She seemed to be lying against the outer wall of a large rectangular hall. Overhead was a vast network of carved and brightly painted rafters, thick with dancing shadows. On the other side of her mat a row of cylindrical red pillars, covered from top to bottom with interlacing cords of twisted gold, ran from one end of the building to the other. Each of these pillars held a bronze sconce, and every sconce a blazing torch. Between the pillars and down a few shallow steps she could see the main floor of the hall, where tall men and bright-haired women in gaily colored cloaks and gowns sat elbow to elbow along a series of polished oak tables. In the center of the floor red embers glowed in the iron grate of an oblong fire pit. In front of the pit stood a raised wooden platform, and on the platform a white-haired man in a dark blue robe was tuning the silver strings of a golden harp.

"My noble friends!" she heard him say as he seated himself at his instrument. "A song!" He cleared his throat, stretched out his arms, and threw back the bell-like sleeves of his gown. *"The Song of the Stone!"*

Men pounded the tables and raised their silver cups. Women tossed their colored scarves into the air. A cheer went up, so loud that the walls and ceiling rang. And then, just as suddenly, a hush fell over the hall. Closing his eyes, the bard raised a hand and ran a finger over the strings of his harp. A bright chain of silvery notes burst into the silent air, went rippling around the bases of the red pillars, and flew up into the shadows among the painted rafters. At last the singer began to chant in a high and plaintive tone:

> *Beyond the wall of sea and sky,*
> *Where hopes and fears and sorrows die*
> *And cast-off dreams slip gently by*
> > *To join the day's descending,*
>
> *An island green laughs in the light*
> *Of golden sun and silvery night,*
> *Unveiling to the second sight*
> > *A joy that's never ending.*

> *There, where the sun goes down to sleep*
> *Below the cellars of the deep*
> *And fairy folk and angels keep*
> > *A vigil o'er its fire;*

> *Out past the waves, beyond the pale*
> *Of circling stream, where white ships sail,*
> *Under the shade of Inisfail*
> > *Ends every heart's desire.*

So sweet was the sound of the voice, so soothing the subtle tones of the shining instrument, that Eny felt herself being carried away on the undulating strains of the song. She closed her eyes and let her thoughts flow out beyond the rafters, out into the night, out past the shining circle of moon and stars. In her mind's eye she saw again a vision of an island—a green island at the meeting place of sea and sky. And still the stream of magical words swept on:

> *A piece of heaven touched the ground*
> *At Heaven's Gate, where Jacob found*
> *A Pillow Stone; and to the sound*
> > *Of Seraphs on the stair*

> *He lay him down and watched his dreams*
> *Fly up to where the starlight gleams;*
> *But when he woke, those golden beams*
> > *Had vanished into air.*

Bold Gathelus, King Cecrops' son,
In Egypt's land where rivers run
Stretched out his hand to seize the Stone
From Israel in Goshen.

With Scota, his betrothed bride,
He dragged it over deserts wide
To Spain, far over the heaving tide
Of the dividing ocean.

Then over the deeps in ships they flew,
Gathelus's Danaan crew,
Breaching bound'ries old and new,
Seeking the final shore;

From Falias and Gorias
To Finias and Murias,
And last to Eire's sea of grass
Beyond the great Muir Mor.

On Tara's plain they set the Stone,
And over it they raised a throne,
That it might roar and shriek and moan
Beneath the king's true heir.

Eny's brain grew gray and hazy, and she turned her face
toward the wall. Slowly she descended into a silent blackness in
which she dreamed of giants and crows and herds of red-eared

deer. She saw herself sitting in the flickering light of a candle, listening intently as her mother read to her from a book. She heard the wildly soaring strains of Simon Brach's red fiddle. She cowered beneath a towering cliff of black stone.

When at last she opened her eyes again, Crucha was sitting on the floor beside her. With a great effort, Eny lifted a hand and touched the old woman's arm. Crucha smiled and laid a finger to her lips. And the poet went on singing:

> But Ernmas's daughter, Morrigu,
> Crafty Anand, cruel, untrue,
> Took up the quarrel with princely Lugh
> And rose in stormy mutiny
>
> When Ith, with all the sons of Mil,
> Came oversea to raze and kill,
> And Ollamh made of Lia Fail
> The exiled Stone of Destiny.
>
> "It must depart," he said. "Its fate
> Lies not with us; I'll not debate
> The point, for either soon or late
> To Inisfail it's going:
>
> Out past the twilight's shimmering shore,
> Out through the sunset's glimmering door,
> Where boiling oceans simmering pour
> Down cliffs beyond all knowing."

He turned away; she stormed and flew,
She raved and ranted, croaked and crew;
To Tory's fastness she withdrew
  Where giants keep the portals.

But Lia Fail passed out of Meath,
And Fairie slipped away beneath
The softness of the hills and heath,
  Invisible to mortals.

"Lia Fail!" whispered Eny. Though her brow was burning and her hair soaked with sweat, she could feel an icy coldness gathering around the roots of her heart. Again she strove to raise herself from the mat. Again she found that she had no strength and fell back with her face toward the wall.

And now she keeps her vigil keen
And rules the Sidhe as tyrant-queen,
Watching town and hill and green,
  To all the world an Enemy;

Thus to and fro she sends her spies
And scans the earth with hungry eyes
Seeking desperately the prize—
  The fabled Stone of Destiny.

"Take some more water," said Crucha, lifting the girl's head into her lap and putting a cup to her lips. Eny gulped the crystal liquid, letting it dribble down over her chin and neck.

> *But if the ancient tales tell true,*
> *The Fomor and the Morrigu*
> *Must one day gnash their teeth and rue*
> > *The schemes of their devising;*

> *For though at length they seize and bind it,*
> *The Stone will crush them when they find it,*
> *Leaving their shattered bones behind it,*
> > *Glorious in its rising.*

Again she tried to sit up. "*Morrigu!*" she coughed, moaning and twisting her body from side to side. "What is it? What does it mean?"

Crucha, however, said nothing, but merely stroked the girl's fevered head and hands.

> *As air beneath the water's flow*
> *Must bubble upward, even so*
> *The heaven-born to heaven must go*
> > *To find a place of rest.*

> *The Stone that fell from sky to earth*
> *Cannot remain within the girth*
> *Of narrow nature: true to its birth,*
> > *It seeks the utmost West.*

And there beyond the sea and sky,
Where hopes and fears and sorrows die
And cast-off dreams slip gently by
　　To join the day's descending,

Shall Lia Fail pass into light
Of golden sun and silvery night,
Where children of the second sight
　　Discern the joy unending....

Once again the bard's voice was fading. Once again Eny's eyelids were growing irresistibly heavy. Seizing Crucha's hand and gripping it tightly, she fell back and lay with the side of her face against the mat.

And then she slept a long, untroubled sleep.

Chapter Fourteen

THE FIR BOLG

She came to her senses atop a heap of sheepskins and rags beneath a wide inverted cone of wooden poles and thatch. Turning her head to one side, she saw Liber crouched in front of a beehive-shaped oven in a low wall of earth and stone, tending a smoky fire of sticks and turf. Rury sat nearby on the hard dirt floor, cross-legged and stitching up a big leather bag with a needle of bone and a thread of tough sinew. Besides the firelight, the only illumination in the little hut came from the gray dawn outside the low-arched door, where Sengann, staff in hand, was standing watch. There was a tang of salt in the damp air. Somewhere in the near distance sea-waves thudded dully on a rocky shore.

"The girl wakes, Liber," said Rury, rising softly and touching his wife gently on the arm. "It's nourishment she's needing. Let you bring food and drink."

Liber stood up and undid the leather flap of the pouch that hung at her waist. Kneeling beside Eny, she reached into the bag and drew out bread and wine.

"Drink, child," she smiled, putting the leather flask to Eny's lips. "It's a good long sleep you've had, being so wearied with adventure and battle and flight."

Eny drank greedily. The wine was rich, heady, and full-bodied. Almost immediately she could feel its bubbling effervescence warming her body and sending out tingling shoots of vibrant strength into her arms and legs and fingers and toes. Eagerly she gulped the sweet liquid, letting the excess spill over her chin and down her neck.

Soon she was sitting up on the pile of fleeces, munching on a hunk of brown-crusted bread, gazing out the door of the hut to where the ocean breakers gleamed in the rising sun and spread their foamy skirts over the red rocks and glistering sand. In the distance the purple swells rippled away to a blazing coppery horizon under a banner of crimson clouds. Across the whole of its restlessly heaving span the surface of the sea was broken only by the abruptness of a single small island of dark rock. The instant she saw it, Eny's heart jumped into her throat.

"That island!" she said, her mouth full of bread. "Is it—?"

"Na, na," laughed Rury, laying his stitching in his lap. "It's only Rachra you're seeing. Tory lies many leagues to the north, over Beinn Meallain, across Mag Adair, through the Hill Forest, and beyond the waters of Camas Morraigu. It's far away you are from them that would do you hurt."

"Where are we?"

"Luimneach, the dun of my brother Seméon. As I told you not three days gone."

"Three days! Have I been sleeping that long?"

"Sleeping and waking, but knowing neither. Sengann and Slanga took it in turns to carry you when you fell senseless. Even among the Danaans, in whose hill-fort we lay hid for two nights, you seemed to see nothing. You lay in a fever and spoke as if you were out of your head."

"Danaans!" Eny felt her jaw drop. "Do you mean to tell me—?"

A shadow fell across the doorway as Slanga, Crimthann, and Anust entered the hut. Anust, her sweet round face radiant as a sunbeam, came and knelt beside the bed of sheepskins. Eny smiled and took the little woman's outstretched hand; but her thoughts were busy chasing after the tail of Rury's last words.

"I've heard lots about the Danaans," she said. "My mom's always talking about them. But she's never once said a word about the Fir Bolg."

"And no wonder," said Rury, "we being a shamed and subject people."

"Slaves, more like," corrected Slanga.

"But what does it mean?" asked Eny. "'People of the Bags?' What are those sacks you carry on your belts?"

"A wandering race we are," said Liber, offering another sip of wine. "In these bags we carry our very lives."

"They're our homes," said yellow-haired Crimthann. "Our barns and our pantries. The tools of our trade. Boats or baggage they might be. Shelter from the storm. Look now!"

With that, he undid his rope belt, removed the bag, loosened a few cords, and began to unfold the leather before her eyes. To Eny's great surprise, it expanded almost magically in his hands. One fold, one crease at a time, he opened it out and spread it over the hard-packed earth until it lay before her, a great mass of supple, workable cowhide.

"It's according to need they serve us," said Anust. "A tent this bag might be. A shield from wind and rain. A creel, perhaps, for gathering food and fuel or transporting wool or fish." As she spoke she unlatched her own leather sack, lifted it with both hands, and dumped its contents—a load of red and purple fruit—out upon the floor. Then, deftly folding and stitching it together, she converted it into a small pouch and reattached it to her belt.

"But a curse these bags became to us long ago," said Sengann, ducking inside from his post at the door, "the time Semeon son of Erglan led the three Nonads of our people into the land of Greece. Then it was with these same bags that the king of that land forced us to carry earth from the low valleys to the high mountains, to make him fields and farms on the tops of the rough-headed hills!"

"Forgetful you are, Sengann," chided Rury, "that these same bags were also our deliverance from that place. *Currachs* they became in our hands, the way that we escaped in them from the land of Greece, sailing over the dark sea in our leather boats."

"Oh, ay," sneered Slanga. "Escape we did—only to find enslavement again in Eire! First under the boots of the cursed Fomorians. Then at the hands of the cruel Milesians, what time Lia Fail vanished and all the fairy folk were driven underground. And now the *Morrigu*!"

Eny shivered. The word sounded familiar somehow, though she could not remember having heard it before. Something about it sent a chill into the marrow of her bones.

"The Morrigu?" she said, drawing one of the fleeces up over her shoulders. "What's that?"

Rury looked up from his stitching with a frown. "I have spoken of her before, not mentioning her name," he said grimly. "Sure it is she who sent her henchmen to fetch you to her tower on Tory Island. She it is, no doubt, who brought you into the Sidhe from the first."

"The daughter of Ernmas she was," said Liber, seating herself beside her husband, "one of the most powerful women of the Tuatha De Danann, and ever more powerful she sought to become. Then came the time that Ollamh Folla, lieutenant to the Danaan Chief Lugh, sent Lia Fail out of the land to protect it from the conquering Milesians. The Morrigu was inflamed with rage. She betrayed Lugh and Ollamh, though he had been her lover. To Tory she went, making herself mistress of the Fomorians, a race of shape-changing giants. With their help she utterly destroyed Tara. As it is written in the ancient book,

> Badb and Macha, greatness of wealth; Morrigu,
> springs of craftiness:
>
> Sources of bitter fighting were the three daugh-
> ters of Ernmas."

"Now she rules the Sidhe," said Sengann. "All of it but the fortress of Baile Daoine Sidhe, where the last of the faithful Danaans are holding out against her."

"And what about you people?" said Eny.

Rury smiled sadly. "It's small account she makes of the Fir Bolg, though laying us under heavy tribute and taxing all our produce: wool, crops, orchards, fisheries. Sorry I am to say that some of our folk serve her willingly. Our little band opposes her as best we may, if not by fighting, then by fooling. When all else fails, it's running and hiding we do best."

"But what does she want?"

"The Stone, of course. Lia Fail. For it is said that the one possessing it is destined to rule. None may be king or queen without it. By its virtue she is hoping to reunite the Sidhe and the Overworld. Her desire is to be mistress over all! Every inch of her power she is putting forth in search of it."

"And yet she is seeking one other thing as well," said Anust, pressing Eny's hand and looking intently into her eyes. "A prophecy there is among the Danaans, and it is what it says: that only a maiden of perfect purity, a maiden of chaste heart and seeing eyes, may ever hope to—"

At that moment another shadow darkened the door of the hut. In came the aged couple, Genann and Crucha, with another Fir Bolg between them, a man Eny hadn't seen before. He was ancient, stooping, and white-bearded, dressed in a sheepskin vest and leaning on a gnarled and knotty staff. His bright blue eyes shone like tiny stars amid the wrinkles of his brown face.

"Semeon!" cried Rury, scrambling to his feet and taking the newcomer by the hand. "Come and see, brother! Our girl is up and awake! Come and see for yourself!"

With that, the old man tottered forward and stood leaning on his staff directly in front of Eny's makeshift couch. Then he bent forward and peered into her eyes. For a long time he studied her face intently, never speaking, never blinking, never moving a muscle. At last he closed his eyes, sighed deeply, dropped his staff, and raised his open palms above his head in a gesture expressive of gratitude and relief.

"Is it not what I was telling you?" said Rury, hurrying to his brother's side. "Is it not what I said when first we brought her to Luimneach?"

Semeon, without taking his eyes off Eny's face, made a slight beckoning motion with the fingers of his right hand. In answer, Liber brought a fleece and a couple of frayed cushions and assisted him to a comfortable sitting position on the floor. Once settled, he drew a long-stemmed clay pipe from his vest and lit it from a smoldering straw that Rury brought him from the oven. Then, puffing slowly on the pipe and releasing a circle of pure white smoke into the dark recesses of the hut's conical roof, he bent toward Eny with his elbows planted firmly on his knees.

"Now it's my turn to be at the telling of a tale," he said.

Chapter Fifteen

THE TALE OF EITHNE

"In the time long ago," Semeon began, "when Eremon, first king of the Milesians, ruled over Eire, and the Tuatha De Danann were gone into exile under the ground, having secreted Lia Fail out of the land, Manannan mac Lir had a daughter named Fedelm, she being given in fosterage to the Danaan prince Angus Og. Now the handmaid of Fedelm, daughter to Angus's steward, was the fairest girl in all the Sidhe, though but a simple servant. One eye of her eyes was as brown as the heifer's, the other as blue as a summer sea, for she was gifted with the double sight, perceiving the world above and the world below. And the name of the handmaid was Eithne.

"This Eithne, for her beauty, was courted by a chieftain of the De Danann, Finbarr by name, but she refused his suit. Then it was by force he would have possessed her. At that rose up the spirit of Eithne like a flame of fire. A keenness for purity and virtue not natural to fairy folk, but pertaining hitherto only to the souls of mortal women and men, awoke within her heart. In the heat of that flame and by its power she rebuffed this Finbarr, and turning away from the life of that world, she began earnestly to desire the life of another.

From that time out she sustained herself no more upon the magical food of the people of the Sidhe, but was nourished instead by the will of God—that, and the milk of two cows brought by Angus from the righteous land in the east.

"Now the Danaan folk, having possessed Lia Fail time out of mind, it being the very Stone of Bethel itself, age not nor die like the sons and daughters of men. In youth they grow from childhood to maturity, but afterwards abide unchanged by the lapse of time. So it was that when fifteen hundred years had passed in the Overland, Laoghaire then ruling in Eremon's place, Eithne went forth from the Sidhe one time to bathe with Fedelm in the River Boyne. For you must be knowing that there are many doors between your world and ours, one of them being the great mound of Brugh na Boyne.

"And when the maidens, having risen from the waters of the river, were arraying themselves on the shore, then it was that Eithne missed her *feth fiada,* the Invisible Cloak of the Danaans that hides them from mortal eyes and lets them pass freely between the land above and the land below. And as she went along the bank in search of this treasure, Fedelm following, she came to a well, and thirteen men sitting around it in robes of purest white with open books before them on their knees.

"'Who are you?' said Eithne in great wonder; for the sight of her eyes told her that these men, being mortal, were yet more than mortal men. 'Is it gods you are, or fairy folk, or men from the hills of the Sidhe?'

"'I am Patrick,' said the one, standing in the midst of the twelve, 'and it would be better for you to believe in God than to be asking who we ourselves are.'

"'What God is it you speak of?' asked Eithne then. 'Whose son is he, and where does he live? Is he young or old? Rich or poor? Strong or weak? Is he one of the ever-living ones? Does he have sons and daughters? May we know his name?'

"Then Patrick took those two maidens by the hand and began to school them in the true faith, urging them with many words to join their lives to the life of the King of Glory. And when he was finished, a great desire came upon Eithne, and she said, 'It is my one wish that I might see Christ, my true husband and the lover of my soul.'

"'That may not be,' answered Patrick, 'except, like Him, you lay aside immortality and embrace weakness, humility, and death.'

"At that word Eithne, being only a servant, but burning still with a passion for holiness and love, rejoiced in heart. But Fedelm, daughter of Manannan mac Lir, the mighty Danaan chief, cast her *feth fiada* about her shoulders and disappeared into the Sidhe. So then, Fedelm being gone, Patrick took some of the water of the well and received Eithne into the church of Christ and the race of mortals with the rite of baptism. And when in later years she slept in death, brought low by a dreadful sickness, the men of Patrick laid her in a bed and covered her over with lilies and white linen, keening her there.

"But it is told among the people of the Sidhe that the death of Eithne was in this manner: that as she sat one time at prayer in a walled garden beside the Boyne, she heard a sound of many voices rushing through the air, lamenting and wailing and calling her by name, as if from a great distance. And she rose up to answer, knowing them for the voices of her kindred, the Danaans, and that they were longing for her and seeking her in vain. For Eithne was well beloved in the Sidhe. Moreover, since her departing, a rumor had gone abroad in the land underground that only a maiden of perfect chastity, such as she was, might bring Lia Fail back to Faery and restore its powers to the Tuatha De Danann, though wiser heads said that the Stone does not return, but must pass on and come at last to the place of its final destiny beyond all worlds. However that may be, Eithne, hearing those voices, was overcome with a desperate yearning and fell down faint and swooning; so that within a few days she lay dead on the breast of Saint Patrick. Yet it is said that she, or one like her, will come to us again in the fullness of time."

The old man's voice fell silent. Eny sat before him with the eyes of all the Fir Bolg fixed upon her, feeling as if she'd been caught in a crowd without any clothes on. A hot blush crept up her neck. Her cheeks and forehead burned. She wanted to pull the sheepskins up over her head, to hide beneath the bed of rags, to find the lost *feth fiada* and disappear. Except for the boom and sizzle of the waves on the beach outside the door there was not a sound to be heard in the little hut. The air was as still, as tense, and as pregnant with anticipation as the atmosphere before a thunderstorm. At last the voice of Rury broke the spell.

"And now that *our* tales are told," he gently urged, "it comes into my mind that, after sharing so many perils and adventures, it is still *yourself* we are not surely knowing. I was at the point of asking when the giants burst forth upon us from the wood, but from that time out I never had the chance. Not a man or woman sits or stands before you now but such as you may truly call a friend, and that to the bitter death. So then, my girl, will you not tell us: What is your name?"

Eny swallowed hard. "It's Eny," she said in a small, quavering voice. "Eny Ariello. That's sort of American—at least my mom always told me so—for *Eithne*."

Chapter Sixteen

THE MAELSTROM

Another long pause followed. Then Eny cried, "I was right! I *told* Morgan we couldn't trust that woman! This is all her doing!"

Crucha gripped her by both arms and looked up intently into her face. "What woman, child? Who is it you are speaking of?"

"Madame Medea, she called herself! She wants that Stone, and she wants *me!* I'll bet anything *she* was that old woman at the Cave of the Hands. *She* sent the crow and made the music! *She* put the vision of the green island in my head! She was there at the ford, too, when the giants were chasing us. I saw her eyes!"

Semeon took a long and thoughtful pull at his pipe. He closed his eyes and blew out another lazily expanding circle of smoke. "If it was a crow you saw, then be sure the Morrigu was near at hand. The bird is her talisman and pet. And it is what I myself am thinking, that she and your Madame Medea are entirely one and the same. She it is drew you here, Eny, the better to lay her hands on you. It is her belief that you are the maid of perfect chastity. If that is true, then the Stone is useless to her without you."

Sengann spit and muttered a curse. "The Morrigu's tower is no place for a slip of a girl like you. Its dungeons are filled with Overlanders taken captive in her quest for Lia Fail, and they in the custody of Balor, the one-eyed Fomorian king. It is not kindly he treats them."

"Sengann tells true," said Rury, casting his eyes grimly around the circle. "So now, whether we live or die, it is clear what course we must take. We dare not let the enchantress find the girl."

It was agreed that Eny and the Fir Bolg from Rury's dun should stay in Luimneach with Semeon's folk until it became too dangerous to remain. Semeon sent scouts to Baile Daoine Sidhe, the Danaan stronghold, to consult with the De Danann and keep an eye on the pass of Beinn Meallain. Meanwhile, watch posts were established throughout the foothills, at the crossings of Inber Domnan and Inber Colpa, and all along the south coast of Mag Adair as far as Taman. Every sentry was instructed to send word to the little village on the seashore at the first sign of approaching Fomorians.

"It is among the Tuatha De Danann you rightly belong," said Semeon to Eny, "and to them you must go in time. But not today. Sure the Morrigu will be seeking you there, her henchmen having seen Rury's band going that way. But about Luimneach and the poor Fir Bolg she will not trouble her head at present."

"Luimneach," repeated Eny, letting the melodious name roll off the tip of her tongue. "That's beautiful. What does it mean?"

"Low-lying," Semeon answered. "For the dun sits in the very mouth of the sea itself."

"And what about *your* village, Rury?" Eny wanted to know. "What's *it* called?"

Rury glanced at Sengann and frowned. "Eba Eochaid," he said. "After Eochy, the brother of us both. But of him we do not speak."

So Eny lived among the Fir Bolg, observing their ways and learning their crafts and trades. She went fishing on the ocean with Semeon's sons, Gann and Erc, in the *currachs* they made from the leather bags at their belts. Soon she gained enough facility in handling these unruly little boats to be able to explore the bays and inlets on her own. Gann and Erc praised her skill and marveled at her quickness. But they solemnly warned her to stay close to the shore, lest she fall into what they called the *Morslogh*, a great maelstrom or whirlpool that spun its dark waters in a powerful spiral round a bottomless black hole not far off the Point of Taman.

When she wasn't on the water, she helped Rury and Crimthann cut birch poles and thatch sleeping shelters and baking huts for the newcomers. Liber taught her to spin and weave. Crucha showed her how to grind grain in a hand mill and bake round loaves of sweet brown bread. Rindail, the village shepherd, took her into the foothills to watch the flocks and shear the sheep. Etar, Semeon's niece, introduced her to the secrets of the potter's wheel. Sengann and Slanga instructed her in the finer points of gathering mushrooms and blueberries and hunting with spear and bow.

But Eny didn't simply learn from the Fir Bolg. She taught them things as well. They had no fiddles, but a few of them were good at piping on simple six-holed whistles and fifes. Once she got the trick of coaxing music out of these primitive wooden instruments—which she did very quickly—she played them every tune she knew, including "The Silver Spire," "The Lark in the Morning," and "The May Morning Dew." She told them stories, too. But the most important thing Eny taught the Fir Bolg was the art of slinging stones.

"You don't need to be afraid of the giants," she told them. "You've got everything you need to fight them right here: plenty of leather and lots of pebbles on the shore. Here, let me show you. Just tie two good thongs to a round patch of leather like this. Then find yourself a smooth stone and put it in the sling—like so. Now swing it around your head really fast—see? Then aim and let go! Wham! Much better than those dinky little spears."

They had to agree. What's more, they concluded that the sling was just what they needed to fend off an impending Fomorian attack. So they took up Eny's challenge with enthusiasm and proved to be talented pupils. In a very short time the Fir Bolg had all become expert slingers and marksmen.

Yet even with so much to keep her occupied, Eny could never completely escape the heartache of her homesickness. Though she loved the Fir Bolg, her longing for Santa Piedra grew deeper with every passing day. Anust seemed to know when her suffering was at its worst, and at such times she would take her by the hand and lead her on long evening walks down the pebble-strewn beach. Around the curve of the little bay they would go, to an upward sloping meadow that rose in soft green terraces from the level of the jeweled beach to the pine-clad heights at the foot of Beinn Meallain. There they would lie on their backs among fragrant grasses and tall-stemmed flowers, gazing up at creamy clouds in a burning blue sky where rainbow-colored birds flew in bright lines and wedges athwart the red setting sun. After that they would stroll through shadowy orchards of yellow-branched and ruby-fruited trees, up the grass-clothed, sheep-dotted hills to a spot where they could turn and look out across the glittering beach and glassy green sea to the distant purple horizon.

In moments like these, Eny came close to forgetting her father, her mother, Morgan, and St. Halistan's Church. Close, but not too close. For stunning though they were, the wonders of the Sidhe never failed to remind her of Laguna Verde and the softly folded hills above Santa Piedra. Often, returning from a walk with Anust, she would say to Rury, "It *is* beautiful here, but I want to go home!"

"And so you should," Rury would reply. "It's there you *will* go if the Fir Bolg have anything to say about it. But what time you do, remember that Rury of the Road has put you under *geis*—a vow and a bond—to do all in your power to keep yourself and Lia Fail out of the hands of the Morrigu. And if ever again you should find the door between this world and your own, I charge you to come back and help the poor Fir Bolg win their freedom!"

And Eny promised that she would.

At last there came a day when she found herself paddling out beyond the breakers to go fishing with Rury, Gann, and Erc. The sea was calm, the morning bright. The sun flashed like fire on the peaks of the wavelets and the tips of the polished oars as they rowed their *currachs* into the salmon-rich waters between the mainland and the isle of Rachra.

"Remember now what it is we told you," called Erc as he tossed a corner of a great hempen net into the bottom of her boat. "Let you and Rury stretch the net and hold your place with the oars. Gann and I are to drop our end in the sea and trawl shoreward. When the net is full spread, it's then we will pull it up on our side, the two of you to follow after. It's a rich haul we should make, the seas being thick with scales and fins this time of the year."

"Myself, I like a line and a hook," shouted Rury with an exaggerated wink at Eny. "Still, it is a good plan, and it may work."

Erc scowled. "It is no plan," he answered, weighting his corner of the net with a large stone and lowering it into the water by a long rope. "It is the way we fish in Luimneach." He bent and tied the rope to the frame of the *currach*. Then he and his brother turned and rowed off in the direction of the land.

Eny watched them go, absentmindedly treading water while Rury, with another wink and a wave, paddled away to a spot about ten yards to her left. Above, below, and all around her stretched the endless soothing blue of sea and sky. The midmorning sun was hot on her hair, the smell of salt pungent in her nostrils. She leaned on her oars and sighed a sigh of deep content.

"Mind you pay attention," called Rury. "Look out for the signal!"

Eny nodded and smiled. Staring off lazily toward the shore, she held the *currach* steady and let her thoughts drift away to Santa Piedra. As she gazed, a hazy veil seemed to fall across the scene. A picture of the tide pools below the Cave of the Hands emerged before her eyes. Slowly, by imperceptible stages, the dazzling strand of Luimneach became the white crescent beach of La Coruna Inlet. The pinnacled tower of St. Halistan's rose up tall against the violet backdrop of Beinn Meallain. Almost choking with a painful yearning, she leaned forward in the boat, imagining her father hurrying through the halls of the church with a bunch of keys at his belt. She heard the voice of her mother taking calls at the switchboard. She saw Simon Brach, a mop in his hand, opening the little green door underneath the tower stairs.

Suddenly the vision ceased and the Sidhe was the Sidhe again. A flock of geese—or were they wild swans?—swooped down from over the mountains of Beinn Meallain. Alighting along the shoreline, the birds lifted their heads and buried their feet in the sand. Once firmly planted, they elongated their bodies and stretched their necks up toward the sky. Then they began to grow. Taller and taller they grew until they were no longer birds at all but trees.

Eny blinked. As she sat there bobbing over the waves in her little coracle, an inexplicable chill took hold of her. A shadow fell over the sun and she shuddered from head to toe. Was she still daydreaming? Or could this actually be happening? Before her very eyes the trees that had been birds were sprouting arms and legs. Their leafy crowns were turning into huge hairy heads. An instant later the transformation was complete, and a host of gigantic human shapes stood ranged along the beach just in front of the little village of Luimneach. Shaking their massive arms and lifting their heavy feet, they lunged forward and stepped into the waves. Eny cried out and looked over at Rury. She knew at once that he had seen them too.

It was in that very moment that Erc turned and began to haul up his corner of the fishing net. He took two pulls at the rope; then dropped it and began gesticulating and pointing and shouting at them.

"Behind you, you squinting clowns! Behind you!" he yelled.

Eny twisted in her seat and looked back. A mist like the one she had seen on the face of Laguna Verde was rolling down upon them, swelling and filling the entire space between the mainland and the steep shores of Rachra. In front of it another troop of giants, as many as ten or fifteen of them, were wading straight toward her through the deep water, so huge that the shining of the waves could be seen between their legs. She dipped her oars and began to pull toward Rury with all her might.

"Not *this* way!" he cried, standing up in his *currach* and frantically waving her off. "Go *that* way! East! Around the head of Rachra! Make for the mouth of Inber Domnan!"

She could see at once that he was right. The Fomorians from the beach had cut off their retreat toward Luimneach and the nearer shore. Already they were so close that the dull flames of their eyes were clearly discernible. Closer and closer they came, their great stomping feet sending up the spray in colossal iridescent fountains. As she watched, they bent down, extended their enormous hands, and crushed the fragile *currachs* of Gann and Erc. They they flung the shrieking Fir Bolg fishermen into the sea.

Eny screamed. Turning back to Rury she saw a huge leg, like the trunk of an ancient oak, come crashing down into the water just in front of his little boat. "Row, Eny, row!" she heard him shout as the ocean rained down around her head in a cataract of foam. She bent to her oars and pulled for all she was worth.

As she came around the wooded point of Rachra her ears were assaulted by a deafening roar, a din like the sound of a thousand oceans thundering over bottomless cliffs at the edge of the world. Trembling and aching, cold and sick with dread, she turned to her right and saw it: the *Morslogh*, the great whirling maelstrom, a seething, steaming tempest of boiling brine, a monstrous glassy green funnel wheeling and spinning endlessly down into the bare, black rocky depths at the bottom of the sea. If only she could steer a course between its inescapable brim and the razor-sharp reefs along the shore! If only she could get to the beach! Once at the river she could hide among the reeds and willows. From there she could make her way upstream to the mountains and the fortress of the Tuatha De Danann. It was her only chance.

Gripping the oars and biting her lip, she began to pull for the shore. Cautiously, hesitantly, her head and her fingertips tingling, her stomach churning with nausea, she rowed steadily toward the small inlet at the mouth of Inber Domnan, constantly shifting her gaze from the right to the left, every moment expecting to crunch up against a rock or fall prey to the irresistible tug of the whirlpool's current.

On and on she rowed. When at last she found the courage to glance back over her shoulder, a lightning bolt of hope flashed through her heart—the shoreline was definitely drawing nearer! But there was something else as well: a black spot between her *currach* and the shimmering strand, a dark shape moving swiftly toward her over the water. She stopped paddling and peered out across the tossing waves.

It was a boat. A big black high-sided, deep-keeled boat with a furled red sail, its lofty prow carved in the shape of a screaming raven. In the bow stood a little man like one of the Fir Bolg, his face averted so that she could not see it clearly. On a bench in the stern, his broad back toward her, sat a huge, round-skulled oarsman. Amidships, leaning on the mast with one slender white hand, stood a tall, dark-haired woman, wrapped and muffled in black to her piercing green eyes.

Eny's heart sank. Salt tears stung her eyes and clouded her vision. Gann and Erc were lost. Rury could hardly have fared any better. The village of Luimneach was doomed, and she had no reason to believe she would ever see Santa Piedra again. In the midst of the darkness and confusion she could think of only one thing: She was under *geis*. She had made a vow to Rury. She had promised that, come what may, she would *never* allow herself to fall into the hands of the Morrigu.

Precious seconds passed, each one like an eternity. The grim black boat drew nearer. The woman's mouth and face remained hidden, but it seemed to Eny that her green eyes smiled.

There was only one thing to do and she knew it. She set her jaw and pictured her father's flashing grin. She remembered her mother's infectious laugh. She thought about her fiddle and the tower stairs. Then, with one last desperate heave, she drove the nose of the *currach* sideways. Tossing the oars overboard, she leaned heavily into the deadly current. There was a howl of whirling winds and a roar of rushing waters. And then her little boat slipped over the edge and went hurtling down into the depths of the *Morslogh*.

Chapter Seventeen

THE LEGEND OF COMPOSTELA

Morgan felt the earth tremble beneath his feet as the church door clicked shut behind him and the sounds of Eny and Simon Brach playing fiddle went silent. At the curb he nearly collided with a dark shape emerging from the mist. It was George Ariellos, just arriving at the church office with a bundle of supplies under his arm.

"Morgan! I'm glad I ran into you!" he said. "Dinner tonight, the Reverend's coming. He can only stay a little while, he's got some kind of meeting at seven. But he especially wants to see you."

"I'm sorry, George, but I can't make it. I have to go somewhere."

"The hospital, eh? Well, we'll save some for you."

He was turning to go when a thought struck him.

"George," he said, "you said there were other stories. Other stories of the Stone?"

George sat down on the curb and motioned for Morgan to do the same. "The old Californios—my people—they also have stories. Stories of missions and miracles. Stories of saints and relics. Stories of signs and wonders." His teeth glinted white in the dusky mist. "You're asking about the tale of La

Santa Piedra and the legend of Compostela." George said softly, "Our story about a Holy Stone. A tale of Old Spain and Old California and Santa Piedra itself. A story that's been in the Ariello family for generations. A story about the Ariellos."

Morgan looked through the mist at the monolithic shape of the church tower. *Another holy stone?* he wondered. *Another stone of power?*

"Well," he said at last, "are you going to tell me about it?"

George leaned back into the grass. Gradually his smile faded, settling into a straight-mouthed, thin-lipped, firm-jawed expression of solemn pleasure:

"It happened during the reign of the second Alfonso, king of Asturias, descendant and heir of Pelayo the Goth— the one who drove the Moors out of Spain. Jorge de Ariel was a poor but pious shepherd who lived in the foothills above Brigantium in Galicia.

"In the early springtime, when the nights were clear and the sky sparkled with a thousand million stars, Jorge penned his flock in a steep and narrow glen at the back of a high meadow overlooking the sea. Then he lay down to sleep, pillowing his head on an odd-looking stone.

"But sleep fled from him—or so it seemed to Jorge. For into his brain came seeping a persistent and swelling light, hot and blood-red behind his tightly closed eyelids. He turned his face to the earth and covered his head with his *manto*. But it was no use. He could not keep the light out. So he threw off the cloak, lifted his head from the stone, and sat up.

"What a sight it was that met his poor, bedazzled eyes! The brightness around him was like the brightness of the night when the heavenly hosts sang the birth of the Holy Child! Jorge knelt trembling on the stony ground, one hand upon the pillow stone, the other shading his eyes against the terrible glare. He swallowed hard and looked up."

"What was it?" pressed Morgan. "What did he see?"

George smiled sublimely. "Angels. Angels going up and down on a golden stairway. It rose from the ground just beside the strange stone and climbed higher and ever higher until it disappeared among the swarms of swirling stars. At the very top shone a single star, more radiant by far than any other, a star to be compared with the star of the Nativity. Down to earth it cast its pure light in a bright, narrow shaft, straight down to a spot of ground at the bottom of the field.

"Up jumped Jorge de Ariel. He wrapped his cloak about his shoulders and ran over the rough ground, through the chill of the night, directly to the place where the star's light touched the earth. There, in a grassy meadow near La Coruna, where the sound of the crashing waves is never far distant, he discovered yet another wonder. For amid a heap of sod and stones, as if it had just been unearthed, stood a marble box like a coffin, milky white and gleaming softly in the heavenly light. Words were engraved on its lid in the Latin tongue: *Reliqua Sancti Iacobi, apostoli, martyri, et fratris Domini nostri.*

"Poor Jorge! Don't you think his mind was spinning like a windmill in a gale? He thought he must be dreaming!

But it was not so. He pondered what he should do, then ran to fetch the priest from the town of La Coruña. The priest examined the marble box and told him that it held the bones of no less a person than Saint James, the brother of our Lord!

"The townspeople built a chapel on the spot and enshrined the marble coffin in an alcove at the back of the chancel. At Jorge's request, the strangely shaped pillow stone was also laid to rest in the little church, just below the altar.

"In time the chapel became a magnificent cathedral. The place was given a name: Santiago de Compostela, 'St. James of the Field of the Star.' For hundreds of years it was the destination of many holy pilgrimages."

The voice ceased. Morgan, like a sleeper waking from a dream, came to himself. George gathered up his supplies and made as if to stand up and leave.

"Wait a minute!" said Morgan. "You can't stop there. You said this story was about Santa Piedra. You said it had something to do with the Ariellos."

George knelt down next to Morgan. "So I did. For centuries Jorge's pillow stone was regarded with great reverence. When the first Franciscan padres came to the New World, they carried it with them in the ship as a holy relic. From Vera Cruz in Mexico they brought it north along the Camino Real. It made stops at San Luis Rey, San Juan Capistrano, Santa Barbara, and San Carlos Borromeo de Carmelo, always under the supervision of a young Franciscan novice named Juan Bautista Alvarado de Ariello, companion to Father

Junipero Serra and descendant of that same Jorge de Ariel of Galicia. Its last known resting place, according to the tale, was in the mission church of Santa Compostela."

George paused and gave Morgan a significant look. "You see what that means, don't you?"

Morgan stared back, bewildered. Perhaps he was just too tired to think.

"It means the stone is here," said George. "Here in Santa Piedra."

And with that he vanished into the church.

By the time Morgan reached Front Street the fog was lifting and a light rain was beginning to fall. The sidewalk was oddly deserted for four thirty in the afternoon; except for the distant boom of the surf and the high, thin cries of the gulls, everything was wrapped in an eerie silence. Turning up his collar, he hurried down the street, not stopping until he stood shivering beneath the swinging, creaking image of the White Hand.

There he paused, chewing his lip while the rain dripped off the end of his nose. Slowly he reached for the doorhandle, then hesitated and pulled his hand away. Maybe Eny was right about the strange woman. Maybe she couldn't be trusted. Then again, Eny might be jumping to conclusions. Madame Medea was an *adept*—an expert in the art of alchemy—and he needed her help. His mother's life was at stake. Eny was too timid, too superstitious.

"*Crrawwcckkk!*"

A brash, grating, cackling noise over his head stopped him dead in his tracks. He froze and looked up. Directly above him, perched on the iron rod from which the wooden signboard hung squeaking in the wind, sat a huge black crow. It cocked its head and regarded him sharply out of a beady eye. Instinctively, Morgan ducked and shied away. But then another sound—a sharp whisper—recalled his attention to the shop entrance.

"Psst! Young mister!"

It was Eochy, the odd little man he and Eny had encountered upon their first visit to Madame Medea's, beckoning to him from behind the red door. "A word with you, sir!" he said. "That's all I'd be asking!"

Again Morgan hesitated. He was about to run when the door of a neighboring establishment—La Coruna Gifts and Cards—flew open and out stepped two painfully familiar figures: Baxter Knowles and his father, the wealthy and highly regarded Brevard Knowles. Except for the pin-striped blue suit that marked him as a formidable man of business, the elder Knowles was just a larger and thicker version of his imperious offspring. Morgan looked from father to son, cursing his abysmal luck. They hadn't noticed him yet, but it was plain they were moving in his direction. There wasn't a moment to lose. With a quick glance up and down the street, he made a dash for the door, pushed past Eochy, and stumbled into the dusky interior of the shop.

"What do you want?" he gasped.

"Just this," said the little man with a cautious sidewise glance. "I'm thinking you'd best be out of this."

"Out of what?"

Before Eochy could answer, a sharp jolt set the entire building rattling from floor to ceiling. The front window clattered. The glassware and ceramic flasks and wind chimes tinkled and rang along the shelves. The door slammed shut as if moved by an invisible hand.

"Who's there?" said a dark, melodious voice.

The strains of harp music, which Morgan had not noticed until that moment, suddenly ceased. There was a sound of clacking beads at the back of the room. A moment later Madame Medea appeared.

"I've been expecting you," she said, a broad smile slowly overspreading her smooth oval face. "Come and sit down. You like hot chocolate?"

Morgan gazed up into her round green eyes. Instantly a throng of hopeful possibilities leaped forward and took possession of his confused and overcrowded brain. He nodded mutely and took her proffered hand. She led him to a chair at one of the wrought-iron tables, lit a candle, and sat down across from him. "Bring us cocoa, Eochy," she said with a wave of her delicate white hand.

She looked different than he remembered her: friendlier, more inviting, more down-to-earth somehow. Gone was her gypsy turban. Her black hair flowed loosely over her shoulders. The robe she wore was soft and white, plain yet elegant in its simplicity. At her throat hung a five-pointed silver star. From her ears dangled two dainty pink nautilus shells.

"Now then," she said as Eochy, head bowed and eyes downcast, set two steaming mugs of cocoa on the table. "What have you come to see me about, Morgan Izaak?"

Morgan took a sip of chocolate, conscious all the while of the unblinking green eyes. When he was finished, he set the mug down, looked straight into her face, and said:

"I think I've found the Stone."

The large green eyes grew larger. As if in answer to their questioning stare, he reached into his shirt and pulled out the sealed flask. Carefully he placed it on the table beside the candle as a single drop of sweat trickled down his forehead. Then he sat back in his chair and looked up at her, a trembly, fluttering feeling rising in the pit of his stomach. He swallowed hard. "That's why I'm here. I was hoping it might be the Philosophers' Stone, but I'm not sure. I thought you'd be able to tell me. I've been slaving over it for a long time. You said—"

She stopped him with a raised finger. Scraping back her chair, she rose to her full height and again held out her hand. "Come with me," she said.

Slowly he got to his feet and followed. "Falor!" he heard her cry as together they ducked through the screen of hanging beads at the rear of the shop. "Prepare the *athanor!*"

Nothing could have prepared him for the sight that met his eyes on the other side of the door. When the last strand of rattling beads had fallen from his shoulders, he found himself standing beside Madame Medea on a pavement of heavy flagstones in a vast echoing hall of carved granite. On an iron perch at his elbow sat the lady's pet crow, its head tucked under its wing. Not far away stood a shapely harp with a tall golden pillar and twenty-one silver strings. On either side seven massive stone columns went marching down the sides of the chamber. Those on the right were inscribed with the symbols of the seven planets. Those on the left bore the names of the seven steps of the alchemical process: *Calcination, Dissolution, Separation, Conjunction, Fermentation, Distillation,* and *Coagulation.*

Morgan rubbed his eyes and looked around. Everywhere were tables and benches crowded with the instruments of the alchemist's trade: tripods and cauldrons, charts and globes, astrolabes, scales, cucurbits, funnels, and sieves. In the shadows between the torch-bearing pillars lurked a confusion of barrels, kettles, ceramic jars, and bronze vats. It was exactly like the pictures of alchemical laboratories Morgan had seen in his father's medieval manuscripts except in one astonishing detail: *It had no roof.* Where the ceiling and rafters ought to have been there was nothing but empty space: an endlessly ascending blackness filled with flaming suns, spinning stars, and pearly silver moons—whether real or merely decorative, he could not tell.

Tightening her grip, the woman drew him down the center of the hall to a wall at its further end. Its right-hand portion was covered with a series of tile mosaics: the Seven-tiered Pyramid, the Signs of the Zodiac, the Mystic Rose, and the Ladder of the Wise. But its left half was dominated entirely by an imposing red-brick furnace: the athanor. In the shadow of the athanor's cavernous copper hood, his broad back bare, his round head glistening with perspiration, stood Falor, pumping a huge pair of bellows by means of a heavy chain. To Morgan, the big man looked like a gilded storm cloud on the edge of a fiery horizon. Except for his shadowy silhouette, there was nothing to shield their eyes from the blinding blaze within the furnace's mouth.

When they had come so close to the athanor that Morgan felt he could no longer stand the heat, Madame Medea stopped and let go of his hand.

"Powders and potions I can make for myself. Let me show you."

Taking a jar from a shelf on the wall, she uncorked it and pushed it into Morgan's hand. He flinched and backed away.

"There's nothing to be afraid of!" she said. "Don't you see what it is? Not the white powder but the *red!* I have a copious supply at my disposal. You know what the red powder can do, don't you?"

Without waiting for an answer, she seized a lump of dull gray metal from a workbench and placed it in a small porcelain receptacle about the size of a coffee cup. Gripping the cup with a long pair of iron tongs, she tossed her dark hair back over her shoulders and approached the furnace.

"Pump up the fire, Falor!" she shouted, thrusting the crucible into the glowing heart of the inferno. "Melt this lead for our young friend!"

The huge man bent to his task with every ounce of his titanic strength. Faster and harder he plied the bellows. Soon the firestorm within the athanor was pulsing with all the swirling fury of a white-hot star. Morgan buried his face in the crook of his arm and stumbled a few steps into the darkness, sick and faint with the overpowering heat. He knew nothing more until the sound of Madame Medea's voice recalled him to his senses.

"Bring the red powder!" he heard her say. "Quickly!"

He turned to face her. She was standing directly in front of him, holding out the smoking crucible at the end of the glowing tongs. The metal within the little porcelain receptacle had become a bubbling, boiling, erubescent mass of liquid fire.

"Now sprinkle some on the top!" she commanded. "What are you waiting for? Not too much—just a pinch! That's right. Now watch carefully. What do you see?"

Morgan stooped down and peered closely into the crucible. As he looked, the seething red-orange molten metal began to change before his eyes. A sequence of color shifts, similar to but distinct from the one he had witnessed inside the alembic, began to appear. The brilliant orange faded to brown. The brown resolved itself into a swirled pattern of cloudy darks and lights, like spirals of cream in coffee. Gradually these whorls paled and lightened, becoming a uniform silvery whiteness. Then the white burst suddenly into all the colors of a peacock's tail. By stages, the lighter and brighter hues of the spectrum began to predominate, until all was a smooth and shining lemon yellow.

Instantly Madame Medea plunged the crucible into a vat of water. Thick clouds of steam rose up and obscured the hall. When the air had cleared, she took Morgan by the arm and led him to the workbench. Picking up the porcelain cup, she turned it upside down and tapped it lightly on the bottom with her finger. What dropped out was a perfect lump of gold—the purest, finest, silkiest gold Morgan had ever seen.

"You see?" she said.

Morgan stared. "Yes," he muttered. "The Red Elixir. Hardly anybody has ever succeeded in making it. Only Alexander Seton and Nicholas Flamel, I suppose. Helvetius, too, maybe. It changes base metals into gold. And if it can do that," he said breathlessly, "it can also—"

She laid a finger on his lips. "No," she said. "It cannot. That is precisely what it *cannot* do. This business of turning lead into gold is fine for children and lovers of bright trinkets. But what does gold really get you in the end? It can't heal disease or grant eternal life. Nor does it contain the power of the stars. That is exactly what so many of the greatest alchemists never understood. A *few* did, of course," she added, gently stroking his hair. Her eyes narrowed and she smiled. "Your father, for instance."

Morgan felt the blood rush to his head. He took a step backward, bumping up against the bench. "What do you mean?" he said.

"Don't you know?" She laughed lightly. "It's the reason I *brought* you here. My sources led me to believe that you know something about the Stone of Destiny. And the Stone of Destiny is the key to everything. It is the one source of the power Paracelsus was seeking. It makes kings and deposes tyrants. Only in its presence can this white powder become the *Elixir Vitae*. It's all a lie, you know—those stories about Nicholas Flamel living to be six hundred years old. Without the Stone of Destiny there is no healing, no extension of life. It is the Satisfaction of All Desire. And you are connected with it somehow."

"Me? I don't know what you're talking about."

"I wouldn't be so sure. It is here, in this place, in this city, somewhere nearby." She took his face between her two hands and looked straight into his eyes. "I asked you to go and find it for me. That is exactly what I intend you should do."

"Look," said Morgan, pulling away, "I came here because I need your help! My mom's really sick, and I want her to get well. If you can't—"

"Oh, but I *can*," said the lady. "But not without the Stone of Destiny. I'm sure you understand. And now I believe our little visit has come to an end. Please come back as soon as you have something to tell me. Not without your pretty friend of course. It would not make me happy to see you again without her. Falor, please be so kind as to see our young friend on his way."

Chapter Eighteen

LAPIS EXSILIS

The Gothic lamp above the tall oak doors of St. Halistan's Church was a nebula of shifting brightness at the top of the hill as Morgan came trudging up Iglesia Street. The rain had stopped, the air had cleared, and beneath the warm circle of light he could see a small cluster of figures standing together and pointing up at the tower. Not until he reached the duplex did he recognize the faces: Rev. Alcuin, the two city inspectors, and Mr. Brevard Knowles. By the time he crossed the street the little group was already dispersing.

"Until tomorrow, then," Knowles was saying as he shook Rev. Alcuin's hand. "Ten o'clock. And please give my offer some serious thought."

"Yes, of course I will," said the Reverend wearily. "Thank you for your time, Mr. Knowles."

Morgan drew up alongside Rev. Alcuin as the three men got into their cars and drove away. "What was that all about?" he said.

"Ah, Morgan!" said the Reverend. "Glad you turned up. I missed you at dinner. I just got the price tag on the repairs for the tower." He took off his glasses, drew a handkerchief from his pocket, and wiped his forehead. "A good deal more than St. Halistan's can afford, I'm afraid."

"So what happens now?"

"Well, without the repairs the tower stands condemned. She'll have to come down. But Mr. Knowles has offered to bail us out. He wants to buy the entire property. For a very attractive sum, I might add."

"Sell the church? You've got to be kidding! What does *he* want with a church?"

"He doesn't. He wants to put up a bed-and-breakfast. But let's not talk about that now, Morgan. I had other reasons for wanting to see you. I wonder if you might like to join me in my office for tea and sandwiches?"

It occurred to Morgan that he had not eaten anything since a half hour before noon. All at once he was struck by a gnawing feeling of ravenous hunger in the pit of his stomach. His knees felt rubbery and weak. To make matters worse, his head was still reeling from the events of the afternoon and evening.

"That sounds like a great idea," he said.

"Good," said Rev. Alcuin. "I've been to see your mother again, and I think we need to talk."

Drab and homey as it was, Peter Alcuin's office had always been surrounded by an aura of near-mythical, almost sacred significance in Morgan's imagination. The boy's strongest notions of his father were intimately connected with the small two-room suite behind the organ loft. Those impressions all came flooding back to him now as the Reverend unlocked the door and led the way inside.

"I won't be a minute," said Peter, tossing his coat over the back of a chair and disappearing into the suite's small half kitchen. "Just putting the kettle on to boil."

Morgan stood on the threshold, breathing in the quiet coolness of the chamber's scholarly, almost monkish, atmosphere. The very smell of the place—a librarylike decoction of worn leather, musty woolen carpet, dusty shelves, and hundreds of old books—was pregnant with images of his dad. He was aware that John Izaak and Peter Alcuin had been great friends. He knew that they had spent long hours together in this room discussing their shared love of language, their common interest in history and legend, and their lively devotion to books. His mother had told him all this many times. But she had also told him that they frequently disagreed, and that their differences could be as sharp and irreconcilable as their friendship was firm and unshakeable.

"Milk with your tea?" called the Reverend from the kitchen.

"Yes, please," Morgan answered.

He couldn't help smiling as he cast his eyes around at the exuberant clutter filling the cramped little room. How many ministers, he wondered, kept a pair of antique wooden Norwegian skis suspended over their doorway like the high crossed spears of an African tribal chief? How many used the cabinet of a vintage treadle sewing machine as a writing table?

What other pastor of what other church had a glass display case reserved solely for treasures like steel-wheeled skates, slingshots, model airplanes, jacks, marbles, and ceramic tops?

"What's your pleasure?" said Peter, emerging with a tray of clinking cups and saucers, a plate of sandwiches, and a steaming pot of tea. He set his burden down on an old wooden milk crate and invited Morgan to take a seat on the sofa under the window. "Ham and turkey or bologna and cheese?"

"Bologna is fine," said Morgan. "Thanks. I'm really hungry."

The Reverend perched himself on the edge of a mahogany Windsor chair and began pouring the tea. "As I mentioned," he said, "I've been to see your mother again. Just this afternoon."

Morgan bit into a sandwich and glanced up. He had a feeling that something unpleasant was coming.

"Funny thing," Peter continued. "With everything else she's going through, it's *you* she's worried about. She wondered why you hadn't been to see her today."

"I'm sorry, but I couldn't. I've been busy working on something."

"I gathered as much." The Reverend paused and took a sip of tea. "That day at the hospital I said I wouldn't ask any prying questions about this project of yours. But now I can't help being curious. You said it had something to do with the tower. Right?"

Morgan swallowed and took another bite. The lab in the tower was a secret he shared with the Ariellos alone. Except for the custodial crew, nobody in the church had any occasion to know anything about it.

"Because the tower, as you know, is almost certainly doomed."

Morgan shoved a stray bread crumb from one side of his plate to the other and said nothing.

"Listen. I'm aware that certain items were left to you at the time of your father's ... death. I have some idea what you've been doing with them. Your mom is very proud of you, Morgan. She knows she can depend on you. But she also fears that you're putting your hopes in the wrong place. To tell you the truth, I don't think she cares half as much about getting well as she does about *you* learning the meaning of faith."

"No offense," said Morgan, twisting uneasily in his seat, "but you and mom could have faith in what I'm doing. She *is* going to get well."

Peter frowned. "Well, the doctor's report isn't very encouraging at this point. You need to be aware of that."

Morgan opened his mouth to speak but nothing came out.

"And there's another thing you ought to know. About your father. His ideas were changing near the end. He'd been reading a great deal—particularly a book by Jacob Boehme called *The Signature of All Things*—about the failure of alchemy. We had several discussions about it right here in this room."

"Failure?" Morgan reached into his pocket and fingered the vial of red powder he'd brought from Madame Medea's shop.

"Yes. Like Boehme, your dad was becoming disillusioned with the quest for the Philosophers' Stone—the quest for *knowledge* and *power*. His thoughts were beginning to turn instead to a spiritual Rock, one that followed the people of Israel in the wilderness. The transformation wasn't complete. But he was moving in that direction. It's funny," Peter added. "The most effective lies are often those that contain an admixture of truth. Yet even that admixture can sometimes be enough to lead a man into the right path."

Morgan didn't know what to make of all this. He'd never heard of Jacob Boehme or *The Signature of All Things*. There was no such book in the library he'd inherited from his father. How could he be sure that the Reverend was telling the truth? Perhaps alchemy was one of those issues about which Peter Alcuin and John Izaak had disagreed. If so, there couldn't be any point in continuing this discussion. He decided to change the subject.

"Rev. Alcuin," he said, reaching for another sandwich, "do you know anything about Lia Fail?"

Peter, who was just getting up to boil more water, froze halfway between a sitting and standing position, his knees bent, his hands still gripping the armrests of the chair. He stared hard at Morgan. "Did you say Lia Fail?"

"Yes. The Stone of Destiny. The Satisfaction of All Desire. Do you know anything about it?"

Rev. Alcuin dropped back into his seat, a surprised expression on his broad, ruddy face. "As a matter of fact, I do. Why do you ask?"

"It's been … coming up a lot lately. In my reading, I mean. For this project."

"Seriously? Because"—the Reverend paused, as if hesitant to say more, then continued—"because, as it happens, your dad brought up the possibility of a similar connection—a connection between alchemy and Lia Fail—in one of the last conversations I ever had with him."

"Really?" Morgan slid forward to the edge of his seat. "What sort of connection?"

"It's rather complicated. He wanted to know why the Philosophers' Stone, which is supposed to be some kind of *powder*, should be called a 'stone' at all. He thought there might be a tie-in with some of the other 'stone' legends that have been floating around western Europe for the past couple of millennia. Like the one about the Stone of Scone."

"What's that?'"

"Supposedly 'the Stone of Scone' is just another name for Lia Fail. It's also been called the 'Bethel Stone,' since it was believed to be the same rock Jacob used as a pillow when he dreamed of the ladder connecting heaven and earth. Gathelus the Athenian is supposed to have picked it up from Scota, Pharoah's daughter, when the Israelites were in Egypt. After that, Celtic folktales say that the Tuatha De Danann—the Irish fairy folk—stole it from Gathelus and transported it to Ireland, where it became known as 'the Stone that Roared.' Much later on the Scots captured it and took it away to Scone in Argyle. Last of all it fell into the hands of King Edward I, who placed it in Westminster Abbey, where the monarchs of England were crowned upon it for centuries. I believe it's since been returned to Scotland."

"Is that where it is right now? In Scotland?"

"Well, as I say, that's *one* of the stories. Another one claims that the Stone of Scone is a fake, and that the real Lia Fail was secretly smuggled out of Ireland long before the Scottish raiders arrived. Interestingly enough, that's where your father's theory comes in."

"How?"

Rev. Alcuin got up and walked over to one of the bookshelves. Climbing up on a stool, he drew down a large leather-bound volume and handed it to Morgan. "You're familiar with King Arthur and his knights of the Round Table?"

"Sure. King Arthur is one of my all-time favorite stories."

"Then you know about the quest for the Holy Grail?"

"Of course. The cup of Christ. What's that got to do with it?"

"I'll show you."

Peter pulled another book off the shelf. "This," he said, "is Wolfram von Eschenbach's *Parzival*. It's one of the earliest of all Grail-quest narratives. German, thirteenth century. Here's what Wolfram says about the knights who kept the legendary Grail castle."

He opened the book and began to read:

> *I will tell you how they are nourished. They*
> *live from a Stone whose essence is most pure.*

It is called Lapis Exilis. *However ill a mortal may be, from the day on which he sees the Stone he cannot die for that week, nor does he lose his color. Such powers does the Stone confer on mortal men that their flesh and bones are soon made young again. This Stone is also called "The Gral."*

"Wow!" said Morgan through a mouthful of bologna and cheese.

"That's not all. This *Gral* was also supposed to have the power to provide food for the hungry—any kind of food they wanted: 'whatever one stretched out one's hand for in the presence of the Gral,' says Wolfram, 'it was waiting.' That's strongly reminiscent of the idea of Lia Fail as 'The Satisfaction of All Desire.' What's more, it could only be handled by a *maiden of perfect purity*." Rev. Alcuin flipped to another passage in the book. "Here. This is from a description of a great banquet at the Grail castle:

A remarkable procession then entered: young girls, marching in pairs with candles, ivory stools, a platter made of precious stones, and silver knives. After these came the Princess. Her face shed such refulgence that all imagined it was sunrise. Upon a cloth of green silk she bore the Consummation of the Heart's Desire, its root and its blossoming—a thing called 'The

Gral.' Such was the nature of the Gral that
she who had the care of it was required to be
of perfect chastity and to have renounced all
things false."

Morgan looked up into the Reverend's face. "So what does it all mean?"

Peter shut the book. "Don't you see? The point is that, in this version of the story, the Grail isn't the cup of Christ at all. *It's a miraculous Stone!* That's the thing that captured your dad's imagination! He came up with the idea that there might be a link of some kind between the powers attributed to the Gral and the powers of the alchemical Philosophers' Stone. He further theorized that this Gral might actually be the real Lia Fail, the legendary Stone of Destiny, secretly sent out of Ireland by the Tuatha De Danann. That's how he interpreted the name Wolfram gives it—*Lapis Exilis*. Some scholars explain it as a derivation of the Latin *lapsit exillis*, 'it came down from above,' or *lapis ex coelis*, 'the Stone from Heaven.' But your dad chose to understand it as *lapis exsilis*: the *exiled* Stone."

"Do you think he was right?"

Peter replaced the book on the shelf and sat down. "I don't know. I'd say it's entirely possible that these fables are all just different versions or mutations of a single myth. But your dad wasn't thinking primarily in terms of fable and myth. He took all of this quite seriously. That was the problem."

"What do you mean—'problem'?"

Rev. Alcuin raised one eyebrow and leaned back in his chair. "Well," he said, "that's where we began this conversation, isn't it? With your mom and her concerns about you following in your father's footsteps. I think you already know why she regards all of this as a 'problem.'"

Morgan felt his cheeks flush—whether with embarrassment or guilt or anger or a combination of all three he didn't know. "As a matter of fact," he said, "I'm not sure I do. I'm not so sure my mom understands. I don't think she gets it. Dad was a brilliant man!"

"Oh, I agree one hundred percent," said Peter. "But brilliance isn't everything. In the end, your money is worth no more to you than the things you choose to spend it on. It's the same with intelligence and knowledge. But I'll grant your dad this much: In some ways, his theory makes a lot of sense. Whether you view it as a simple question of folklore or as quest for an actual artifact, his ideas really do fit the evidence. We can trace the progress of the various 'stone' stories across the face of Europe. They start in Ireland and stretch in a wide arc through Britain, over into France, from France to Germany, from Germany to Switzerland and Italy, and finally down into Brigantium and Santiago de Compostela in Spain. The popular impressions they've left behind, and the apparent correlation between some of their most striking features and the parallel legends of the Philosophers' Stone, are altogether—"

Morgan felt as if someone had just slapped him on the side of the head. His ears were ringing, his heart pounding.

The wheels of his mind began to spin like a yo-yo on the end of a string. His thoughts raced back to that morning. *The last known resting place of the Stone,* he heard George say, *was in the mission church of Santa Compostela* … here in Santa Piedra. Then came the voice of Madame Medea: *It is nearby. Very close to you, I think.*

"… but as far as I'm concerned," Rev. Alcuin was saying, "these stories are intended to point to something beyond themselves. They're *images* of a greater reality. We all know that the Philosophers' Stone can't give anyone eternal life. And it's obvious that Lia Fail has never satisfied anybody's deepest longings and desires. That distinction belongs to Someone else. Your father was beginning to see that. Your mother wants you to see it too. I hope you'll give some serious thought to …"

But Morgan wasn't listening. It was as if Peter Alcuin and his office and his books and his teapot and the tower of St. Halistan's and the rest of the entire world had all faded away into an engulfing gray mist. He could see nothing, nothing at all but the flowering courtyard and tall Romanesque facade of the Mission Santiago de Compostela.

"I'm sorry, Rev. Alcuin," he blurted abruptly, "but I've got to go. Thanks very much for the tea and sandwiches."

And with that he was out the door.

Part 3

Chapter Nineteen

THE MISSION

On Monday afternoon, while Eny was sitting above Laguna Verde and gazing out into the mist, Morgan was on his knees in the school bike racks fumbling with his combination lock. It was late. He'd had to stay after class to make up a bungled math test, and now he had less than an hour before the Mission was scheduled to close. Haste, anxiety, and the damp cold combined to make his fingers stiff and clumsy. Twice he tried and failed to open the lock. A third time he spun the dial and struggled with the shackle. *Come on, you stupid thing!*

"Nice catch out there today, Robot-Mouth!"

His hands jerked at the unexpected sound of a voice next to his ear, and the lock snapped open. Looking up, he found himself staring straight into the face of Baxter Knowles.

"Wait a minute," said Baxter with a grin. "You *didn't* catch it. That's right! Sorry, my bad!"

This was followed by a chorus of laughter. Morgan looked around and saw that he was hemmed in on every side by a gang of Baxter's buddies.

"I guess you've heard the news," Baxter went on. "About my dad tearing down your old church, I mean. To put up a new bed-and-breakfast. Looks like you'll have to find some other place to do your magic tricks from now on."

Morgan got to his feet and yanked the chain through the ringing spokes. "Don't tempt me, Baxter," he said.

"Ooh! A tough guy!"

Morgan said nothing but turned away and began wrapping the chain around the seat post of his bike. In the next instant Baxter was upon him, gripping him by both arms, shoving him hard up against the jangling chain-link fence. Grunting with the effort, Morgan twisted to one side in a desperate attempt to escape, but Baxter stuck out a foot and tripped him. His feet flew out from under him, the sky spun over his head, and he fell heavily, his backpack bursting open and spilling its contents over the blacktop: books, gym clothes, the remains of his lunch … and a small flask of fine white powder.

"Look at this!" said one of Baxter's accomplices, picking up the little bottle with a triumphant smirk. "What is it?"

"Let *me* see!" commanded Baxter with a scowl.

Morgan scrambled to his feet and made a grab for the flask as it went flying in a wide arc over his head. "Give it back!" he shouted as Baxter snatched it out of the air just in front of his face.

"Why? Is it some kind of magic potion?"

"I said give it to me!" Morgan lunged forward and flung out a hand, but two boys seized him from behind and dragged him back. "It's medicine! For my mom!"

A shade of doubt crossed Baxter's face. "What kind of *medicine?*"

"That's none of your business!" Morgan fumed. "You can't just—"

But he never finished the sentence. A burst of wind and a storm of black feathers fell from the sky, thrusting itself directly between him and his bullying tormentor. Baxter threw up his hands as a huge crow, wings fluttering, beak clacking, and talons flailing, flew screeching into his face like a howling banshee. The other boys released their grip on Morgan and scattered like dry leaves in a gale. Dropping the flask, Baxter fled with a cry of terror.

Left to himself, Morgan retrieved the jar and returned it to its place in his backpack with the rest of his fallen gear. As far as he could tell, not a single grain of the precious white powder had been lost. *Looks like somebody's watching out for me after all.*

The mist had lifted and become a ceiling of low-hanging clouds by the time he made the turn from Mission Street onto Compostela Road. Far to the west a thread of bronze sunlight crept in at the edge of the curtained sky and cast a strangely muted, almost surrealistic orange luminescence over the scene. The bright reds and purples of the bougainvilleas above the door seemed to glow with a phosphorescence all their own as he pedaled up to the Mission visitor center. Dropping his bike beside the wall, he shouldered his pack and stepped into the gift shop.

"I'm sorry, young man," said the woman at the counter, glancing up with a smile. "The last tour of the day is already in progress. You can come back tomorrow morning if you like. We open at ten."

Morgan's cheeks burned. "I'm not here for the tour," he stammered. "Can I just look around for a while?"

"That's fine. But you won't have much time. The Mission closes at six."

He made his way to the back of the store and began thumbing through a rack of souvenir postcards. There were pictures of the Mission church, the cloisters, the cemetery, the chapel, and the gardens. There were cards bearing portraits of Father Junipero Serra and Father Juan Crespi and photographs of the restored cells and kitchens of the monks. There was even an entire section devoted to the high altar in the main sanctuary and the ornate gold and silver service used by Father Serra to celebrate the Mass. But there was nothing about a legendary Stone.

Near the door leading into the courtyard he picked up a color brochure bearing the title *Welcome to Mission Santiago de Compostela*. Opening the little booklet he read:

> *The Mission of La Iglesia de San Sebastian y Santiago de Compostela was established by Padre Junipero Serra during the summer of 1782, just two years prior to the founder's death. A young Franciscan named Juan Bautista Alvarado de Ariello was instrumental in aiding*

*Father Serra in this work, his longtime friend
and companion Padre Juan Crespi having
passed away at the beginning of the year.*

Ariello. So George was right. There *was* a connection
between the Ariello family and the Mission. And Juan
Bautista Alvarado de Ariello was the very name he'd given to
the friar who once had personal custody of the miraculous
Stone from Spain. Apparently the trail was getting warmer.
Morgan shoved the brochure into his pocket and sauntered
outside.

Except for the gentle murmur of the water in the fountain, silence reigned in the Mission courtyard. Fragrant
flowers—roses, lavender, jasmine, gardenias, honeysuckle,
clematis—grew in rich profusion on every side of the
square. Red salvias, pink hibiscus, blue hydrangeas, and
orange poppies cheered the dullness of the damp gray afternoon. The all-enfolding quiet was comforting and almost
palpable.

Morgan stood in the light of the gift shop's grated window
and studied the gardenlike enclosure. The entire west end of
the quadrangle was taken up by the basilica, a towering structure of gray and yellow stone with a domed bell tower on the
left, a square pinnacle on the right, and a four-pointed rose
window in the center of the high arching facade. In the far
corner grew a mournful-looking cypress, while close at hand
an ancient ficus cast its shade over a wisteria-covered wall.
Apart from the trees and flowers, almost everything in the

place was of stone: the walls, the fountain, the grave markers and monuments in the narrow cemetery, even the borders surrounding the flower beds. In spite of this, Morgan saw nothing that looked even remotely like a Stone of Destiny— at least not as he imagined a Stone of Destiny ought to look.

He was about to cross over to the museum, a small adobe building on the opposite side of the square, when its door creaked open and a solitary figure emerged: a small, angular, bald-headed man in a shabby black suit. Morgan recognized him at once. It was Eochy, Madame Medea's assistant shop-keeper. *What's he doing here?* he thought. *I don't have time to talk to* him *right now!* Averting his face, he scurried across to the basilica, hoping the odd little man hadn't seen him. As discreetly and quietly as possible, he opened the big iron-studded door and slipped inside.

As the door shut softly behind him, Morgan found himself standing at one end of a long, high-ceilinged, deeply shadowed space, somewhat smaller than the sanctuary of St. Halistan's but far grander and more cathedral-like than any church he'd ever been in. The air was thick with an odor of incense that reminded him somehow of honey and milk. His footsteps echoed tentatively among the arched stone rafters as he scuffed over the pavement, past a basin of water and a brightly painted wooden statue of a pale-faced woman with a naked child on her arm. Six small chandeliers and a series of high narrow windows cast a dim light over the ranks of dark wooden benches ranged on either side of the center aisle. In the chancel at the far end of the building yellow candles glowed in a gallery of gilded niches recessed into the wall. Above the candles hung a carved crucifix, and under it, on a platform of stone, stood an ornate table draped with a linen cloth and decked with gold and silver vessels. A small group of tourists stood huddled at the base of the platform.

"And this," the tour guide was saying, her voice reverberating from one end of the hall to the other, "is the high altar, the heart and life of Mission Santiago de Compostela. The monstrance is made of pure gold and was brought all the way from Toledo in Spain. The two figures flanking the crucifix represent Saint Francis of Assisi and Saint James of the Field of the Star."

The high altar! Like a bolt of lightning, another line from George's story flashed through Morgan's mind: *Jorge's pillow stone was laid to rest in the little church ... just below the altar.* If they had placed the Stone under the altar while it was in Spain, they must have done the same thing here in California! If only the tour group would leave so he could get a look behind the table! Slowly he edged his way down the center aisle.

"Unfortunately," the guide continued, "the basilica hasn't always been this beautiful. What you see today is the result of a long process of reconstruction and restoration. The California missions were 'secularized' in 1834, and over the next several decades Santa Compostela fell into a state of ruin and decay. To make matters worse, local ranchers and developers took to plundering the buildings for construction materials as the town of Santa Piedra grew. Many of the structures built in this area during the 1870s and '80s actually contain pieces of the original Mission church.

"Now if you'll all follow me," she concluded amid a buzz of muffled voices, "we'll just take a quick look around the cloisters before bringing our tour to a close. This way, please."

As the group exited through a door to the left, Morgan darted to the front of the church and leaped softly up the three stone steps leading to the altar. He found it separated from the nave by a low wooden railing and a gate of ornate Spanish ironwork. Feeling for the latch, he flipped it up. But even as he did so the double doors at the back of the sanctuary swung open, and a dull gray light spilled into the hall. He spun around and saw a silhouette on the threshold—the shape of a small, thin, bald-headed man. Him again! Morgan dropped on all fours, crawled down from the platform, and hid behind the first row of pews.

Seconds passed, and all remained still. He was about to lift his head when he heard the sound of footsteps. Slowly they approached, with a measured and unhurried tread; closer and closer they came, straight down the center aisle. He held his breath, hunched himself into a ball, and jammed his body more tightly into the space beneath the bench. In the next instant a figure crossed the narrow space at the end of the row of seats—not the figure of Eochy, but a tall, dark-haired priest in a long black robe. Morgan breathed a sigh of relief.

He slid to the end of the pew and peeked out. As he watched, the priest opened the little iron gate, knelt before the altar, crossed himself, and then stood for a long time with his head bowed. At last he took a long-handled, bell-shaped snuffer from the table, extinguished all but two of the candles, and turned to descend the steps. Morgan ducked. Again the footsteps passed, this time in the opposite direction. After what felt like an eternity their sibilant echoes died away and the great oak doors closed dully behind them. A deeper darkness fell over the sanctuary.

Immediately he was on his feet, skipping to the top of the platform, jumping over the low wooden railing at a single bound. Slipping behind the altar, he got down on his knees and lifted a corner of the richly embroidered linen cloth. The flickering shadows cast by the candlelight made it difficult to see clearly. With pounding pulse and bated breath he thrust his head beneath the table for a closer look. What he saw made him gasp in surprise and disappointment.

There was nothing under the altar. Nothing but a hole. A smooth-sided rectangular hole in the stone pavement. A hole about four feet long and two feet wide.

Morgan vaulted over the railing and ran straight out the back door of the church.

"Come back when you have more time," smiled the clerk at the counter as he rushed breathlessly through the Mission gift shop and out into the street.

Though the gray sky was far from dark, it seemed to Morgan that the shadows had deepened during his time inside the Mission. They looked especially dense just below a large elm that stood opposite the Mission on the far side of the road. With one eye on this strange patch of blackness, he grabbed his bike and pulled it away from the wall.

"*Hsst!* Young mister!"

Morgan started violently and nearly dropped the bike. "*You* again!" he cried, his heart thumping as Eochy, eyes shining and hands twitching nervously, emerged from the gloom beneath the vine-covered porch. "Why are you stalking me?"

"It is what I've been waiting to tell you," said the little man. "Are you not noticing that great clumpish creature over there"—he pointed to the shadow across the street—"and you all alone, and the night coming on?"

Morgan peered closely at the dark spot beneath the tree. As he did, he had the impression that it was slowly taking on a more definite shape: a massive body with powerful arms and legs and a small round head set low between wide, bulky shoulders.

"Is that Falor?" he asked. "Your friend from Madame Medea's?"

"Falor it is but no friend of mine. He is not sent on friendly business."

Morgan swung onto his bike. "What do you mean? Didn't he come with you?"

"That he did not. And a sorry thing it would be, him to see me here and speaking with you like this. True it is we serve the same mistress. But then some serve willingly and others not. Others only *seem* to serve—for reasons of their own."

"Well, that's interesting, but I have to go now. So please stop bothering me. When I have some information for your boss I'll let her know."

He put his foot to the pedal and prepared to push off. But Eochy reached out and took hold of his arm.

"That you must not do," he said. "Twice have I said it, you not heeding at all. Now I say it again: You're best out of this altogether."

Morgan shook him off. "When I want your advice I'll ask for it," he said.

With that, he rode off into the gathering twilight, laughing under his breath at the little man's wheezy voice and comical warnings. He couldn't help laughing right out loud when he imagined the bent and balding figure tracking him through the streets of Santa Piedra, chasing him across the Mission courtyard, and following him into the basilica. He must be crazy.

He was about to laugh again when a curiously cold and knife-edged wind ruffled his hair and made him tremble. A great black bird swept over his shoulder and went soaring on ahead like the vanguard and herald of the coming night. An inexplicable chill fell over him, a nameless dread like an all-engulfing cloud, and he found himself shivering uncontrollably. Leaning forward on the handlebars, he shifted gears and began to pedal faster.

As he rode on, he was increasingly possessed by the feeling that he was being followed. When he reached the corner of Compostela and Mission he twisted in his seat and looked back. There, not a hundred feet away, was the gigantic form of Falor, pounding down the road after him like a pile driver with great wide-flung, ground-devouring strides of his immense tree-trunklike legs. Morgan felt as if an icy lump of lead had dropped into his heart. He bit his lip and bent into the wind, racing downhill with all his might toward the distant shining sea.

At Front Street he swung to the right and put on a burst of speed. After making the turn, he glanced back over his shoulder. Falor appeared to be gaining on him—either that, or the big man was actually growing larger at every step. *That's impossible!* he thought as he zipped past Alta Drive and Vista Del Mar, the shops and house-fronts swirling by in a multicolored blur. His legs were aching and his lungs burning, but he could not stop and dared not take the direct route home. He had to find some way to evade this relentless pursuer!

Beyond the business district, Front Street curved westward and veered closer to the pebble-strewn, wave-swept beach. On the left hand heaved the long gray swells of the Inlet. On the right glittered the windows of the houses on Vizcaino Hill above Iglesia Street. Through the mist and the sweat in his eyes he could just make out, at the far end of the crescent shoreline, the whirling lights of the Fun Zone Ferris wheel and the warm glow of the restaurants on Fisherman's Wharf. One more time he turned in the saddle. Falor was even closer now—or bigger—looming like a thundercloud just above Morgan's head. He could see the ugly grimace on his heavy face and the red gleam in his burning left eye. He could hear the shattering thuds of his jackhammer feet upon the quaking asphalt. He almost fancied he could feel his hot breath on the back of his neck. He closed his eyes and shifted into high gear.

With the scent of sand and brine and kelp in his nostrils, Morgan flew like the wind past clanging bells and private docks, past rocking boats and swinging masts, past rocks and gulls and rusted huts, past sea lions barking in the darkness under the barnacle-encrusted pier. At last he came to the Fun Zone Midway, where the air was redolent with funnel cakes and kettle corn and cotton candy. Ditching his bike alongside the railing, he dived into a crowd of children who were waiting in line to ride the Ferris wheel. Without ceremony or apology he ducked down behind a couple of little girls who were busy slurping snow cones.

Looking up from this place of refuge, he could just see Falor hunkering down in the shadows beyond the carousel and the bumper cars, cowering before the light and the probing eyes of the children. As he watched, hardly daring to breathe, the great shape shuddered and shook itself. Then it got up and began moving away, diminishing in size as it went. In a few moments it was gone. Though he strained his eyes, Morgan could see nothing but the vague outline of something like a small black cat disappearing into the distance or sinking into the ground. He wiped the sweat from his eyes and collapsed in a heap.

"No cuts in line," said one of the snow-cone girls.

It was beginning to get dark when Morgan finally reached the duplex. Weary and shaken, he walked his bicycle up the steep sidewalk and leaned it against the side of the house. Then, with a bleary-eyed glance at the lighted tower of St. Halistan's, he shouldered his backpack and stumbled up the steps. Fumbling in his pocket for the key, he stepped forward into the shadows, groping for the door. Then he stopped and stared, stunned by what he saw.

There on the doorstep in front of him stood Eny, dressed in rags and dripping from head to toe.

Chapter Twenty

OISIN

Before Morgan could think of anything to say, the left-hand door opened, and Moira peered out.

"Well, I never!" she exclaimed, squinting at them through the screen. "Where in the world have *you* two been? Your supper will be ice cold by now! I could have kept it hot on the stove, but how was I supposed to know when you might show up? I didn't want it to burn to a crisp!"

"Sorry, Mrs. A," Morgan said sheepishly. "I guess I lost track of the time."

"I guess so! And look at you! You're an absolute mess. Covered with grime and grease and sweat—like you've been in a fight or a football game or a high-speed chase or something! What would your mother say? And *you*, Eny! Did you decide to go for an after-school swim? In a *burlap sack*? What happened to your clothes?"

Eny shook her head wearily and ran her fingers through her streaming hair. There was a haggard look on her face, and she stumbled slightly when she took a step toward the door. "I can explain, Mom," she said in a small, quavering voice. "But you've got to promise to believe me."

Morgan glanced at Moira. He saw her forehead pucker as the expression on her face shifted suddenly from one of irritation to alarm. When he looked back at Eny, his heart was struck with something like a shock of cold dread. Never had his friend appeared so thin and worn and sad. Even in the half-light he could tell that her olive-brown face was colorless and wan, as if all the blood had been drained out of it. Except for her one blue eye, which gleamed like the evening star in a winter sky, all the fire had gone out of her normally radiant countenance. She took another step, then stopped and lightly touched her forehead, swaying uncertainly. Morgan put out a hand to steady her. Moira banged the screen door open and rushed out onto the porch.

"Help me get her inside, Morgan," she said, catching Eny before she could fall, and supporting her on her arm. "Over there, on the couch. I'll have George call the police!"

"No!" protested Eny. "*Please* don't do that! All I need is a blanket and something to eat and drink. Then I'll tell you everything."

Moira hustled out to the kitchen and put their dinners into the oven to warm. Then she came back and carried Eny straight to the bathroom for a hot shower and a change of clothes. Within half an hour they were all three together again in the living room, Morgan wolfing down macaroni and cheese at the coffee table, Eny sipping chamomile tea on the sofa, Moira hovering over them like an agitated mother hen. Moira came and laid a hand on her daughter's forehead.

"You don't feel feverish," she said after a moment's pause. "Thank heaven for that! I was worried when you didn't show up for supper, but when I saw you looking like that on the doorstep—! Well, that *really* gave me a scare! You kids just don't know what you put your moms through sometimes! Can you tell me yet what happened?"

Eny put down her cup and looked straight into her mother's eyes. Morgan saw her bottom lip began to quiver. But instead of crying, she sat up straight, lifted her chin, and spoke in a strong, steady voice. "Mom," she said, "I know it's going to sound crazy. And I know you must have been worried sick, and I'm really, really sorry about that. I was afraid you might have given up on me by now, but there was nothing I could do! *I was in the Sidhe!*"

What happened next was like nothing Morgan had ever witnessed between parent and child before. Moira didn't become angry. She didn't shout at Eny or tell her to stop lying. She didn't demand a serious explanation. She didn't even appear to be anxious about the girl's sanity or health. Instead, a strange sort of light dawned in her hazel eyes, and a faint smile played around the corners of her mouth. She smoothed back her wild auburn hair and laid her glasses on the coffee table. Then she drew a footstool up to the couch and sat down facing her daughter.

"The *Sidhe*," she said. "You've been there?"

"Yes," said Eny. "That's what you call the Irish fairyland, isn't it? In your stories, I mean?"

"Of course. But you're telling me that you *went* there?"

215

"Yes. That's why I was gone so long. For weeks and weeks!"

Morgan gaped at Eny in surprise. He'd seen her just yesterday playing fiddle with Simon Brach in the church. But Moira merely leaned forward and rested her chin in her hands. "What was it like?" she said.

"Lovely in most ways. Absolutely beautiful! I heard music, and that led me down to the Cave of the Hands. Then I found a tunnel and followed it a long way into the earth. After that I fell into a sea of light and woke up on the shore of a green ocean. I learned a lot about the people you call Danaans—"

"You *did?*" breathed Moira.

"Yes, and I met some other people, too, people you never told me about. The Fir Bolg. They rescued me and helped me. They gave me the clothes I was wearing. They took care of me and protected me."

"Protected you? From what?"

"That's the most important part!" said Eny, shaking with excitement. "I was chased by giants!"

Morgan froze in the middle of a bite and dropped his fork.

"There was this terrible, evil woman called the Morrigu, and she wanted to get her hands on me, so she sent the Fomorians—that's what the giants are called—to hunt me down. Sometimes she's young and slender and dark and beautiful, but other times she looks like an ugly old hag. She has this crow, and the crow goes out on all her errands—"

Morgan swallowed hard, almost choking on his food.

"—and she keeps prisoners—people from the world aboveground—in a tower on an island. She seems to think I'm somebody called *Eithne*."

Moira's smile faded, and a cloud darkened her face. "I named you after her," she said softly. "It just so happens that I know a bit about the Morrigu too. 'The Battle Crow' she's called in some of the tales. Very subtle and very dangerous. She can assume many different guises."

"I know! I know!" cried Eny. "It was horrible what she did! Gann and Erc were drowned, and the village was destroyed, and I'm not sure what happened to Rury!" Again her lip trembled, and she slumped down into the cushions of the couch, pulling the blanket up under her chin. Morgan could see tears welling up at the corners of her eyes. "I would have given anything to get home if only I'd known how," she went on after a moment, "but there was nothing I could do. Then one day I was out on the ocean and I fell down into a huge whirlpool and … and … well, I can't explain how, but here I am! And I'm so, *so* sorry for being gone such a long, long time!"

Moira bent forward and kissed Eny on the forehead. "The important thing is that you're home," she said, stroking her hair. "That's all that matters now. As far as I'm concerned, that's the most marvelous and miraculous thing of all!"

Morgan's mind was reeling. Crazy as Eny's narrative sounded, it had undeniable affinities with some of his own experiences of late. What's more, Moira seemed to believe it.

To a certain extent, he could understand her reaction. Eny was no liar. During all the years of their lifelong friendship he had never known her to tell so much as a little white fib. She was as faithful as the day was long: honest, pure-hearted, and trustworthy in everything she said or did. She could be dreamy and imaginative, it was true, but never once had she tried to deceive him. In fact, she came as close to being the perfect friend as anybody he'd ever known or even heard of. Why wouldn't a mother believe a daughter like that?

He had doubted her, of course, when she told him about the giant in the mist and the old woman down by the tide pools. But that was only reasonable. At the time, anyway. Since then, things had happened that cast a whole new light on certain details of her story. He shivered as he thought about Falor and the frantic chase down Front Street. Maybe there was something in what she was saying after all. But *fairyland? That* part he *couldn't* believe. He didn't *want* to believe it.

He had his reasons.

"Excuse me, Mrs. A," he said, tapping Moira on the shoulder, "but nobody's been gone for weeks and weeks. Eny just missed dinner—that's all. Like me! She's probably been playing around down at La Punta Lira, right? She's always playing around down there."

Moira regarded him solemnly. "The time element is the very thing that makes Eny's story so believable."

Morgan felt as if his head was about to explode. "What are you talking about?"

218

"Eny says she's been in the Sidhe," Moira explained. "In Faery. Now in all the tales I've ever heard, time in Faery is completely different from time in our world. That's one of the reasons it's so perilous to go there. You never know how the air of that land will affect you. A thousand years on one side of the divide can be like a single day on the other, and a single day like a thousand years. It works both ways, and there isn't any rhyme or reason to it. That's why people who stumble into the Sidhe from the land aboveground hardly ever return. If they do come back, there's no telling when they'll come back or what they'll find when they arrive. You remember Rip Van Winkle? Well, there have been others like him. I'm thinking of one very famous case in particular. An Irish hero named Oisin."

Morgan saw Eny sit up straight on the sofa. He himself had an idea what was coming, so he pushed his empty plate aside and leaned back in his chair. Moira folded her hands in her lap, as she often did when preparing to tell a story.

"Oisin was the son of the chieftain Fionn MacCumhail," she began. "His birth and lineage were uncanny and miraculous, for his mother was one of the people of the Sidhe. But that's a subject for another time. My tale begins when he was a young man still in the bloom of youth—a warrior and poet of great renown in Ireland.

"One summer morning Oisin went hunting by the shores of Lough Lena with his father, Fionn, and his father's men, a band of bold heroes known as the Fianna. Searching about for game, Fionn became aware of a dark spot in the fog. As he watched, this shadow came closer and took on the form of an approaching rider. Then a window opened in the haze and a bright figure emerged: a lovely golden-haired maiden on a tall white horse. Her dress was white and her belt green. Her four-folded cloak was dark brown, fastened at the shoulder with a gem-studded brooch, and embroidered from top to bottom with silver stars. On her head she wore a circlet of gleaming gold, and in her hand she held a blossoming hawthorn branch. Straight up to the Fianna she rode without flinching or blinking an eye. She stopped in front of Fionn and bowed her head in greeting.

"'Do you know who I am, Fionn son of Cumhail?' she asked.

"'And how should I be knowing that?' answered Fionn.

"'I am Niamh of the Golden Hair, daughter of the king of Tir-Na-nOg, the Land of Youth which is in the Green Isle of the West. I have come a long way to find you.'

"'There was little need,' said Fionn. 'What is it you want of me?'

"She smiled. 'The love of your son Oisin,' she said.

"Oisin was standing spellbound at his father's side, dumbstruck and overwhelmed at the sight of the maiden's unearthly beauty. She turned to him and said, 'Will you come with me, Oisin, to my father's country?' Then she began to sing:

> *Delightful is that land beyond all dreams,*
> *There all the year the fruit is on the tree.*

Nor pain nor sickness knows the dweller there,
Death nor decay come near him never more.

"The young man never hesitated. Without so much as a glance at his father, he took the girl's hand and swung up into the saddle behind her. Then, as the Fianna watched, Niamh of the Golden Hair shook the bridle, wheeled the horse about, and dashed away with her love, down the ringing glade and through the parting mists. It was the last time Fionn ever saw his son alive on earth.

"As for Niamh and Oisin, they rode till they came to the western ocean, where the white horse sprang lightly into the air and went racing over the surface of the sea, his silver shoes skimming the foaming tips of the restless waves. Through sun and shower they sped, beneath rainbows and over clouds, past rocks that shone in the rain like glittering jewels. Time and times and half a time they journeyed until Oisin no longer knew if he were waking or in a dream. At last there came a breach in the eternal mists through which they glimpsed a distant vision: a green island under a blazing sun at the edge of a blue horizon.

"Thus they came to the land of Tir-Na-nOg, where they received a royal welcome. There they were wed, and there Niamh's father the king feasted them in his high hall a full three weeks to the sounds of harps and pipes and drums. They spent their days hunting in the greenwood and swimming in the surf and the sparkling streams. At night they dined on fresh fruits and slept in a bower of twining branches underneath the winking stars. At all times their hearts were filled to overflowing with pleasures and amusements of every imaginable kind.

"Oisin soon came to see that Niamh had spoken the truth: So great were the joys and delights of that land, so complete the satisfaction of his every need and want, that he nearly forgot Ireland and his father and the Fianna. Nearly, but not quite. For in the silent midnight watches, softly glimmering reminders of home often stole into his secret thoughts. At such times his heart came close to breaking with the pain of its longings.

"At last he asked his bride for leave to visit the land of his birth. 'It is not long I will stay,' he promised, gazing into her deep green eyes. 'Just long enough to greet my father and assure him that I am well.'

"At first she would not hear of it; but when he did not relent, but persisted in his pleadings, she reluctantly granted his wish. 'Take my horse,' she said then in a sorrowful voice. 'The white steed knows the way to carry you over the sea to Eire. But heed this warning: Whatever you do, you must never alight from off his back. For the instant your foot touches the soil of that world, you will be lost to me and I to you forever.'

"So he gave her his word and mounted the horse, and once again crossed the mystic ocean. Time and times and half a time he rode, until the horse touched down on the shores of the Emerald Isle, his hoofs striking silver fire from the gray rocks. From the western coast they sped like the wind until they came into the regions of Kildare. But when they reached the Hill of Allen, where Fionn's hall used to stand, Oisin could only stare in fear and wonder. There was nothing left of the place as he had known it. The walls, the court, the sheds and stables, every last vestige of the great house was entirely gone. Only furze and clumps of course grass could he see growing on the hilltop.

"Then terror gripped him and he fled until he came to the eastern ocean. On a hill overlooking the sea he came upon a group of farmers—oddly small and feeble men, he thought—who were struggling to clear a boulder from their field. Being a poet, a nobleman, and a gentleman as well, he rode straight up to them and offered his aid; but they, seeing what they took for a mighty warrior or an angel from heaven looking down at them from the horse's back, moved away from the stone and regarded him uneasily from a distance.

"'What ails you?' said Oisin, setting his hand to the rock. 'It is no difficult task to move such a stone.' Then with one great thrust of his arm he sent the boulder rolling down the hill. But such was the force of that mighty heave that the girth of the saddle burst and he was pitched headlong to the ground. As soon as he touched Irish soil his youth and beauty departed, so that when the farmers, seeing him in distress, came to raise him up, they found him a white-bearded, decrepit old man with barely the strength to stand on his own two feet. The fairy horse was nowhere to be seen.

"'What is this?' cried Oisin, staring down at his hands, now withered and scarred with age. 'What has happened to me? Where is my father, Fionn MacCumhail? Where are his men, the Fianna, and the high hall of the Hill of Allen?'

"'Now you're raving, old man!' they exclaimed, backing away from him with awe in their faces. 'Either that, or you've been entirely bewitched! Fionn MacCumhail has been dead these three hundred years—if any such person ever lived at all!'"

Moira fell silent. Then she looked at Eny with glowing eyes and said, "So you see what a fortunate young lady you've been. You're one of a chosen few. To have spent weeks and weeks in the Sidhe only to return safe and sound the very same afternoon—well, that's an experience not many people can claim to have had!"

Morgan jumped to his feet with a gasp of exasperation. "That doesn't make any sense at all: Anybody can claim anything. If she'd come home gray-haired and looking like an old woman it would be obvious that something weird was going on. But she's no different! How do you know she's not just making up excuses?"

Eny glared at him. There was a look in both her eyes, brown and blue, that reminded him of a wounded deer he'd once seen out on the Point. He winced and glanced away. Moira smiled a patient, knowing smile and opened her mouth as if she were about to speak. But just at that moment the front door opened and in walked George, two big bunches of keys jingling at his belt.

"So *here* you are!" he exploded good-naturedly, whisking

off his cap and mopping his forehead with a red bandanna. "I've been hunting everywhere for you two!"

"I'm sorry, Dad," said Eny, leaping up and throwing her arms around him.

George's eyebrows shot up in surprise. He stared at his wife wide-eyed across the top of his daughter's head. "It's all right, *mi hija*," he stammered, gently peeling her off and holding her by the shoulders at arm's length. "I wasn't coming after you with a stick or anything!"

"You didn't call the police, did you?"

"No, no! Nothing like that! I figured you and Morgan were together all along. Into some kind of mischief maybe," he added with a wink, "but no real serious trouble." Then, frowning deeply, he wrinkled up his forehead and shot another glance at Moira. "What's this all about?"

Moira got up and took Eny by the hand. "Nothing, George," she said briefly. "She's just glad to see you, that's all. She's had a busy day. We can talk about it later. Right now I think I'd better help her into bed."

George looked bewildered. "Bed? At this hour?"

"Shush, George." Moira scowled, turning to escort Eny from the room. "Can't men understand anything?"

George turned to Morgan as Moira and Eny disappeared down the hallway. "Do *you* understand?" he said.

Morgan just laughed. "Mrs. A really takes her stories seriously, doesn't she?" he said. He knew how things went between George and Moira, and he had no desire to get drawn into one of their squabbles.

"Stories?" said George. "So that's it! She's been telling stories again and doesn't want me to know! Oh yes, she's *very* serious about them. Those pagan myths and fables!"

"Do you believe *your* stories? Like the one about the Stone of Compostela?"

George shoved the red bandanna into his back pocket and eyed him closely. "What's your point?"

Morgan opened the front door and put his hand on the screen latch. Then he looked back at George.

"I went to the Mission today," he said. "I was looking for it. I remembered what you said about the little chapel in Spain—how they kept the miraculous pillow stone under the altar. So I sneaked inside the basilica and hid until nobody else was around. Then I got up on the chancel and looked underneath the table."

For once George appeared to have been stunned speechless. His mouth dropped open and there was an expression of dull incredulity on his honest face. At the same time a faint light, as of a hope that hardly dared to hope, glimmered in his dark brown eyes.

"It's not there," Morgan concluded, shouldering the door open and pushing his way out into the darkness. "There's *nothing* there. Nothing at all. Nothing but a big square hole."

Chapter Twenty-One

ELIXIR VITAE

That night Morgan tossed and turned for what felt like hours. Try as he might, he could not force down the insistent patter of his heart. Faces whirled before his mind's eye. Voices sounded in his ears: *This is the high altar.... I have come a long way to find you.... You are seeking the Stone.... Somewhere nearby ... in the church, perhaps ... under the altar...*

The clouds above Santa Piedra parted, and crazy trapezoids of yellow moonlight fell slanting through the window, splaying themselves rudely across the calico squares of his quilt. He squeezed his eyes shut and burrowed under the covers until sleep and darkness took him.

Gradually the moonlight faded. A thick mist streamed in through the open casement, collecting in luminous pools at the foot of the bed. He found himself rising and wading through it, stumbling over wet grass and cold gravel, down past the lights of the spiraling Ferris wheel to the endless, sunless sea.

At the corner of Front Street a woman stepped from a darkened doorway with a naked baby on her arm. She spoke his name and laid a hand on his shoulder, but he averted his gaze and walked on. Finding his bike at the foot of a vine-covered wall, he mounted it and rode away.

Through the night he sped, up a hill and down an ancient Roman road bordered on either side by megaliths of lichen-covered granite. Straight along this course he flew while fairies zipped past on dragonfly wings and lean wolves slunk from shadow to shadow in pursuit of little red-hooded girls. Between the megaliths shimmered the shop fronts, and in every shop window burned a pair of green eyes. One of the shop doors opened and a bald little man rushed out, frantically waving his arms. Glancing back, Morgan saw that the megaliths had sprouted arms and legs and were thundering after him over the slippery flagstones. He gritted his teeth and pedaled harder.

Ahead loomed a forest of cylindrical columns like the pillars of a vast Greek temple. Each was engraved with the name of one of King Arthur's knights: *Sir Sagramore, Sir Gawain, Sir Gareth, Sir Gaheris, Sir Percival.* In the space between the last two pillars, which bore the names *Sir Galahad* and *Siege Perilous,* Morgan caught sight of a fleeting glimmer of gold: *the Holy Grail.* He leaned forward and threw himself into the chase.

On and on he pedaled, past the docks and pier, past the barking sea lions, past the taunting henchmen of Baxter Knowles. At last he found himself wheeling to a stop before the star-studded, candle-lit chancel of a high-arched cathedral. Above his head a gilded crucifix twisted and turned in the thunder-charged air. Beyond it bright angels ascended and descended upon the rungs of a golden ladder. He dropped the bike and leaped up the altar steps.

Where the altar should have been there stood a rough wooden door labeled *Room 247*. Presently it swung wide and out hopped a huge black crow. After the crow came a slender nurse in dark green scrubs. Her green eyes sparkled in her long, oval face. "You can come in now, young man," she said.

He followed her into the room. On a long wooden bench lay the form of his mother, pale as a ghost, thin as the night wind, stiff as a straight dried reed. Her eyes were closed, her jaw set, and she was wrapped from toe to chin in a gauzy white shroud. Morgan reached out to caress her hair, but the nurse gripped him hard by the elbow. From a shelf above his head she pulled down a big canvas sack, ripped it open with her scarlet nails, and dumped its entire contents—a coarse powder the color of blood—over the motionless figure.

"*Elixir Vitae!*" intoned the nurse, waving her hands in the air like a sorceress casting a spell. "Elixir of Life! Elixir of Life!"

The doctor—a short, slight, balding man with a long crooked nose—came in and laid a clammy palm on Morgan's forehead. "No fever," he murmured, checking his watch. "No pulse. Nothing but a hole. A big square hole." Then, with a wink, he drew Morgan's face down next to his own and whispered, "You'd best get out of this, young mister!"

Suddenly the door crashed in and a burly, round-headed orderly clattered into the room pushing a wobbly, lopsided gurney. His one eye flared fiercely as he seized Morgan by the shoulder, but the nurse waved him aside.

"Prepare the athanor!" she shouted.

Releasing Morgan, the orderly swept the shrouded figure from the bench to the gurney. Then out of the room he exploded, weaving and banging his way down the echoing hallway at a frenetic pace. Morgan followed, shouting and calling after his mother.

At the far end of the corridor burned a pulsing red light. Into that lurid glare the hulking orderly drove his fragile cargo, recklessly bouncing the stretcher from one side of the white-walled passage to the other. Morgan's legs were aching, his face streaming with sweat. At every step the light grew harsher and the heat more oppressive. At length the hallway opened into a reverberating hall of stout red brick. At its further end, like the maw of a beast, gaped a smoke-blackened arch, and within the arch roared a tempest of flame and red-hot coals. Beside it stood the nurse, calmly rotating a small golden crucible in her hand.

"Now into the crucible!" she cried. "Into the athanor and the purifying flame!"

Out of the blackness swooped a huge crow with a pair of gigantic tongs in its talons. "*Calcination!*" rasped the crow. "*Dissolution! Distillation!*"

As Morgan watched in disbelief, the orderly grabbed his mother's body and stuffed it into the little gold cup in the nurse's hand. Then the crow, flapping and hovering just above the nurse's head, gripped the crucible in the tongs and flew with it like a bat out of hell straight into the raging fire.

"No!" screamed Morgan, pounding the orderly's broad chest with tightly clenched fists. He fell to his knees, weeping uncontrollably and pressing his forehead to the floor. But a hand seized him by the collar and jerked him to his feet.

"Look now!" commanded the voice of the green-eyed nurse. "Look into the flames and tell me what you see!"

He dried his eyes on his sleeve and peered into the heart of the athanor. At first he saw nothing but a blinding white blaze like the sun shining in its strength. But then a window opened in the midst of the flames and a figure emerged: a golden-haired maiden on a tall white horse. So stunning was the loveliness of her face that he thought she might be an angel from heaven. Her eyes were like stars, her cheeks like roses, and there was an aura as of a golden halo above her head.

"Mother!" he cried. "I see my mother! It's me, Mom! Morgan! I'm here!"

She rode straight up to him, smiling like the sunrise. "Will you come with me, Morgan, to my Father's country?" she said.

Then came a din of thunder and a flash of lightning. The next thing he knew he was tumbling backward, falling helplessly through empty space. Down, down like a rock he plummeted, but soon the velocity of his descent began to diminish. Then slower and slower he fell until it seemed to him that he was a bit of thistledown spiraling earthward in a light summer breeze. At last his head came to rest against something soft, like a pillow. Fearful of what he might find, he opened his eyes and rubbed them with his knuckles. Trembling and panting, his forehead damp with sweat, he sat bolt upright in bed and looked at the clock.

It was 4:53 a.m.

"You may go in now, young man," said the nurse.

Fingering the flask in his jacket pocket, Morgan crossed the hall and approached the door to his mother's room. He was about to go in when he heard the faint sounds of singing. Very far away they seemed, as if they were coming from the next floor, or perhaps from a room at the other end of the corridor. Gently he pushed the door open and stuck his head inside.

His mother was sitting up in bed with two pillows at her head. Her eyes were shut, and her blue-veined hands were lying still in her lap. The voice he had heard was hers, and the words she was singing were these:

> *Thy bountiful care what tongue can recite?*
> *It breathes in the air, it shines in the light;*
> *It streams from the hills, it descends to the plain,*
> *And sweetly distills in the dew and the rain.*

He knew at first sight that she had grown worse since his last visit. Her hair, or what was left of it, floated nebulously about her head like a cloud of white filament. Her face was drawn, her skin transparent, and all her limbs looked brittle enough to break at a single touch. Pitifully small, pale, and bloodless she appeared in the midst of the bright bouquets and potted plants that surrounded her bed, the most prominent of which was a young ficus tree that stood just at her elbow, green and glowing, with a small white card dangling from its branches: *Get well, from George and Moira.*

For a moment he stood there listening to her singing. Then he stepped softly inside, trying not to disturb or interrupt her, but the door creaked and clicked behind him, and her eyes popped open at once.

"Morgan!" she said, her voice a fragile wafer of sound floating in the thick, heavy air. "You've come! I'm so glad to see you!"

He slipped up to the bedside and took her hand. "Rev. Alcuin told me you'd been asking for me. I'm sorry it's taken so long. I've been—"

"Don't!" she said, beaming at him as if her delicate features would break with the strain. "Just let me look at you. I feel as if I could eat you up! My beautiful freckle-faced boy!"

Morgan felt his neck burning. "You don't have to get so mushy," he said, rubbing his nose. "I've been busy, that's all. Working on something to help you—"

"Hush. Not another word until you've heard what *I* have to say. Working on something!" She laughed lightly, but her laughter quickly became an extended fit of coughing.

When she was able to go on, she said, "You're always working on something, aren't you? Always something to help me. That's what I wanted to say to you, Morgan. Why do you love me so much?"

He stared at her in shock. She was smiling, but there was a look of sincere wonder and mystification in her eyes.

"Y-you're my mother!" he stammered.

"Any woman can be a mother. I don't think very many are so deeply loved. That's what has me puzzled. Why me? What have I done to deserve it? I never had time to ponder it before—I've been too busy working. But these last few days …"

Her voice trailed off, and her eyes strayed to the window. Morgan sat holding her hand. After a few minutes she started again.

"Have you ever noticed, Morgan? Rev. Alcuin and the others are forever telling us how important it is to love. Love God with all your heart, soul, mind, and strength. Love your neighbor as yourself. They're right, of course. But I haven't heard them say a whole lot about the staggeringly beautiful and impossible and life-changing marvel of *being* loved! Have you? What does it mean? Where does it come from? Who can explain it? Lately I feel so blessed that sometimes I'm afraid I'll die of pure happiness. That's why I wanted to ask you to forgive me."

"*Forgive* you? I—I don't know what you mean."

She took both of his hands in hers and looked him in the eye. "If only I'd realized it before! Think of the years we've had together. What a gift! I don't believe I ever told you, Morgan. I didn't help you to understand. I never understood it myself. But life is a miracle! Love is beyond comprehension! If only we knew this! If only we really felt it, we could have paradise on earth, right now, today! Forgive me for not helping you to see this!"

"Mom, I …" Morgan faltered, but his voice faded into silence. He was at a complete loss. Loneliness and fear were gathering like chill, stagnant water in the hollow spaces inside his chest. He was beginning to feel as if he didn't know this person.

A nurse came in with a tray containing Jell-O, chicken broth, a cup of tea, a pitcher of water, and a clear plastic cup. Morgan stood aside as she set it on the little table beside the bed and began adjusting his mother's IVs.

"This is my son," his mother said proudly with a smile that lit up the whole of her colorless face.

The nurse smiled too. "Yes, I know. We've met. How are you today, Morgan?"

Morgan blushed and looked at his shoes. "Good, I guess," he said.

"He's not 'good,'" his mother said decisively. "He's better than good. He has a loving heart."

The nurse smiled again and nodded kindly. After taking his mother's temperature, checking her blood pressure, and consulting her other vital signs, she sat down and recorded all of her data on a clipboard at the foot of the bed. Then she looked up and said, "Is there anything more I can get for you, Mrs. Izaak? Are you comfortable?"

"I'm fine," said Mavis. "Morgan's here, and we have lots to discuss."

"Good. You two have a good talk. The doctor will be in to have a look at you as soon as visiting hours are over. Until then, just ring the nurse's station if you need anything."

"I have everything," said Mavis. "Everything and more. Thank you."

All this while Morgan was standing and looking intently at the cup and pitcher on the little tray. When the nurse had gone, he sat down beside the bed, picked up the pitcher, and poured out some water. Then he drew the flask from his pocket.

"Mom," he said in a low voice, his eyes on the door. "Do you trust me?"

"I know that you love me," she said.

"This is what I've been working on," he said. "I want you to try it. Until you do, I can't be sure of its powers. I followed the instructions precisely—everything, from collecting the dew right down to the final steps of distillation and coagulation."

Mavis's smile faded. "Morgan," she said, "I thought we talked about your father's books and instruments."

"We did! But what do you expect? I can't just let you lie here and die. Not while there's something I can do! Something that might actually help! Besides, this isn't the only thing I've brought!"

Uncorking the flask, he carefully shook a small amount of his white powder into the cup. Immediately the clear liquid

236

began to boil and swirl with snaking corkscrews and spirals of maroon and vermilion. Violet bubbles collected along the sides of the clear plastic, then rose to the surface and burst with a light effervescent fizz. Morgan took it in both hands and held it out to his mother.

"It contains all the power of the stars! It's the *Elixir Vitae*—the Elixir of Life. And that means it can heal diseases. All the books say so!"

Mavis frowned. She looked down at the cup, and a confused, bewildered expression took possession of her features.

"Won't you just try a little? For my sake?"

He leaned across the bed and put the cup of red liquid into her hand.

"You know I'd do anything for you, Morgan," she said. "Anything I could. But sometimes there are things we *can't* do. Not for ourselves or anybody else. Sometimes we just have to pray and trust. We have to trust that we're *loved.*"

Footsteps sounded in the hall. Morgan cast another nervous glance at the door. When he turned back to his mother, he could see that the cloud of confusion was dissipating and the light was dawning again in her face. She pushed back against the pillows, and as she did so her hand—the hand that held the cup of Elixir—drooped nearer to the bed-sheets.

"We have to trust," she continued, "that the One who loves us knows what's best for us, and that He's doing everything that can be done. Haven't I told you all this before?"

"Yes, you did, but—"

"I *know* I did!" Her eyes grew bright, and a warm glow rose from her neck into the hollows of her cheeks. "I told you that life is a miracle and that love is paradise on earth!"

The footsteps drew closer. His stomach churning, Morgan tried to motion to her to hurry and drink the cup, but she closed her eyes and allowed her hand to fall a little further.

"Do you remember," she said, "what I told you the last time you were here? About longing to follow the sunset down over the edge of the world? Well, I don't feel that way anymore. What I think now is that *today*, this very moment, is all I need. One day, one hour, one minute is more than enough."

As she spoke, Morgan heard the door open. He turned to see the nurse coming back with the doctor just behind her. When they saw that Mavis was not merely talking with her son, but actually speaking with great fervor and intensity of feeling, the two of them stopped and stood listening.

"All my life," Mavis was saying, "I've been surrounded by God's beauty and glory. I've experienced the miracle of being loved without deserving it. I never understood why. Even now I don't understand it. I know it sounds silly, but I never even noticed it until they brought me here. I wish I could—"

At that, her hand dropped to the bed and the cup tipped sideways, spilling the entirety of its precious contents into the potted ficus. She laid her other hand across her heart and sighed deeply.

The doctor stepped to the bedside and touched her lightly on the shoulder. "Good afternoon, Mrs. Izaak," he said. "How are you feeling today?"

As he spoke, the nurse took Morgan by the arm and drew him gently to the door. "I think it would be best," she whispered, "if you go on home now and let her get some rest. As you can see, it's—well, it's beginning to affect her mind."

Morgan nodded. He searched for something to say, but words failed him. The nurse opened the door, and he stepped out into the hallway. But before turning to go, he took one last look at his mother where she sat conversing quietly and earnestly with the doctor. What he saw caused the breath to catch in his throat.

The ficus tree had withered, and its crumpled leaves were already falling to the floor.

Chapter Twenty-Two

JACOB'S LADDER

Ding!

The elevator doors slid open, and Morgan stepped out into the hospital lobby, his mind a barren wilderness, his emotions a maelstrom of darkness and light, heat and cold. The sun was shining in through the front windows, glaring off the highly polished floor. Momentarily dazed by its brilliance, he staggered uncertainly toward the exit. But before he was halfway across the room, someone came up from behind and touched him on the shoulder.

"I had a feeling you'd be here."

He turned and found himself face to face with Eny. Her brows were knit, and there was an urgent light in her eyes. She brushed a few coppery strands from her face and jammed a forefinger into his chest. "All day long at school I was looking for a chance to talk to you, but you kept slipping away. Are you avoiding me?"

Morgan forced a laugh. "Why would I do that?"

"I don't know," she said, her eyes narrowing. "Why?"

"Look, Eny, I don't have time for this right now, okay?"

He turned, but she grabbed him by the sleeve. "Don't walk away from me! You have to listen!"

"Listen to what? What's your problem?"

"Didn't you hear what I told you and my mom last night?"

"Of course I did. What about it?"

"I'm not lying, Morgan, and I'm not out of my mind! I know it's hard to believe, so I don't blame you for laughing, but there's a lot more I have to say. Things my mom wouldn't understand. But you would, and you need to, so you've got to hear me out!"

"Why me?"

"Because it concerns you. It concerns you more than anybody else I can think of!" She brushed a tear from her nose and glanced over her shoulder. Then she whispered, "I'm convinced of it now. Your Madame Medea is the Morrigu."

"My Madame Medea!" scoffed Morgan. "She's just a stupid alchemist!"

"No, she isn't. I've seen her in her true shape. I know what she's all about. She's not just a shopkeeper. She's … something else. I felt her power. I saw what it can do. She killed my friends! She destroyed a whole village! And it was all because she was trying to catch me. What's worse, I'm afraid she hasn't given up yet!"

Morgan ran the tip of his tongue over his braces. "And that's my problem because…?"

Eny's eyes flared. "What a thing to say! I thought we were friends! But if you want to know, I'll tell you. What she's really after is Lia Fail—the Stone of Destiny. Because whoever possesses the Stone of Destiny gains the power to rule everything."

"Uh-huh," Morgan said dully. "I seem to have heard that before."

"Well, what you haven't heard is that the Stone is useless to the possessor unless it's under the care of a young girl— a pure and blameless young maiden like Eithne. For some reason, she thinks *I'm* that girl!"

"Funny, huh?" said Morgan. But no sooner had the words passed his lips than he heard the voice of Rev. Alcuin rising up unbidden at the back of his mind: "*A maiden of perfect purity and perfect chastity* ... having renounced all things false...." In that moment Morgan suddenly knew in his heart of hearts that faithful, honest Eny could very well be that maiden.

"It's not funny," said Eny. "And it's not the only thing I have to tell you. Maybe you don't care about anybody but yourself. But if that's the case, then you should know that, in my opinion, she's after *you* as well."

"Me?" Again Morgan tried to laugh, but the result of his effort sounded more like an asthmatic wheeze. "What for?"

"I'm not sure. I only know that, for some reason, she dragged the two of us into this thing *together*. She seems to think that you're looking for the Stone of Destiny too, and that you know something about it. She said so the very first time we met her. Maybe *you* understand what she meant, but I don't. My guess is that it has something to do with your dad and his books and your alchemy experiments."

Suddenly Morgan felt as if he were about to choke. "She was talking about the *Philosophers'* Stone," he spluttered.

"You should know that, Eny. I've told you a hundred times!" He coughed and yanked himself free of her grasp. "Look, I'd love to continue this discussion, but I really have to go. There's a lot to do at home. I'll see you later."

With that he spun on his heel, walked out the front door, and jumped on his bike. As he pedaled down Vista Del Mar, it occurred to him that the sky was clear and the sea sparkling for the first time in days.

On one point Morgan had been entirely truthful with Eny. He did have a lot to do at home. The last day of school was less than three weeks off, and there were tests to study for, reports to write, and homework to finish. If he didn't buckle down, Moira would know, and Moira would tell his mother. It was crucial to make a good show of hitting the books. So when he arrived at the duplex, he ducked his head in at the Ariellos' and told George that he wouldn't be joining them for dinner. Then he boiled some water, whipped up a pan of instant macaroni and cheese, and got down to work.

Once summer vacation comes, he told himself as he grappled with a particularly difficult algebra problem, *I'll start all over again. I'll build my own athanor. I'll follow Flamel's recipe this time. Morrigu or not, Madame Medea's no alchemist. How could I let myself be fooled by such a quack?*

After dark he put his homework aside and ran across the street to St. Halistan's, intending to spend the rest of the evening searching his father's books for answers to the questions crowding his brain. *Who knows?* he thought, reaching into his pocket for the little brass key—*I might even sleep in the lab tonight.* But when he opened the door at the base of the tower, a sound drifted out that stopped him dead in his tracks. The sound of fiddle music on the stairway.

Eny and Simon. Again. Morgan groaned. *Who died and made them owners of the tower stairs?* Holding the door open just a crack, he stood hesitating on the threshold, peering into the dimness within, trembling somehow at the thought of facing her again. *This is ridiculous,* he thought, shaking himself and slipping quietly inside. *She probably won't notice me anyway. She's got her music—and her new friend—to keep her busy.*

But she did notice. No sooner had he closed the door and stepped onto the mat than the music suddenly ceased. In the dusky, empty silence a single light shone above the stairs, faintly highlighting the reds and blues in the stained glass window and casting a crown of pale luminescence over the heads of the two musicians. They were sitting together, just two steps below the landing, their fiddles on their knees, their eyes fixed expectantly on his face. Morgan wished there were another way to get to his lab.

"Well, now," said Simon with a tip of his bow. "Mr. Morgan Izaak. I'm glad to see you. Very glad indeed. I told you once that I came here in need of your help, and I have a feeling that tonight is the night."

Morgan advanced a few paces into the shadows. "Help with what?" he asked. But before Simon could answer, a sharp jolt shook the tower, sending a small cascade of loose mortar, plaster, and gravel skittering down the stony face of the front wall.

Someone whistled in the darkness. Footsteps echoed from the door leading to the sanctuary. Then a diagonal beam of light sliced the gloomy air and lingered over a large patch of broken masonry high up in the corner above the street entrance.

"We aren't taking this step a moment too soon," said the voice of Rev. Alcuin. "Sorry as I am to have to say it."

Morgan looked over his shoulder and saw George, Moira, and the Reverend standing in a huddle about ten steps to his left. Rev. Alcuin was squinting up at the wall while George kept the light trained on the cracked stonework.

"I'm afraid you're right," said George. "These tremors are a bad sign. We could get a *really* big one any time, and we don't want that to happen when we've got people in here."

"No, no," sighed Peter. "Of course not. I suppose it's all for the best. Maybe the Lord Himself has sent Mr. Knowles to minister to our needs in this time of distress."

Moira clucked her tongue. "God's ways aren't that mysterious," she said.

Simon waved his bow at them from the top of the stairs. "A good evening to you, folks!" he called. "Now don't you worry, George. I've given that window a good cleaning"—he jabbed a thumb over his shoulder in the direction of Jacob's Ladder—"and finished the scrubbing and buffing in the main hallway, too. This is just a bit of a break we're having.

The little lady has agreed to scrape out a few tunes with me over my dinner hour. Then it's straight back to work."

"I hope so," said George, "because we're really slammed with work. Cleaning out the tower is job number one for the rest of the week. We'll have to start tonight if we're going to finish in time. Everything goes, and that means everything. They've given us until Monday. Then the wreckers are moving in."

"I know," said Simon. "I've already mentioned it to the lad," he added, nodding in Morgan's direction.

Morgan stared. So the tower was really coming down! His lab was actually about to become a thing of the past! Like birds released from a cage, his plans for the evening flew out the window. He'd have to act quickly if he wanted to salvage anything. If he didn't start packing and moving right away, there would be no more books to study, no more pestles and mortars to pulverize the ashes of his immolations, no more alembics and Bunsen burners with which to test his theories and confect his elixirs. He could see that Simon's lips were moving again, but he wasn't listening to the old gray janitor. He pressed his palms to his temples and began thinking out a course of action.

George, Moira, and Rev. Alcuin were making a slow circuit around the base of the tower, examining the seams between the huge blocks of stone, shining their light up into shadowy angles and corners, talking together in low, serious tones about structural weaknesses and square footage and the future of St. Halistan's Church. But Morgan's thoughts were only for his lab. *I know where to find some boxes on the fifth floor,* he thought, doing some quick calculations to determine how many he'd need. His stomach churning, he started up the stairs, taking the first three steps at a single leap. But even as he did so, Simon and Eny shouldered their fiddles and raised their bows.

"A set of jigs," proposed Simon. "How about 'Tripping Up The Stairs'? After that we'll go into 'The Silver Spire'—in honor of the tower."

Eny nodded and they began to play. They played as Morgan had often heard them play before, but this time there was something different about the music. The instant the old man touched horsehair to strings, a fragrance like that of honeysuckle and lilacs came pouring down the steps. It washed over Morgan's head, it caressed his face, it flooded his nostrils. Then his skin began to tingle and the hair rose up at the back of his neck. The air itself, though very still, seemed charged with invisible sparks, and the stained-glass picture of Jacob's Ladder pulsed with color as if illuminated from behind by a chorus of dancing candles. As in the past, the soaring melody filled his brain with a wordless song: *Cease striving. Let go and trust.* He understood without looking back that the others knew what he was seeing and feeling—that George, Moira, and the Reverend had fallen silent and were watching the scene unfold with blank upturned faces.

Like a traveler doggedly braving a storm—a storm of rose petals or honeyed mist—Morgan pressed forward up the stairs, resolved to reach his lab at all costs, determined to overcome any obstacle no matter how enchanting or sweet. As he climbed, he could see the ivory inlay on Simon's fingerboard glittering like cold flame. He could see the light leaping from the tip of Eny's bow and shimmering on her hair like a summer sunset. She blushed and turned away at his approach. But Simon smiled and got to his feet as the boy drew nearer, plying his bow furiously all the while. And when Morgan made it clear that he wanted to pass, the old man hopped up lightly to the next step—the last stone step before the landing. That was when everything changed.

First came a dreadful shock like the blow of a celestial hammer. The walls shuddered so violently that great pieces of rock broke loose and fell crashing to the stairway and the floor. Then, with a horrible splitting sound, a huge black crevasse opened on the street side of the building and gaped from the ceiling to the door. "It's the big one!" shouted George in a terrified voice, but Morgan knew it wasn't; for in the next instant it became plain beyond the shadow of doubt that this was no ordinary earthquake.

The stone step on which Simon stood fiddling began to quiver and vibrate like the tailpipe of George's rattly old pickup truck. Then it burned with russet fire and glowed with a silvery sheen. At last it shook itself like a living, breathing creature and let out a deafening roar. It roared like a lion. It roared like a jet engine. It roared like the raging sea. Morgan cringed and covered his ears. But Simon stopped playing, bowed his head, and let his bow drop to his side.

What happened next Morgan could never clearly recall. It was as if there had been no beginning and could be no end to the tempest of images that swept around his head and drowned his reeling senses. He was aware of nothing but a galactic hurricane of blinding illumination, a monsoon of eddying color, a deafening squall of ear-splitting sound.

Somewhere in the midst of this dreadful swirling cyclone a shaft of hot white light shot like a spear straight down through the center of the stained-glass window and fell sizzling upon the face of the trembling, roaring stone. No sooner had it touched the step than its dazzling beam assumed the shape of Jacob's golden ladder. As Morgan watched, the ladder stretched and grew. Up from the stairway it rose, crashing straight through the ceiling, piercing all seven stories of the tower, rocketing skyward, flinging itself out into the wide spangled night. Higher and higher it soared until its topmost rung exploded like a nova and became a distant blazing star. Then the tower's stone walls melted like wax and dropped away like a veil of evening rain.

After that came angels—not rosy-cheeked, ringleted cherubs like those depicted in the stained glass, but terrible, burning seraphs only vaguely or partially human in aspect and form. They burst upon Morgan's view in a great variety of shapes and sizes, some with the faces of men and women, some with the burnished feet of bulls and calves, some with the heads of eagles or lions or lambs. All had wings like wind-blown banners, some two, some four, some six. With these pointed pennons, rainbow-hued, eye-speckled, and broad as the fantails of peacocks, they beat the air and whipped the stars from one end of the heavens to the other. Those who possessed six wings used two to veil their faces, two to cover their feet, and another two to caress the tips of their neighbors' plumage. Every angel shone with a brilliance so unbearable that it was impossible to tell whether they were dressed in some kind of glowing raiment or whether it were merely their unclothed bodies that burned with the heat and glory of a raging furnace. Morgan could not see them at all unless he shaded his eyes and glanced aside. Up and down the golden stairway they flew, surrounded by bright-tailed comets and rings of red fire, chanting words he could not understand, singing in voices like thundering waterfalls and restless winds.

How long all this went on Morgan had no idea, but when next he turned his eyes in Simon's direction the old man's appearance had been altered beyond all recognition. No longer was he bent and gray and tattered, but straight, tall, and golden-haired. A voluminous cloak of purple satin flowed from his broad shoulders, and he wore a fine white silk shirt fastened close to the body with hooks of shining gold. A chain of tiny golden apples and a ruby-encrusted brooch secured the rustling cloak at his shoulder. Around his neck gleamed a twisted silver torque, and upon his head a band of filigreed gold. Instead of a fiddle he held in his left hand a silver shield rimmed with gold and embossed with precious stones of every color; and at his side, where his bow had fallen, flashed a gold-hilted sword with a sharp blade of bright blue steel. He was standing in the middle of a group of angels, speaking with them earnestly, nodding vigorously, emphasizing his unheard words with broad and forceful gestures.

Morgan looked away, and immediately it was as if he were falling freely through space, spinning out of control, cartwheeling through a matrix of shifting shadows and shapes and sounds where there was no longer any up or down, no in or out, no this way or that—only a bewildering sense of everything getting inextricably mixed up with everything else while he himself went careening madly right through the center of it all. At intervals he got brief glimpses of the familiar and recognizable: the brass railing on the stairway; Rev. Alcuin's dimly glinting spectacles; a pigeon on a window ledge; Moira with her hands stretched high above her head; a leather-bound book on a stained and pitted workbench; George with his eyebrows raised in alarm; George gaping openmouthed for wonder and joy and dismay.

At last he caught sight of Simon again—not the golden-haired Simon of the purple cloak and flashing sword, but Simon as he had always known him: a gray-haired man in baggy pants and a drab gray coat. Once again the fiddle was on his shoulder, and once again he was coaxing torrents of sweet sound out of it with darting and skittering bow. Morgan could see Eny at his side, sawing away at her own violin as if she had been doing so from all eternity, her brows tightly knit, her mouth a thin, straight line. After a few moments of this Simon threw off his last bow stroke with an expansive flourish. Then, brandishing the bow above his head like a conquering hero, he jumped down from the last stone step.

Morgan blinked and looked around. He was lying at the foot of the stairs, and everything had suddenly returned to normal. The angels were gone. The stars had disappeared. Jacob's Ladder was dim and small within its black and narrow frame. The walls of the tower stood grim and silent in the high-arching shadows, shaken but not much the worse for wear. The gaping crack above the door had somehow been erased. Eny and Simon were sitting quietly on the second step below the landing, their faces placid, their bows and fiddles resting in their laps.

"What happened?" said the voice of George. It sounded husky and shaky and unusually tentative in the lofty echoing spaces of the tower. Morgan rolled over on his side and saw the chief custodian, scrunched and crumpled as an old rag doll, sitting on the floor between his wife and Peter Alcuin. All three had their backs to the wall and their feet splayed out in front of them, as if they had been flung against the stones by the sheer force of the vision. Their faces were pale and pasty, etched with expressions of recently fled and slowly fading terror.

Simon grunted and labored to his feet. "I had a feeling you were going ask me that," he said. "And I suppose you really do deserve an explanation. Well then. It's like this. This step," he said, turning and pointing his bow at the last stone step beneath the landing, "is Lia Fail."

Chapter Twenty-Three

OLLAMH FOLLA

Moira was the first to speak.

"If that stone is Lia Fail," she said, pushing herself up from the floor and shoving a handful of auburn hair out of her face, "I mean, if the Stone of Destiny has been here on this stairway, right here in St. Halistan's church, under our very noses, for all these years, and you knew it all the time—why didn't you say so?"

Simon rubbed the back of his neck and chuckled. "Well now. Would any of you have believed me? Would anyone have cared?"

"*She* would," said Eny. "She believed *me* when I told her I'd been in the Sidhe."

"Ay!" muttered George.

Simon's intractable black eyebrows arched upward to mingle with the fringes of his limp gray hair. "You've been in the Sidhe, missy? Well, there's a piece of news worth knowing; though I might have guessed it—if not by your eyes, then by the way you played that last jig! But there's a simple answer to your mother's question. I didn't tell because I *didn't know*. I *couldn't* know until the Stone revealed itself. Before this night, I had nothing to go on but bits and pieces. Theories and suspicions. Hints and clues."

Morgan sat up, his ears tingling. "What sort of hints and clues?"

"As it happens," Simon replied coolly, "they had mainly to do with your father. That's right. You needn't look so surprised. He was very close to uncovering the secret himself. So I came looking for him. But I came too late. That's why I said I'd be needing *your* help!"

Instantly an avalanche of doubts and fears tumbled into Morgan's brain. Heady with the thrill of unsuspected possibilities, he got up and stood gazing into the old man's lined face and twinkling blue eyes, silently sifting through the scores of questions that came crowding in upon him in rapid-fire succession. How much had his father known? Did he actually believe, as Peter Alcuin suggested on that earlier occasion, that this Stone of Destiny and the Philosophers' Stone were connected? Was he really "disillusioned" with alchemy? Had he discovered another, better way to achieve his goals? Morgan opened his mouth to voice his jumbled thoughts, but before he could speak, the Reverend stepped to the base of the stairway and laid a hand on the brass rail.

"I appreciate a good story as much as anybody else," he said, looking up at Simon Brach. "But I have some questions about this one. For one thing, if that step is Lia Fail, then who are you?"

Simon sat down and laid the red fiddle in its velvet-lined case. "Now that's a tale that will take some telling," he said, spreading his large-knuckled hands over his big bony knees. "Plenty of telling, since it's all tied up with the story of the Stone itself." He paused a moment, as if looking for the right place to begin. Then he said, "I'm a man of the Tuatha De Danann."

Moira let out a squeal and skipped over to sit on the bottom step at Peter Alcuin's feet. "We're all ears," she said, smoothing her skirt and adjusting her glasses on her nose.

"*Caramba!*" grumbled George.

Simon took a long, slow breath. "I have been in this world a long while," he said, "seeking Lia Fail. My people lost track of it after sending it into exile, and I've been given the job of hunting it down. I've been known by many different names in different times and places: Dan Sheehan, Jamie Friel, Jeremy Bran; Bedivere and Baruch, Galahad and Brendan, Irial Faidh and the Fisher King. Where I come from, they call me Ollamh Folla."

"Ollamh Folla!" said Eny, brightening. "I know that name! You're the one who smuggled Lia Fail out of Ireland!"

"To save it from the invading Milesians," offered Moira.

"And once it was safely away," continued Eny, "you went underground, where your enemies couldn't find you, with King Lugh of the Long Hand and the rest of the Danaans. That was the beginning of the Sidhe."

The old man smiled and nodded. "Your knowledge of the subject is good," he said. "But not complete. I didn't send Lia Fail out of Ireland simply to save it from the Milesians. I sent it because it *had* to go. That was its *destiny.*"

"Because of the prophecy, you mean?"

"That's one way of putting it. But there's a reason behind every prophecy. The Tuatha De Danann were never the Stone's rightful owners. They acquired it by *stealing* it from others. They usurped its powers for their own gain. And though, as the ages rolled by, they attained immortality simply by virtue of its presence in their midst, they also discovered that the penalty for their theft lay in the treasured prize itself. To this day many of them still crave the Stone's gifts and call it 'The Satisfaction of All Desire.' But the wisest among them know that the power of Lia Fail is a terrible burden. They have learned that unending life within the circles of the created worlds is a bitter, grinding weariness. That's why the king's closest advisers eventually counseled him to send Lia Fail away—beyond the edge of the world, to the Land of the Sun's Going, as it had been foretold. I was a member of that group. We were twelve in number, and in this we were all agreed. All of us, that is, but one."

"The Morrigu," whispered Eny. Morgan flinched at the name.

Again Simon nodded. "Now these things happened, as Moira rightly says, at the time of the Milesian conquest of Ireland. Not so very long ago, as the Danaans reckon time. But this isn't the whole story. Not by a long shot. No, if you want to understand what Lia Fail really is and where its destiny truly lies, you have to go back to the beginning. You have to go back to Bethel." He glanced over his shoulder at the stained glass window above the landing.

As if at a predetermined signal, Rev. Alcuin removed his spectacles and cleared his throat. Closing his eyes, he pinched the bridge of his nose and began to recite, very slowly and distinctly, in his best preaching voice:

> *And Jacob went out from Beersheba, and went toward Haran. And he lighted upon a certain place, and tarried there all night, because the sun was set; and he took one of the stones of that place, and put them for his pillows, and lay down in that place to sleep. And he dreamed, and behold a ladder set up on the earth, and the top of it reached to heaven: and behold the angels of God ascending and descending on it.... And Jacob awaked out of his sleep, and he said, Surely the LORD is in this place; and I knew it not.... And Jacob ... took the stone that he had put for his pillows, and set it up for a pillar, and poured oil upon the top of it. And he called the name of that place Bethel.*

The Reverend opened his eyes and looked around. "Bethel," he said. "That's Hebrew for 'House of God.'"

"Exactly!" said Simon. "As if God could live in a rock! Though I suppose that's not so surprising when you consider that some of Jacob's descendents believed He could live in a *box!*"

Moira sighed. "That's a Bible story," she said. "I thought we were talking about the Tuatha De Danann."

"I believe we are," said Rev. Alcuin. "Though I'm interested to see how Simon is going to weave the threads of his tale together."

"Patience," said the old man with a wink. "Now no stone can be God's house, as the Reverend knows perfectly well. But *this* Stone had been touched by the divine power, and there were some unusual properties associated with it. So Jacob and his sons took it with them when they went down into Egypt. That's where it fell into the hands of Scota, Pharaoh's daughter, at the time of the Exodus. One of Scota's suitors, a man named Gathelus, had filled her head with the notion that the Bethel stone was the source of Moses' powers. She sent her servants into Goshen to lay hold of it. They seized it by force from the house of Reuel, one of the Hebrew chieftains. And when Pharaoh and his army were drowned in the Red Sea, Gathelus and Scota took the Stone and fled to Spain, where they founded the ancient kingdom of Brigantium, first home of the Tuatha De Danann. Gathelus, you see, was a Greek—one of the people Homer calls *Danaoi*. The Danaan race takes its name from him."

Rev. Alcuin looked thoughtful. "I don't consider myself an expert," he said slowly, "or even a believer. Not necessarily. But as I was telling Morgan just the other day, folklore is rich in legends about stones of virtue and power. The evidence—primarily *philological* evidence—indicates that these tales may be interconnected. It was a subject of special interest to Morgan's father. British and Irish traditions have always maintained that Lia Fail and the Bethel stone were one and the same, so that part of Simon's account doesn't surprise me in the least. But what I *don't* understand is how either one of them could have ended up *here*. That's the thing that doesn't make any sense. I'm not familiar with a single story that would explain it."

"But you are!" said Morgan.

Peter regarded him strangely. "I am?"

"Yes! When we were talking in your office that night, you said something about Santiago de Compostela. Don't you remember? It was almost the very last thing I heard you say!"

"Of course I remember," said the Reverend. "But I don't see how—"

George was at his elbow in a flash. "The Legend of Compostela!" he said, his voice cracking with excitement. "I told it to the boy myself! 'A story of Old California,' I said. 'A story about the Ariello family and Santa Piedra!'"

Peter shook his head. "That's not the way I heard it. The version I know comes from medieval Spain."

"Yes, of course!" said George, barely able to contain himself. "It begins in Spain. But it ends here! Why do you think the town is called *Santa Piedra*—holy stone? Why do you suppose Father Serra named our Mission after Santiago de Compostela?"

Rev. Alcuin raised an eyebrow and fell silent. One by one, the rest of them turned to Simon, as if expecting him to provide the answer. But Simon's face showed that he, too, was still seeking a solution—that the wheels of his brain were spinning madly in an attempt to fit the pieces together into a consistent and meaningful whole.

Moira rubbed her nose and frowned. "Brigantium," she mused. "It was from Brigantium in Spain that the Danaans set out with Lia Fail in their flying ships. But that was ages ago, when they were fleeing from the Gallaeci of the East. From Spain they went to Falias, from Falias to Gorias, Finias, and Murias. Westward, always westward they set their sails:

> *For being but few to journey on the land, they*
> *would move on the face of the waters, to the*
> *extremity of the world, to the land of the sun's*
> *going, as they had heard.*

"The last place they landed was Ireland," she concluded. "The stories I know don't say anything about California!"

George was fuming. "How many times have I told you, Moira!" he said, beads of perspiration glistening on his broad, brown forehead. "Those tales of yours are nothing but pagan fables! I'm talking about the tradition of the Holy Church! And the tradition of the Church says that the Franciscan padres brought the miraculous Stone to the New World as a holy relic of Santiago de Compostela! From Vera Cruz in Mexico they sent it north by sea to Alta California. It traveled from mission to mission until it arrived in Santa Piedra. Its final resting place was in the Mission—underneath the altar!"

Moira glared at her husband over the rims of her glasses. "Has anyone ever seen it? Has anyone even looked?"

"I did," said Morgan.

Every eye was on him in an instant. "And?" pressed Moira.

"You can ask George. I already told him. There was nothing there. Nothing but a hole." He paused and inclined his head in the direction of the stairway. "A hole just about the size of one of these steps."

"Seriously?" said George. "A step the size of *that* one?" He pointed at the last stone step below the landing.

Morgan nodded.

"But *how?*"

"I think I understand that, too," Morgan replied. "When the Mission fell into ruin, the people of Santa Piedra started using pieces of it to build other stuff around town. Houses, sheds, barns. Churches, too, I guess. Back in the 1870s. That's what the tour guide said."

Peter looked at George. "Well," he said, "we've all seen the inscription on the cornerstone. St. Halistan's was built in 1873."

"So that accounts for the *last* leg of the Stone's journey," said Morgan. "From Spain to Santa Piedra."

"And *I've* given you the first," said Moira—"*from* Spain *to* Ireland, a long, long time ago. But what happened in between? If the Stone from the Mission is really Lia Fail, how did it get from Ireland to Compostela?"

Morgan locked eyes with Peter. "I think Rev. Alcuin has that piece of the puzzle. Remember what you told me about the Grail legends? How the Gral was originally a Stone, and how different versions of the Gral story can be found all across Europe—from England to France, from Germany to Italy, and finally even in Spain? *That* must be the path Lia Fail followed! That must be the route it took after Simon—I mean, Ollamh Folla—sent it out of Ireland."

Simon beamed at him. "I think you've got it, lad!"

Morgan felt his head and chest beginning to swell. Could he actually have played a part in finishing something his father had begun? He looked up at the two fiddlers. Eny was smiling down at him from her place at Simon's side, her blue eye sparkling in the dim light like a sunlit sea. Morgan's cheeks and forehead burned. He bent down and turned his face away.

"Isn't it marvelous?" Simon went on. "Apparently the Stone has been seeking its *own* destiny all along—moving toward it, inexorably, since the very beginning. Gathelus stole it from the Hebrews thinking he'd made himself its master, but it wasn't so. The Danaans were never anything but the agents of its designs. Once we let it go, it found its own way. Against all hope and expectation, it overcame every obstacle and came at last to the westernmost edge of the world. Its long journey is nearly over. Only one thing more remains to be done."

"What do you mean?" said Morgan, a strange tightness rising at the base of his throat. "Lia Fail is here. We've found the Stone of Destiny! What else is there to do? Isn't that the end of the story?"

Simon shook his head. "Not quite. The Stone can't *stay* here. Nothing can that has been truly touched by the hand of

God. Not for long, at any rate. While it *does* remain, it retains an aura that, despite all the miraculous signs and wonders it produces, can only deceive and disappoint. It makes grand promises it can't fulfill. That's why it must go on and complete its course. It has to pass beyond the circles of the world until it reaches its destination: Inisfail, the Green Island in the West, the Land of the Sun's Going. I'm not the one to take it there, but I *can* escort it to the threshold. That's what I've been sent to do."

Eny set her fiddle aside and took Simon's hand. "I'll help you," she said. "I *have* to help you. If you don't succeed, Lia Fail may fall into the hands of the Morrigu, and I promised a friend that I'd never let that happen. I know where we can find a boat—down at Harp's Haven, near the old whaling station out on La Punta Lira."

The old man smiled and bowed his head in gratitude.

Rev. Alcuin seemed worried. He took a handkerchief from his pocket and mopped his brow. "I don't know who the Morrigu is," he said, "or where you're planning on going in a boat. All I know is that it sounds extremely dangerous, and I'm not sure I approve. George, Moira—what do you think?"

George glanced up at Eny with a grin. "What can I say? We've seen miracles tonight. I have no idea what should be done about them. But my little girl seems to know."

Moira looked disgruntled. She frowned at Simon. "I believe in the stories, and I know what has to happen. But as far as I'm concerned, you still haven't answered the most important question! You may be a Danaan, but you're no king. So why should Lia Fail roar for *you?*"

"I think I know the answer to that one," Eny offered. "It's because you're the king's *representative,* right? The Fir Bolg told me that Ollamh Folla is King Lugh's lieutenant and right-hand man. Is that the reason?"

Simon stroked his chin. "It's a possibility, missy," he said thoughtfully. "Then again, maybe not. I think we've seen that Lia Fail has a mind of its own. It might be that the Stone roars whenever it wants to for whomever it chooses. It might be that the one 'destined to rule' is the one we least suspect. Perhaps real power and kingship aren't what we take them to be. If you ask me, there's a mystery here—a mystery that's best left unexplained."

Rev. Alcuin was fingering the cross that hung around his neck. "There's no need to explain," he said. "That part of the story was explained a long time ago."

At that, Simon leaped to his feet and rubbed his hands together. "Well," he said, "I think we've had enough talk for tonight. There's work to be done! Am I right, George?"

George slapped his forehead. "More work than ever!" he exclaimed. "Not only do we have to clean out the tower, we've also got to figure out a way to remove that step and shuttle it down to the old whaling station!"

"A big job," Simon said, laughing as he descended the stairs and laid a hand on Morgan's shoulder, "a big job indeed. But there's no need to worry. We've got good people on our side. The lad's going to help us. Right, Mr. Izaak?"

Morgan looked up. It was as if he were peering at the old man's face in a distorted mirror or through a clouded glass. For some reason his stomach was shifting uneasily. He wasn't sure how he should feel or what he ought to say. To make matters worse, Simon's words were whirling through his brain like a swarm of angry bees: ... *can't stay here ... beyond the circles of the world ... promises it can't fulfill ... a mystery best left unexplained.* He tried to speak, but the words caught in his throat. He coughed and rubbed his nose and tried again.

"I'm sorry," he heard himself stammer in a tremulous and distant voice. "I'd like to help, but I really can't stay. Not tonight. I've got lots of stuff to do at home."

Chapter Twenty-Four

HARP'S HAVEN

Numb, dazed, and frazzled, Morgan stumbled into the darkened apartment and threw himself blindly on the couch. Eager as he'd been to start packing up his lab, the events of the past hour had drained him of every last ounce of energy and strength. George and Simon would have to draft somebody else for their cleaning crew. Tomorrow would be time enough to retrieve his father's books. As for the rest of the stuff, it was replaceable. Replaceable *and* irrelevant. Who needed alembics, cucurbits, and tinctures now? Lia Fail had been found. The Satisfaction of All Desire had come.

It would be difficult, of course—maybe even impossible—to bring his mother into direct contact with the Stone. He'd probably have to come up with some other way of accessing its power. He still had a few ounces of the white elixir in his backpack, and if Madame Medea were telling the truth, then Lia Fail was the key to unlocking their healing virtues. Exactly *how* it was supposed to work, he didn't know. But he could sort out the details in the morning. With a sigh and a yawn, he rolled over on his stomach and pressed his face into the corner between the cushions and the back of the couch. So profound was his exhaustion that he fell asleep at once. And as he slept, he dreamed another dream.

The sea—dark purple, banded with green and gray. Overhead a moldy yellow sky. On the sand a dying king, sword in hand, visor down. Near the king a tall, trembling knight, and at his side a willowy woman in white. She sat on a stone step, mending bleeding wounds with needle and thread. Her head was bent, her hair dark, her face shadowed, but her eyes at fleeting moments flashed deep green. Morgan stood on the sand, a small, carved wooden cask in his hands.

"Bedivere," said the king, "I have tarried overlong. Take Excalibur my good sword and cast it into the deep. Then come and tell me what you see."

"Good, my lord," the knight replied, "I hear and obey."

So the knight took the sword and went his way. But as Morgan watched, he slipped aside and hid Excalibur beneath a tree.

"Well?" asked the king when he returned.

"My lord Arthur," the man answered, "I saw naught but the wind and the waves."

"Seek not to betray me," said the king. "Go and carry out my command!"

Once more the knight contrived to hide the sword, and all transpired as at the first. But the third time, seeing Arthur could not be deceived, he took Excalibur and heaved it far out over the water. Immediately an arm and hand burst upward from the surface, caught the sword by the hilt, and drew it down. Then a boat, shrouded in black and filled with weeping women, appeared beyond the rolling breakers.

Bedivere came and told this to the king. Then he, too, wept. "What shall become of me, my lord, now that ye go and leave me alone among mine enemies?"

"Comfort yourself," said Arthur. "In me is no trust to trust in. I will cross the sea to Avalon, there to be healed of my wounds."

The boat came to shore. Three women got out, lifted the king, and laid him inside with his head upon a cushion.

"Wait!" shouted Morgan, running to the water's edge. "Don't go! Not yet!" He opened the cask and pulled out two flasks, one filled with white powder, the other red. "See?" he said. "I have the cure! You can't leave now!"

Quick as lightning, Sir Bedivere snatched the flasks from his hands. Then, just as he had done with the sword, he whirled them over his head and hurled them out into the ocean.

"What have you done?" screamed Morgan, choking with rage and drowning in tears. "You idiot! You've taken our last best hope and thrown it away!"

"I'm sorry," said the knight, unlacing his helmet. He lifted the visor, and his face was the face of Simon Brach. "It's too late," he sang, "too late for grand promises. They all pass away, pass away, pass away. They all pass away to the Land of the Sun's Going." He smiled warmly, then turned and walked off.

"Come back!" shouted Morgan as the boat put out from shore. But the ladies paid no heed. Only the white-robed, green-eyed woman seemed to care. Silently she rose from *the stone step and wrapped her arms around him, brushing away the hot tears with her cool, smooth fingertips. But he pulled free and splashed out into the waves, shouting and weeping and flailing his arms.*

"Don't worry, Morgan!" called a voice from the boat—the voice of the king himself! "Be comforted! Remember! One day is enough!"

With that, the wounded monarch sat up in the barge and removed his helmet. To Morgan's surprise, the head thus revealed was not the head of a king at all, but that of a beautiful woman. The shining hair, cascading over the shoulders like a river of molten gold, was the hair of Niamh, daughter of the Lord of Tir-Na-nOg. But the face was the face of his mother....

The following day, after the usual amount of bickering and squabbling, George and Moira agreed that Eny should go with Simon after school to Harp's Haven, an abandoned small-craft harbor at the base of La Punta Lira near the old shore whaling station. At first, George insisted on going with them—not out of fear for Eny or distrust of Simon, but because he dearly wanted to carry on the Ariello family tradition by playing some part in the last chapter of the story of the miraculous Stone. Moira, of course, disagreed. She took the position that Lia Fail was the special concern of the Tuatha De Danann, and that it's always best, if possible, to keep out of the business of the people of the Sidhe. Naturally, her view prevailed in the end.

As things turned out, Eny and Simon had a perfect afternoon for their outing. The morning fog burned off by midday, and at three thirty the two trekkers were making their way out onto the Point under brilliant sunshine. Eny went with high hopes, her heart lightened by the fragrant brightness of the world around her, her spirits buoyed by the thought that Lia Fail would soon be beyond the Morrigu's reach.

There was a boat down at the Haven that she practically considered her own: nothing but a hull, a bench, and two oars, but it was sound and seaworthy, and she had often used it to make short excursions around the Point and across La Coruna Inlet. It was just what Simon needed, she thought, for the successful fulfillment of his mission: a reliable means of water transport and a hidden point of departure. They had all agreed it would be best to avoid the busy docks near Fisherman's Wharf.

As they crossed the bridge over Pillar Creek, Eny could see the sparkling jade waters of Laguna Verde on their right and the dark green mass of the pine hill forest on the bluff directly ahead. Below and to the left lay a wide expanse of humpy, scrub-covered yellow rock. Leaving the lagoon behind, they turned and followed the left-hand trail past the forest fringe and across Arroyo del Mar. Gray squirrels chattered at them from the tops of the pines. Red-winged blackbirds and white-breasted nuthatches dropped snatches of song from the lower branches of the poplars in the arroyo. Gulls screamed in the salt sea air.

"It's supposed to be shaped like a harp," Eny explained as they trudged through a spiny patch of wild blackberry bushes and sticky yellow monkey flowers. "That's why the Spaniards called it La Punta Lira. It's a triangle. Pillar Creek runs pretty much straight north and south. It's the pillar of the harp. On the side facing the ocean, the land slants seaward, like the soundboard. And on the north, along the Inlet, the shore is curved like the harp's neck. Roughly speaking, anyway." She laughed. "So it's a kind of musical place. In more ways than one."

"You come here often, do you?" asked Simon, stumping along beside her.

"All the time. It was here—at the Cave of the Hands— that I found my way into the Sidhe."

He rubbed his chin. "Interesting. I know most of the portals, but I have never heard of that one until now. Perhaps it wasn't *permanent*. Some of them are—like Brugh na Boyne and the Catskill vales and the forest of Broceliande. But others can open and close at any time. Without warning or reason or rhyme. Especially if *she* has anything to do with it." He looked up uncertainly as a shadow passed over the sun.

"The Morrigu?"

Simon nodded.

"She chased me," said Eny with a shiver. "She sent the Fomorians to catch me. I lived in fear of her the whole time I was in the Land Underground. She's after Lia Fail, but she wants me, too! She thinks I'm the fulfillment of a prophecy."

"Of course. The prophecy of Eithne. She's seen it in your eyes. If she knew your heart, she'd be even more certain. But that's beyond her grasp."

They walked on in silence until Eny said, "The Fir Bolg—the little people I met in the Sidhe—they told me that Ollamh Folla had been her *lover*." She shot him a tentative glance. "Is that true?"

Simon smiled. "We both served the king. That meant we were often at court together. I admired her, and she knew it. But she came to hate me when I sent the Stone away."

"Didn't she realize the danger?"

A spot of darkness darted across their path; something rustled in the leaves above their heads. "She was always as proud as she was beautiful," said Simon, scanning the branches with narrowed eyes. "A relentless foe. Implacable to anyone who displeased her in any way. She cares nothing for danger. She'll risk anything to get her way."

"But did you love her?"

It was a long time before the old man answered. "That would be hard to say, missy."

"Did she ever love you?"

"No. I don't think so. I don't believe she's capable of it. No one can love whose heart is set on power. To such a mind, everybody else is expendable. Everything can be sacrificed, thrown away. Everything can be made to serve a single end."

"But love is about sacrifice, too. Isn't it?"

"Not that kind of sacrifice. Love sacrifices to give, not to gain. It throws *itself* away to serve another."

"But what if that was a person's whole reason for *wanting* power? What if they were going to use it to help somebody else? What if they worked really hard to get it just so that they could save someone's life with it? Wouldn't that be a good thing?"

Simon gave her a penetrating look. "In my opinion, missy," he said, "the person you have in mind is in far greater danger than he suspects. But he's not without hope. There's always hope for any heart that loves with that kind of love. He may come through all right in the end. Yet perhaps as if it were through fire."

Even as he spoke there came a violent snapping and crashing among the treetops and a sudden spot of feathered blackness dropped down out of the foliage upon his head. Without so much as blinking, Simon lifted a hand and batted it away as if it were a fly or a bit of cotton fluff. The bird flew off with an angry screech, winging its way far out over the Point. Her heart pounding, Eny stumbled backward and pressed herself tightly against the slender trunk of a young pine.

"The Morrigu?" she said, searching the old man's face.

"The Morrigu," Simon nodded.

Soon they came to the top of a rise covered with live oak and low-growing green-and-purple scrub. Below them stretched the heaving expanse of the blue ocean. At their feet a rocky trail wound down to a narrow beach where the gray and rotting remains of a pier and some old docks straddled the foaming surf. A small houselike structure and a few ramshackle huts and sheds stood scattered about on the shore.

"When I was a little girl," said Eny, leading the way down the cliff, "I used to hang around here on summer afternoons just to see the fishing boats come in. They'd bring back huge marlins and sailfish and hang them up on that dock down there. The square building in the middle was the Anglers Club. It had a cupola on top with a bell in it, and they'd ring it to let everybody know how many big fish had been caught. On a clear day you could hear it chiming all the way up in town."

"It sounds lovely," said the old man.

"It was. Come on, I'll show you. My boat's covered up underneath the pier."

But when they reached the pier there was no boat to be seen. There was nothing but a broken rope, a shredded blue tarp, and some very large tracks in the wet sand.

"Gone!" moaned Eny. "I don't understand it! No one else has ever used that boat! No one even knew it was here! Some kids must have taken off with it!" But no sooner had the words left her lips than a chill of doubt pricked her scalp and ran tingling down her spine.

Simon shook his head. "No, missy. You know better than that. Just look at the size of those footprints. That's a

Fomorian, that is. She's on to us. Somehow she's got wind of what we're up to."

Eny trembled as she lifted up the remnants of the tarp. "Whoever it was, they dragged it down into the water," she said, pointing to some lines in the sand. "They could have smashed it up, but they didn't. Maybe they rowed it farther up the coast. They might have hidden it in one of the caves. Let's go and see."

For more than an hour, then, they scoured the pebbly shoreline, working their way gradually north toward the great Rock of La Piedra. It was arduous going. In many places the soft white sand gave way to huge heaps of gray stone where gulls and cormorants sat hunched in noisy squawking battalions. Sea lions sprawled on flat-topped boulders, their grunts and barks echoing forlornly off the heights. From time to time sharp masses of bleached rock rose up directly across their path, forcing them to leave the waterside and take to the trail above the cliffs. When they were able to climb down again, their progress was slow and tedious, for the rock face along this stretch of shore was honeycombed with deep holes and dripping grottoes and tiny inlets of every imaginable shape and size. Searching for a small rowboat in such a place was like hunting for a needle in a haystack.

At length they came to the towering mass of the Rock itself. Here they were obliged to forsake the beach once more and clamber up a narrow track that skirted the base of the formation and snaked its way over the tip of the Point to the northern shore. Following this path, they came at last to the tide pools below the Cave of the Hands.

"There it is," said Eny, panting and leaning on Simon's arm. "*La Cueva de los Manos*. This is where I saw the crow for the first time. There were voices at the back of the cave that day, and when I ran to escape, *she* was standing right here—washing something in one of these pools."

Simon grunted. "One of her most common disguises," he observed.

"The next time I came, I saw a vision of the Green Island in the West. It seemed so real, but it must have been one of her enchantments. There were strands of light and strains of music. I was sitting on a rock, way up there on that cliff, slinging stones into the ocean, when—"

"*Hsst!* Young miss!"

Eny stopped short, nearly gagging on the tail end of her unfinished sentence. The voice was ominously familiar, and it had come from the direction of the cave. She turned and squinted up at the cliff. *La Cueva de los Manos* was like an empty eye socket in the glaring yellow face of the sun-drenched rock, and from out of the shadows under its low-arching brow a slight, spindly figure was leaning down and beckoning to her with a knobby-fingered hand.

"*Eochy*?" she gasped. "The little man from the alchemy shop?" She turned to Simon, clinging to the lapels of his coat to keep from falling. "He's one of them! He works for *her*!"

"Eochy son of Umor?" A slow smile spread over Simon's weathered face. Then he, too, glanced up at the cave entrance.

"Eochy of the Fir Bolg of Eba Eochaid?" He slapped his thigh and laughed aloud. "Now there's a stroke of good luck!"

Eochy was waving frantically and scowling like a thunderstorm. "Hush, man!" he hissed. "Not so loud! Do you want the bird to be hearing?"

"Luck!" choked Eny. "What do you mean? What are you talking about?"

"You poor, silly child!" he laughed, gripping her by both shoulders and almost lifting her off the ground. "He doesn't work for her! He works for *me!*"

Chapter Twenty-Five

BROKEN TRUST

"How is that possible?" gasped Eny as Simon took her by the elbow and tugged her gently up the bank toward the mouth of the cave. "I *know* who he is! I've seen him in Madame Medea's shop. *She's* the Morrigu, and *he's* one of her slaves! He obeys her like a little puppy dog!"

"Patience, missy," whispered Simon. "All now mysterious shall be bright at last."

But once inside the cavern, Eny pulled away and threw herself against the wall near the door, glaring at the little man who cowered in the shadows on the far side of the chamber. "You don't understand!" she said. "I heard his name in the Sidhe! He's the brother they don't talk about! That's what Rury said! I know what he meant, too, because he told me that some of the Fir Bolg serve her willingly! I'll bet *he* took the boat!"

Eochy stepped timidly to the center of the chamber. "True it is," he said, "that some serve willingly. But others have no choice. Such a one was I. A spy she wanted, to keep watch on the Danaans. She would have destroyed my dun and killed my people. So I went and did her bidding—for their sake."

"That's no excuse!" said Eny.

"Excuses," said Simon, "are of no use. Answers are what's needed. A way out, a plan of escape." He folded his arms and inclined his head in Eochy's direction. "He came to me in Baile Daoine Sidhe, and we devised one. That's how he started working for me."

Eny looked from one narrow, craggy face to the other. A haze passed over her eyes and she slid to a sitting position on the floor. "I don't understand," she said.

Simon gave her a wink. "Do you know what a double agent is, missy?"

She stared and nodded slowly. But Eochy clapped his hands and jigged from one foot to the other.

"The worm turns!" he almost sang. "The spy spies on his mistress!"

Simon laughed. "And a good job he makes of it too! He's the reason I'm here. I had a notion of what John Izaak was up to, but the Morrigu knew far more than I did. Eochy told me everything. I came on his advice, and I saw at once that giants were in the land. But until this moment I had no idea that *she* was in Santa Piedra herself. She must be close to uncovering the secret."

"Close!" exclaimed Eochy. He hopped over to Eny and leaned down until his nose was nearly touching hers. "*This* is how close she is! And it is what she hopes, that the prize will soon be falling into her hands. Exactly where and when, she has not yet guessed. But Lia Fail is near, and she knows it."

"Not just near," said Simon quietly. "It is found."

The little man's mouth fell open, and he dropped to his knees.

"Yes," Simon added. "In St. Halistan's Church. On the tower stairs."

"Great Rindail!" cried Eochy, clasping his hands above his head. "So it is! So it *must* be! I see it all now! But if this is true, she'll soon be knowing! If not by the crow, then by the son of Izaak—your young gentleman friend."

"Morgan?" said Eny. "I don't believe it!"

"Believe what you like. He cares not for my warnings. Already he is deeper in her snares than he supposes. But however it is with *him,* you must realize that the Morrigu will stop at nothing to keep the Stone from crossing the sea. Nothing! That is why Falor, the great galumphing oaf, has taken your boat. She knew about it! She suspected how it might be used! From this point out, her accursed bird will be watching all your doings with an unsleeping eye. If, as you say, the Stone is found, then I fear she will soon be making off with it to her fortress under the ground."

Eny sat listening to all of this with her head between her knees. Slowly a great heaviness descended upon her, as if a hundred-pound yoke of iron had been laid across her shoulders. Simon and Eochy seemed to feel it too, for they both fell silent. For a long time there was no sound inside the Cave of the Hands except the pounding of the waves on the shore and a ceaseless drip at the back of the cavern. After a while, dimly curious about the source of that interminable trickle, Eny lifted her head and opened her eyes. A faint light

285

was welling up between the two boulders in the far corner of the chamber.

"Look!" she shouted. "It's the tunnel! The portal is opening again!"

Simon followed her gaze. "I believe you're right, missy!" he said.

Then came the dawning of another light—this time inside her mind. "The Fir Bolg!" she cried. "*They* could help us! One of their little skin *currachs* wouldn't be enough, but think what we could do with a whole bunch of them! We could float Lia Fail to the Green Island on a huge cushion of leather bags!"

Eochy looked mournful. "Boats and bags they have indeed," he said, "but not for me. I think you know they won't be hearing *my* appeals!"

Eny scrambled to her feet and pushed the little man toward the tunnel entrance. "They'll listen to *me!*" she said as the light strands entwined her arms and legs like the tendrils of a luminescent vine. "This is my chance to help them win their freedom! Come on, Simon! Let's go!"

When Morgan woke in the morning, there was nothing left of his midnight dream but a thin, lingering fragrance. But that residue, vague as it was, had power to drive his thoughts and direct his actions.

I don't care what the others think, he told himself over breakfast, hardly knowing what he said or why he said it. *It's shameful to waste a thing like that—to just take it and throw it into the sea! Nothing good can come of that!*

After eating, he went early to St. Halistan's Church, rustled up a few boxes, and removed his father's alchemical books from the tower lab. Once the entire collection was safe under his bed, he grabbed his backpack, jumped on his bike, and headed off to school.

It was always difficult to concentrate on schoolwork during the final weeks of the semester, but today he found it impossible to corral his scattered and wandering thoughts. All day long they went bounding from horizon to horizon across the jumbled plain of his inner mindscape, spinning and looping through the aftermath of the previous night's cataclysmic visions. As a result, he failed a pop vocabulary quiz and missed six words, including *magnanimity* and *renunciation,* on a spelling test. When asked to name one of Shakespeare's plays, he answered "Medea." He told his math teacher that the first two steps to solving a geometry problem were "distillation and calcination." He dropped three fly balls in right field before the gym coach finally sent him to the bench. Everywhere he went he heard the deafening roar of Lia Fail. Everywhere he turned, his eyes were blinded by the light of Jacob's Ladder. And through the midst of all these confusing mental pictures, like a thread through a string of beads, ran the single most disturbing image of all: the face of his mother, wan and hollow-cheeked, crowned by a halo of thin, wispy hair.

By the time the final bell rang he knew exactly what he had to do. Stuffing his dirty gym clothes and a few books into his backpack, he slammed his locker and ran directly to the bike racks without speaking to a single soul. While unlocking his bike, he caught sight of Eny. She was standing just outside the fence, and she seemed to be waiting for someone. But he didn't call out to her, and he didn't let her see that he was there. Once outside the gate, he rode as fast as he could straight down the hill to Front Street and Old Towne.

Madame Medea's shop looked strangely forlorn and barren as he leaned his bike against a post and stepped in under the squeaky, swinging signboard. Far out over the ocean a thick gray line of fog lay like a sleeping serpent on the horizon. Gulls screamed in the distance and a stiff shoreward breeze ruffled the choppy swells just beyond the foam. Morgan looked up and saw the White Hand swaying in the wind. He felt as if it were motioning to him—whether beckoning him closer or waving him off he did not know. It didn't really matter in either case. He had already made up his mind what he was going to do.

He walked up to the door and found it standing ajar. The little bell tinkled softly as he touched the handle and pushed it open. It was very dark inside—dark, silent, and empty. There was no little man on the threshold to greet him or scold him or shoo him away. There was no crow perched above the signboard to screech or caw or clack its beak at him. There was no giant lurking in the shadows, no Baxter Knowles emerging from a neighboring storefront to frighten him off. There was nothing but a soft ripple of harp music and a faint flicker of flame at the rear of the shop, back behind the dusty display cases and the ramshackle shelves of bottles and jars.

Slowly he made his way down one of the cluttered aisles, bumping into things that rattled or jangled in the darkness, keeping his eyes fixed on the guttering yellow candle at the end of the row. On every side of him the endless ranks of brass tubing, glass globes, and copper pans flashed uncertainly in the intermittent glow. He could see her clearly now, sitting beside one of the café tables, just in front of the screen of shimmering wooden beads, the light of the taper glimmering palely on the wire strings and polished pillar of the harp. The tune she played was gentle, soothing, and familiar, though he could not think of its name. He walked straight up to her and bowed stiffly.

"I have something to tell you," he said.

Madame Medea played on until the tune came to an end. When she looked up at him, it was with an expression of bland disinterest.

"Where is your friend?" she said coldly. "Didn't I tell you not to come back without her?"

"You don't understand!" said Morgan. "I've brought the news you've been waiting to hear!" So violently was his heart pounding that he found it difficult to speak. He closed his eyes and clenched his fists to keep himself from trembling. When he spoke again, his voice was not much more than a whisper. "The Stone of Destiny has been found!"

Her full red lips curved slightly upward at the corners. Folding her long-fingered hands in her lap, she lifted an eyebrow and inclined her head to one side. For a moment she regarded him in silence, her brow as calm and clear as a sheltered bay on a sunny summer afternoon. But her green eyes glittered, and it seemed to Morgan that her breath came more rapidly. A flush of pink appeared at the base of her throat, just above the neck of her blue satin gown.

"Is this true?" she asked quietly.

He nodded. "In St. Halistan's Church. On the tower stairs. It's actually one of the steps—the last stone step below the first landing, under the stained-glass window."

Her smile broadened and two tiny sparks appeared in the black circles at the centers of her eyes. "It is as I suspected," she said. "You have done well to tell me."

"Yes. And now that I've found it, I was hoping we could talk about my mother. You said you'd help me cure her cancer."

The smile faded. She rose and laid a shapely hand on the curved neck of the harp. "We have been over this," she said, glaring down at him. "I've already told you. Without the Stone, the Elixir is worthless. Without the maiden the power of the Stone cannot be unlocked. Why have you not brought her?"

"I couldn't! You don't know Eny. She wouldn't have come! Besides, I don't see what difference—"

"Be silent!" The white face remained as smooth as marble, but the green eyes darkened. "If you have told me the truth, then the Stone of Destiny is already mine. But it is not enough. I must also have the girl."

"But you promised! You said that if I found the Stone, you'd help me heal my mother!"

"Did I?" She lifted her hand from the harp and studied her glossy red nails. "I said I could. But then why should I? I told you from the beginning what I required of you. The Stone of Destiny and the maiden."

There was nothing he could say. He stared up into her face, at a complete loss for words. But as he did so, it seemed to him that a veil was somehow lifted from his eyes. For the first time, he thought, he could see her as she really was: hard and cold as ice; unwaveringly intent upon a single thing—the power of Lia Fail. In that instant he realized that she cared nothing for him or his mother or anyone else.

"I swear to you," Madame Medea was saying, "that these are the last kind words you will ever hear from me if you do not return with the girl before this night is out. I will not bear to look on your face again if you come without her. She is essential! I must have her! Now go! And do not prove as useless as your father!"

As she spoke, something snapped inside his brain. Chains and steel bands seemed to break and fall away from his mind and heart with a dull ringing sound. Suddenly Eny's fears and pleadings and warnings all came back to him in a rushing torrent. He remembered what she had said about the giants and the Morrigu and the prophecy of Eithne. He pictured her eyes shining with tears. He tried to imagine what it would mean for his good and gentle friend to fall into the hands of this scheming, calculating woman.

From somewhere in the region below his rib cage a surge of red-hot anger boiled upward into his chest, rushed up through his throat, and gushed out through his eyes and nose and mouth. He took five backward steps, extended an arm, and raked an entire row of bottles, jars, and flasks from one of the sagging shelves. The glassware fell to the floor in a shattered heap and scattered across the carpet in a fan of glittering sparks, leaving trails of steaming and smoking tinctures and essences in its wake. Retreating another step, he laid hold of the edge of a thick oak table and flung it over on its side, sending globes and tongs and shovels and spoons clattering from one end of the shop to the other. Then he turned to face her, brushing a strand of damp yellow hair out of his eyes.

"That's what I think of you and your demands!" he said, shaking like a live wire. "I kept my part of the bargain, but you lied to me! You may think you have Lia Fail, but you can't have my friend! And you won't get me either!"

He turned to run. At that instant the screen of wooden beads burst apart, and Falor thundered into the room like an avalanche. Blind with frenzy, Morgan dashed down the aisle in the half-light, leaping over shards of broken glass, banging his elbows against the sharp corners of cabinets and shelves, stumbling through piles of mortars and pestles and shattered alembics. He could hear the giant's labored breathing just over his shoulder. He could feel the walls and ceiling shudder and tremble as the mountainous man's tree-trunk legs and pile-driver feet pounded after him over the creaking floor.

Morgan reached the front of the shop and flung himself desperately at the door with Falor close on his heels. His heart was in his mouth, his hand was on the handle, his fingers were on the latch. But just as he was about to squeeze and pull, a glint of gold caught his eye in the umbrella stand at the entrance to the shop: a long blue sword with a large gilded pommel.

Quick as thought, he whipped it out and spun around to face his adversary. To his great surprise, the giant skidded clumsily to a halt, blundered against a post, and retreated several paces. Astonished at the success of his bold maneuver, Morgan brandished the blade threateningly, yanked the door open, and leaped over the threshold. The earth shook violently beneath his feet and the sign of the White Hand rattled above his head.

"Let him go, fool!" he heard Madame Medea shout as he fled out into the street. "I have a far more important job for you this evening!"

Once in the open, Morgan crossed Front Street and ran north along the seafront until his legs and lungs gave out. Then he threw himself over the railing and fell facedown in the sand, chest heaving, limbs quivering, eyes dark with exhaustion, fear, and hopelessness. For a long time he lay there gasping and gulping the air, twisting his head miserably from side to side, expecting at any moment to feel the huge hand of Falor on the back of his neck. When at last he looked up, he saw that the dark line of fog had moved ashore and that the whole of Santa Piedra was shrouded in a cloud of gray drizzle. Overwhelmed with emotion, he wept.

"I'm sorry!" he cried between broken sobs. "I tried my hardest, but my best is never good enough. I did everything I could to save my mom, but I failed. I'm so, so sorry! You know I'd do anything for her, but I just can't betray Eny! I can't go that far! If my mom has to die, then I guess that's the way it is! There's nothing more I can do!"

He had no idea how long he lay there. As far as he knew, no one saw him. No one came near. When his tears were spent, he got to his feet, empty, chilled, and shaking. Brushing the sand from his clothes and face, he picked up the sword, tucked it under his arm, and turned to the east.

He was standing at the base of Vista Del Mar Avenue. Through the thickening mist and fog he could just make out the lights of the hospital twinkling at the top of the hill. Instantly he was seized with a desperate longing to see his mother. He ached with the desire to hold her hand and look into her face again. There was no way to tell how much time he might have left with her, but he knew it wasn't much. So many precious days had already slipped away! Nothing could be done to change that now, but there was still today, and today would be enough. She had told him so.

Gripping the sword tightly, he climbed the railing and dropped down onto the sidewalk. Then he recrossed the street and set off for the hospital.

Chapter Twenty-Six

THE BATTLE FOR THE STONE

He quickly came to the conclusion that he had been lying on the beach for a very long time; for as he labored up Vista Del Mar, regretting the loss of his bike and sweating under the burden of his backpack and the heavy sword, darkness rose up in the east and crept seaward across the lowering gray sky. The drizzle turned to light rain. Brooding clouds pressed down upon the hills, obscuring the hospital and veiling the houses on either side of the street.

At the corner of Alta Drive he was startled by a flash of lightning. As the thunder sounded, a dreadful cacophony of croaking and squawking burst over him like a shower of hailstones and a swift black shape swept down across his path. Dodging to one side, he heaved up the sword and swung it wildly above his head. There was a *swish* and a *snap* and the shape hurtled away, leaving two or three inky feathers fluttering in the wind.

Morgan pressed on to the hospital. As he neared the main entrance, it seemed to him that the ground began to roll and shift. In the glare of a second bolt of lightning he could see telephone and power lines quivering violently and scattering large drops of water helter-skelter through the air.

Hitching up his backpack, he reached out and put his hand on the door.

It was locked. *How can it possibly be that late?* he wondered. *I guess I'll have to use the emergency entrance.* But as he was turning away he caught sight of someone inside the lobby, just on the other side of the glass—a frumpy, dowdy, gray-haired woman in a dingy gingham dress. She was down on her hands and knees, scrubbing the floor with a brush and a bucket of water.

"Hey!" yelled Morgan, banging on the window. "Can you please let me in?"

She lifted her head and looked round at him. Her face was old and wrinkled as an ancient map, but the eyes in the deep-set sockets were green and luminous like a cat's. She stared at him briefly and went back to her work.

"I'm here to visit my mother!" he shouted, raising his voice and pounding even harder. "I didn't know they closed the main entrance so early! Can't you open it for me?"

With a great effort the old woman struggled to her feet and tottered over to the door. For a few moments she stood frowning at him in silence. Then she opened her mouth and began to speak. Morgan saw her lips moving slowly and distinctly on the other side of the glass; but it was inside his head that he heard the sound of her voice.

"Go home, foolish boy," she said. "Your mother is dying. The hospital is closed and the doors are locked. Go home and don't come back." With that, she picked up her pail and brush and disappeared down a dusky corridor on the far side of the lobby.

Again the earth trembled and the glass doors rattled. Seething inside, Morgan splashed away through the wet blackness of the parking lot. *I'll go to the church and find Rev. Alcuin*, he thought. *He'll help me get in.*

The rain increased as he turned the corner and headed up the hill toward the tower of St. Halistan's. High and stern it stood amid the storm, looming like a pillar of solid shadow above the rain-dark roofs of the town. Concerned about the sword, he paused in a sheltered doorway and wrapped the blade in his jacket. Then he plodded on, skipping over puddles and leaping the small rivulets that ran in the driveways and gutters.

He had nearly reached Vizcaino Street when an all-too-familiar voice hailed him:

"Going somewhere, Strawhead?"

He spun on his heel. Immediately five dim figures rushed out of an alley and rammed him hard against a soggy wooden fence. Lightning flashed, and there stood Baxter Knowles and his crew, laughing, shouting, grinning, green-eyed. The sword was out in an instant, tracing a blue arc in the air just in front of their astonished faces. The gang fell back at once, and Morgan fled under a volley of curses and threats.

On and on he ran until he came to the corner of Alta and Iglesia. There he stopped, blinking in disbelief, supposing that his eyes must be playing tricks on him in the doubtful light, for when he looked up toward the church he seemed to see not one but *two* towers standing side by side—one of them tall, straight, and still, the other hunched and bent and slightly swaying. As he watched, the shorter of the two grew larger and appeared to draw nearer. Then it shook itself, bent its head, and raised a gigantic arm toward the sky.

Falor! Morgan's heart dropped like a stone into the cold pit of his stomach. The apparition turned, swinging its heavy face into full view, and he saw that he had not been mistaken: Madame Medea's one-eyed henchman, grown to an impossibly immense size, was stalking down out of the foothills above Santa Piedra, moving closer to St. Halistan's with every shuddering step.

Then up from the sea came a chorus of harsh, wild cries. Looking back over his shoulder, Morgan saw twenty-one broad-winged, long-necked geese beating up from the beach in a long white veil. Down through the slanting rain they dived, fluttering and splashing to earth just in front of St. Halistan's Church. Once on the ground, they planted their feet, stretched their necks, and grew upward, assuming the shape of straight-stemmed firs and pines. When they were as tall as Falor himself, the trees sprouted massive heads and arms; and in the next instant a troop of twenty-one broad-shouldered, round-skulled Fomorian giants stood roaring and stamping like thunder in the middle of the street.

Chilled to the core, fearing to be caught up and crushed at any moment, Morgan backed slowly down the street, keeping his gaze fixed on Falor's beetling black brow. As he did, the clouds parted above the giant's head and a patch of sapphire blue appeared in the sudden opening. In the middle of the patch blazed a silver star, so bright that the pinnacle of the tower gleamed like white fire in its radiance. Instantly the beams of the star became a shining silver chain, and the chain became a golden stairway linking heaven and earth. Then out of the star itself, as if through a celestial portal, streamed rank upon shimmering rank of six-winged seraphs—golden-headed, flame-eyed, rainbow-bright. The stairway rippled and swung beneath their brazen feet like a glittering gold band. So great was the splendor of their burning countenances that the dismayed Fomorians flinched and cowered before its light.

Shielding his eyes from the brilliance and the heat, Morgan turned and looked out to where the heaving expanse of the sea sparkled like blue-green glass all the way to the horizon wall. So intense was the light of star and stair that he could clearly discern every wrinkle and swell, every wave cap and curl on the face of the deep. Among the foaming reefs he glimpsed a fleet of tiny round boats dancing up over the breakers along the strand like dry leaves on a tossing breeze, each one carrying a single passenger. As the small craft scraped up on the glistening sand, the little people jumped ashore, folded their boats into small bundles, and charged up the beach in waves.

As he was studying this strange new development, squinting shoreward through prisms of color and shrouds of shining rain, there came another clap of thunder, followed by a different kind of tumult in the air. Creaks and groans and jumbled voices sounded in the midst of the storm. Then a high-prowed wooden ship crested a cloud and bore down upon the startled

Fomorians from out of the swirling sky. At its mast billowed a square red sail, and along its carved and painted gunwales clattered overlapping rows of glittering round shields. Down from the rigging and over its bulwarks leaned the figures of the airborne mariners, all of them armed with bows, all of them wearing burnished shirts of mail beneath their brightly colored tunics and cloaks. They nocked their arrows and pulled back on their bowstrings. A deadly shower rained down upon the heads of the fuming giants.

Morgan felt the ground tremble as Falor stomped and shouted and beat the air with his arms. Screaming with rage and pain, the giant's huge companions staggered and lumbered blindly from one side of the street to the other, swearing and threatening and plucking feathered darts from their shoulders like porcupine quills. More arrows poured down and a second flying ship appeared in the clouds, followed by a third and a fourth. And then a voice called out from somewhere behind Morgan's back:

"Look! It's the Danaans! The Danaans have come to help!"

It was Eny. She was standing at the corner, rain pouring from her dark hair, her face upturned and radiant in the dazzling light. At her side stood Simon Brach, a gnarled hand shading his eyes and a broad smile covering his narrow, craggy face. And next to Simon, glaring straight at Morgan with a sort of knowing smirk on his thin lips, was Eochy, the irritating little man from Madame Medea's shop.

What are they doing here? thought Morgan, suddenly deaf and blind to the tempest seething above his head. *And why is* he *with them?* But in the next instant he realized that these three were not alone, for at Eochy's elbow hunched another crooked little man who looked almost exactly like him except that he was dressed in soiled and shapeless rags. And behind *that* little man stood another, and yet another behind *him.* There were, in fact, rows and rows of little men and women, all of them with grim expressions on their lean and wrinkled faces and bulging leather bags at their belts. Suddenly it dawned on Morgan that these were the people he had seen disembarking from the small round boats on the shore.

"Come on, everybody!" he heard Eny cry. "This is why we came!"

Morgan shouted and waved at her, trying desperately to get her attention, but she didn't seem to notice him. She was carrying a fluttering blue banner in her left hand, and she turned and raised it before the dwarfish army at her back.

At that, each little man and woman dipped into his or her bag and drew out a long leather sling and a smooth, round stone. Fitting stones to slings, they spread out across the street and began to whirl the leather thongs above their heads. Then, at another command from Eny, they let their missiles fly. The Fomorians stumbled backward and gave way before the withering hail of stones.

"Looks like they're on the run, missy!" said Simon Brach with a laugh. Then he looked up to where one of the flying ships hung rocking in the wind-currents above the church tower, and he jumped to the top of a low wall and flagged it down with a wave of his hand. Like a descending shadow the vessel's curved keel dropped out of the sky, discharging another storm of arrows as it came. When it was no more than twenty feet from the ground a shining rope fell over its side and Simon, leaping from the wall, seized it and swung aboard. Then the ship rose swaying into the turbulent air. Once above the tower again it shifted sail and tacked around the base of the golden stairway in a wide arc. Following it with his eyes, Morgan caught a glimpse of Simon in the bow, looking just as he had seen him on the tower stairs: straight, tall, and strong, a purple cloak flying from his shoulders, a tall helmet flashing on his head, and a sword like a fierce flame glittering in his right hand.

It was the voice of Eny that brought him back to earth. "Let them have another round!" he heard her shout, and at that the slingers let loose with a second volley. The giants writhed and twisted in a grotesque dance, raising their arms to shield their faces as a flurry of rocks and stones pummeled their bodies and cracked their skulls. One of them fell with such a bone-rattling thud that the whole earth shook and the tower trembled. Bellowing like a mad bull, Falor stepped over the roof of a house and motioned to the others to follow. A shout of triumph went up from Eny's little army as the Fomorians began to lumber off toward the hills.

Seeing his chance, Morgan elbowed his way through the crowd and laid a hand on Eny's shoulder. She whipped around to face him, dripping and panting with exertion, a pale fire burning in her one blue eye.

"Morgan!" she said, laughing and hugging his neck. "I'm so glad you're here! Did you see that? I taught them to sling stones and they made the giants run!"

"Yes, I saw!" yelled Morgan above the howl of the wind and rain. "But who are they? And what in the world is going on?"

"The Fir Bolg! Eochy's one of them. He's on our side! Rury's his brother—he wasn't drowned after all! Simon and I went down and fetched them up from the Sidhe. Another long story. But they're here to help us rescue the Stone of Destiny from the Morrigu. What *I* don't understand is how she found out where it is!"

Morgan felt his face turn pale. There was a pause as they stood there together, the cold rain dribbling off their noses. Then he said, "I know the answer to that. I told her."

Eny's eyes popped. "You did *what?*"

"It's true," he said, dropping his gaze. "This whole thing is my fault."

She let go of him and backed away. "How could you? Eochy said you might, but I didn't believe it! Never in a million years would I—"

"Eny! It's because of my mother!"

She shook her head. "I know, Morgan. I understand. You'd do anything—sacrifice anything—to help her. But this?"

"No. Not anything. I went too far, and I'm really sorry. But I didn't go as far as *she* wanted me to go. I couldn't."

She looked at him uncertainly. "What do you mean?"

"I mean you," he said. "I couldn't betray *you*."

Her face softened. The corners of her mouth twitched, and she looked as if she were about to speak. But she said nothing.

At that very moment there came a lull in the storm, and an uncanny stillness descended over the entire scene. The rain stopped. The thunder rumbled away into silence. The wind dropped to a whisper, and the sails of the flying ships fell slack in the dead air. And then a small black winged shape hurtled down out of the clouds athwart the blaze of the golden stairway and came to rest on the top of St. Halistan's tower.

Immediately a screen of darkness, like an explosion of impenetrable smoke, fanned out into the air on every side of the shape. It swelled and spread, damping the brightness of the angels and veiling the light of the star. A piercing wail, as of anger mingled with agony, burst from the center of the growing shadow; and in the next moment Morgan and Eny saw a figure standing on top of the tower—a dark-haired woman, cloaked and muffled in black, her arms extended above her head, the fingers of her hands outstretched toward the heavens, her eyes glittering green. She cried out a second time, and the retreating Fomorians turned on their heels and charged back down the hill, setting earth, church, houses, and trees trembling beneath the din of their onslaught.

And now the tide of battle, which up to that instant had been with Eny and her friends, began to shift. The giants converged on the church like a raging sea. With crushing blows of their iron-shod feet they drove the Fir Bolg back toward the Inlet. Eny broke away from Morgan's side and rushed in among the little people, plucking at their sleeves and blocking their path, calling each one by name.

"Wait, Rury!" she shouted. "Eochy! Sengann! Come back! We can't quit now! Give them another round! We did it before, and we can do it again! "

At the sound of her voice a number of them stopped and stood their ground, firing off a few more stones. But so feeble and halfhearted was the volley that the Fomorians hardly seemed to notice. Undaunted, one of the giants lashed out with the toe of his boot and sent several Fir Bolg spinning through the air and slamming into the wall of the white duplex. Then the rest of the Bag People fled in a disorderly rout.

As they ran, another cloudburst of arrows rained down from the becalmed ships. The Danaan archers, it seemed, were doing their best to cover the retreat of the little people; but in the dusky light their aim was poor, and from such a great height they could do little to fend off the renewed ferocity of their gigantic enemies. Instead of flinching, Falor reached up and broke off a pointed stone pinnacle from the top of the tower, heaved it into the sky, and struck one of the Danaan craft in the side, snapping its mast and smashing a gaping hole in its deck and hull. With a terrible groan the ship heeled over, scattering shields and shining warriors through the air like copper pennies. Morgan hid his eyes as ten or twelve armored Danaans crashed heavily to the ground before his feet.

Eny stumbled over to him, one hand on her forehead as if she were in great pain. She looked haggard and spent, and he could see tears brimming at the corners of her eyes. Morgan reached out and touched her.

"What now?" he asked.

But before she could answer the gathering darkness was lightened momentarily by a faint flash overhead. This was followed not by thunder but by a war-whoop. They looked up and saw Simon Brach leaping over the side of one of the flying ships, sweeping down through the murky air, clinging with one hand to a long rope and brandishing a flickering sword in the other. Down to the top of the tower he swung, landing on his feet directly in front of the Morrigu.

Morgan and Eny cheered, for the enchantress was clearly taken aback by this bold and unexpected stroke. She recoiled before Simon, shielding her eyes with her cloaked left forearm and flinging her right hand straight out in front of her face. Seeing his advantage, the Danaan thrust at her with the sword. But she lifted her hand, and the blade, as if caught on the edge of an invisible shield, glanced to one side and struck ringing against a stone pinnacle. She laughed and spread her fingers wide. Immediately the wind came up, the rain fell in torrents, and the storm returned with redoubled fury.

Then stroke by stroke, blow by blow, the two godlike figures bore down upon each other with such violence that the sky itself shuddered from end to end. Above their heads screeched the circling black crow. From every side the surging winds swept round them with all the force of a gathering cyclone. Morgan and Eny clung together, watching as the Danaan ships, their sails bellying to the point of bursting, drew aside and heaved to in the calmer air beyond the center of the storm, holding their fire lest Simon should be struck by a friendly arrow. The Fomorians, too, backed away and stood motionless with their great heavy faces turned up toward the top of the tower. It was plain that everything depended upon the outcome of this single combat.

Again and again Simon swung the shimmering sword. Again and again the Morrigu parried with a mere wave of her hand or a flick of her fingers. They could hear her laughing in the midst of the gale, as if she cared but little for the prowess of her formidable opponent. And yet as the battle progressed it became obvious that the Danaan was slowly driving her back. Morgan looked on, his heart in his mouth, as she gave way before him, step by step. She was up against the parapet now, leaning backward over the edge of the tower, her eyes gleaming, her dark hair loose and flying. Simon heaved up the sword—and then a mighty blast of wind tore the blade from his hand and sent it spinning like a straw out into the roiling blackness of the storm.

"Morgan!" screamed Eny, tightening her grip on his arm. "Do something! You've got to do something!"

"What do you expect me to do?" he yelled. "I can't do anything!"

Then he remembered the sword in his jacket. Yanking it loose, he flung its wrappings aside. Lifting the blade high overhead, he swept it from side to side in a wide arc. As he did so, hope surged in his heart like a fountain of living water; for the sword glowed with a dark sheen in the surrounding gloom, and he could see the terrible Fomorians cowering in its pulsing light. Again he waved it in the air, shouting with all his might. At his signal one of the Danaan ships shortened sail and descended out of the clouds. A rope dropped over its side and fell dangling near to his hand. He cried out:

"Simon! Simon! Take my sword! I'm sending it up to you!"

Simon heard him. He looked down. His eyes met Morgan's. And in that brief instant, while the face of the Danaan hero was turned away from the face of his enemy, the Morrigu grappled him in her arms, wrenched him off his feet, and flung him over the side of the tower.

The wind rose, screaming like a banshee. Lightning flashed, thunder cracked, and it seemed to Morgan as if all the glass in all the windows of the world rattled and shattered beneath the shock. With a laugh like the rumble of an avalanche or the groan of an iron gate, Falor stepped away from the wall of the church and started to grow. He grew until his great round head rose above the highest pinnacle of the tower. With one vast hand he picked up the Morrigu and set her on his shoulder. With the other, he broke off the top of the tower, reached down inside, and pulled out Lia Fail, the Stone of Destiny.

Then, as what remained of the tower of St. Halistan's crumbled and collapsed in a steaming heap, he bowed his mountainous shoulders and stalked off toward the sea.

Chapter Twenty-Seven

LOST AND FOUND

When next he knew anything at all, Morgan was lying on his back under a bloodred sky, looking up into the furrowed brow of George Ariello. George's back was to the east and his face in deep shadow, but his grin flashed like a crescent moon emerging from a cloud the moment Morgan opened his eyes.

"Hey, look!" he called over his shoulder. "He's awake! I think he's going to be all right!"

Morgan raised himself on his elbows and looked around. He was lying on a canvas tarp in the middle of the little patch of grass between the sidewalk and the duplex, cold and wet, his clothes caked with mud, his hair stiff with grit and grime. Moira was standing on the front porch. Beside her sat Eny, a blanket around her shoulders and a steaming cup in her trembling hands.

As soon as Morgan lifted his head, Moira hurried down the steps. Kneeling over him with a look of deep concern in her hazel-green eyes, she tucked a clump of hair behind her ear, adjusted her glasses on the bridge of her nose, and examined him with the air of a trained physician, turning his head this way and that, peering into one eye and then the other, laying a hand on his forehead, feeling his arms and legs and rib cage for breaks and contusions.

"Stop that!" whined Morgan, twisting away from her. "It tickles!"

"Well, you can thank heaven it's no worse than that!" she said, raising an eyebrow and curling her lip. "After what you've been through! Do you kids have any idea how worried we were?"

He blinked and rubbed his eyes. Across the street St. Halistan's sanctuary was all but hidden by a small mountain of gray rock and rubble, its jagged slopes and peaks tinged with the orange glare of the rising sun. The ground on every side was covered with broken bits of stone and mortar and concrete, piles of splintered timbers, ashen heaps of gravel and plaster, and the twisted wreckage of iron girders. Voices hummed in the air, interrupted now and then by the hiss and crackle of radios and walkie-talkies. Shovels scraped. Hammers pounded. Chain saws revved. Backhoes groaned. Glancing to his left, Morgan saw a shiny red hook and ladder, a couple of ambulances with flashing lights, and several black-and-white police cars parked helter-skelter over the sidewalks and the lawns of neighboring houses. Everywhere were men in hard hats, helmets, and fire-fighting gear.

"What happened?" he said.

"Earthquake," said George, pouring hot cocoa from a thermos flask into a styrofoam cup. "A *big* one! That and the worst thunderstorm anybody can remember in Santa Piedra. Together. At the same time. Really strange."

"And you two out in it!" exclaimed Moira.

"I've never seen anything like it," George continued, handing the cup to Morgan. "The church is okay, but the whole tower came down. Most terrifying sound I ever heard. Like a freight train falling off a cliff."

"What in the world were you thinking?" Moira persisted, grabbing Morgan by the chin. "Don't you even have enough sense to come in out of the rain? We searched all night, only to have you turn up in our own front yard! Were you here all along?"

Too weary to explain, Morgan asked, "Is everybody okay? What about my mom? Was the hospital damaged?"

"The hospital is fine," said George. "They were gearing up for a flood of emergencies, but so far there hasn't been a single case. That's the strangest part of the whole thing. It seems there were only two places in town where the earthquake did any damage at all: St. Halistan's and Front Street. Even here at the house—right across the street—we had nothing but some broken dishes and a few cracks in the ceiling."

"Rev. Alcuin's safe, too," said Moira, taking a seat on the porch and refilling Eny's cup. "The rectory, the sanctuary, the church offices—they're all perfectly sound. But Mr. Brach is missing. I can only hope he was somewhere else when the quake hit. His little apartment under the stairs is buried under tons of rock right now."

Morgan and Eny looked at each other. Eny reached up and took her mother's hand. "Mom," she said. "It wasn't like that."

"Not like what?"

"I think you know," Eny answered softly. "You know about the Morrigu and Ollamh Folla and Lia Fail. You saw what *we* saw on the tower stairs." She glanced over at George, then turned back to Moira. "There was a battle."

Moira looked at Morgan. Morgan nodded.

"Simon was in the thick of it," Eny continued. "The Danaans, too, with their flying ships. And the Fir Bolg, and the angels, and the golden ladder. Things went pretty well for a while, but in the end—"

She stopped and stared down at her cup.

"In the end we lost," said Morgan. "The Stone of Destiny was taken."

Moira's mouth fell open.

"Taken?" said George. "What do you mean 'taken'? Isn't it buried somewhere in that pile?"

Morgan shook his head.

"I assume we're still talking about the Stone of Destiny?" said a new voice. It was Peter Alcuin. He was peering over George's shoulder, his face gaunt and unshaven, his shoulders stooped, his black coat covered with a thin layer of dust. Though his smile was broad, there were dark rings under his eyes as he slapped George on the back and stepped into the center of their little circle.

"Yes, Rev. Alcuin," said Morgan, pushing himself up into a kneeling position. "The Stone of Destiny. Lia Fail. We lost it. *She* got it—"

"Morgan!" the Reverend interrupted, as if noticing him for the first time. "Found at last! Eny too! And both in one

312

piece! Well, that *is* good news! I can't tell you how glad I am to see you. Please don't get up! You look like death warmed over!"

Morgan grunted and struggled to his feet. "I need to get to the hospital right away. Can you help me? They wouldn't let me in last night."

Peter frowned. "Yes, I'll help you. I was planning on taking you over there in any case. Just as soon as we've had some refreshment. It's been a long night for everyone, and I've arranged for a bit of breakfast in my office. Go home and get cleaned up. Ah, but first, there's something you *have* to see. Over here!"

Together they followed him through the wreckage, Morgan limping with stiffness, George mopping the back of his neck with a red bandanna, Eny still sipping cocoa, and Moira holding the blanket around Eny's shoulders. Over mounds of rubble and around heaps of rock they picked their way, avoiding pits in the pavement, stepping carefully over nail-studded two-by-fours, and skirting huddles of earnestly conferring firefighters.

At last they stepped up onto what had once been the corner of the sidewalk in front of St. Halistan's Church. Rev. Alcuin stopped in the middle of a clear, open space that was surprisingly free of stones and other debris and pointed at something. It was a block of glossy black marble, about three feet square, smooth, sleek, and darkly gleaming in the morning sun.

"The cornerstone," beamed the Reverend. "Amazing, isn't it? Not a single stone of that whole tower was left standing on top of another. And yet the cornerstone is still here. Right where it's always been."

Morgan bent down and peered closely at the stone. He'd known it all his life. He'd passed it coming and going a thousand times. Never once had he stopped to give it a second thought. But now he studied it closely, as if seeing it for the very first time. Somehow he had the odd sensation that he was examining it for clues. He ran his fingertips over its cool, silky surface. He felt the sharp edges of the ornate Gothic letters carved into its adamantine hardness. He read the words of the inscription over and over again to himself:

St. Halistan's Church

1873

"Jesus Christ Himself being the chief cornerstone."

After a few moments he turned away, wrapped in a cloud of confused and conflicting emotions, and as George, Moira, and Rev. Alcuin continued to marvel over the miracle of the cornerstone, he slowly made his way back to the duplex, his eyes to the ground, his hands in his pockets, his thoughts dark and troubled. He was picturing his mother dying in the hospital. He was trying to imagine what life would be like without her. He was thinking about the cornerstone, the Philosophers' Stone, and the Stone of Destiny—struggling heroically to understand how they all fit together, fighting to unravel the tangled threads of the past several weeks' events, striving unsuccessfully to weave them all together into some kind of meaningful pattern. He was wondering how it was all going to end. That was when something caught his eye.

He stopped and looked again. No, he hadn't been seeing things. It was still there, winking out at him incongruously from beneath a bleak mound of gravel and crumbling concrete: a hint of gold, a flash of bright blue steel, clear and luminous as the dawn sky. He bent down, shoved the debris to one side, and wrenched the glittering object out of the dirt.

It was the sword.

The sword! Morgan smiled faintly and rubbed his chin. In the pain and anguish of the battle's terrible climax he'd hadn't even realized that he'd dropped it. And now here it was again—almost as if it were following him and seeking him out. Looking this way and that, he thrust the blade beneath his muddy jacket and hurried home. There he stashed it under the bed alongside his father's books.

By nine o'clock, cups and saucers were clinking in the restful brown seclusion of the minister's second-floor study. The ruddy morning light poured in through the dirty yellow window panes, scattering spots of orange and copper and burnt umber over the dark furnishings and ceiling-high banks of books. Veins of liquid fire ran along the polished edges of the Norwegian skis above the doorway; sparks of gold danced among the jacks and marbles in the glass display case and on the pendulum of the antique mantel clock. George and

Moira were seated on the sofa. Morgan and Eny had pulled a couple of chairs up to the little coffee table.

"More tea, anyone?" asked Rev. Alcuin as he made the rounds with the pot and a pitcher of milk. Then he slipped briefly into the kitchenette and reappeared carrying a tray laden with scones, toast, a stack of blue bowls, a crock of oatmeal, and a jar of orange marmalade. Setting his burden on top of the vintage sewing machine, he collapsed into a high-backed Windsor chair, removed his glasses, and sighed deeply.

"You'll have to excuse me," he said. "Like you folks, I've been up most of the night. Looking after the needs of my parishioners. Funny thing was, most of them didn't have any."

George cocked an eyebrow at Morgan.

"They felt the quake all right," Peter continued. "And they were plenty shook up by the violence of the storm, especially the kids. But as far as I've been able to ascertain, nobody suffered any real damage except for one family. Unfortunately, it was *significant* damage."

Moira looked up from her efforts to spread a piece of toast with a lump of rock-hard butter. "Well? Who was it?"

Returning his glasses to his nose, the Reverend folded his hands in his lap and gazed slowly around the circle. "The Knowles family."

Morgan started and nearly spilled his tea.

"It wasn't their home," Peter hastily added. "Thank the Lord, no one was hurt. But their business interests took a terrible hit."

"Front Street," said George. "What did I tell you?"

"Quiet, George," said Moira, elbowing him sharply. "Let the Reverend talk."

"I'm afraid George is right," said Rev. Alcuin. "That whole block was leveled. Uncle Pritchard's. Mr. B's Formal Wear. The Knowles Book Knoll. La Coruna Gifts and Cards."

"All Knowles-owned establishments," put in George.

"Yes. And all gone. The quake pretty much reduced it to powder."

Morgan could feel Eny's eyes fixed on his face. "What exactly does that mean for Mr. Knowles?" he wanted to know.

"For one thing, his deal with St. Halistan's is off. He can't possibly afford to buy us out anymore. We may never rebuild the tower, but we still have our church. Mr. Knowles, on the other hand, is ruined."

Morgan bit into a scone to keep from smiling. "So what'll he do now?"

"We spent a long time discussing that. I offered to help in any way we could, but he turned me down. He's off to New York—he and his wife. Apparently he has friends in the financial sector. Meanwhile, they're sending Baxter to live with an aunt in Needles."

"Needles!" muttered George. "*Dios mio!*"

"Precisely," said Peter. "But enough of my gab. I want to hear from you people. Tell me about the Stone of Destiny."

There was a long pause. Morgan squirmed, feeling for some reason as if everyone was expecting him to say something. But Eny spoke first.

"I wouldn't know where to start," she said, setting her cup and saucer on the table. "It all happened so fast that I hardly know what to think or feel. It's like Morgan said. The Stone is gone. And Simon—"

She hid her face. Morgan twisted in his chair and opened his mouth to offer an explanation. But before he could get a word out she raised her head and said, "Do you honestly mean to tell me that none of you saw what happened? You didn't see the battle?"

No one answered.

"That makes it even harder," she went on. "You probably think I'm crazy. You all saw the golden ladder and the angels on the tower stairs. Why not this?"

"You know better than that," Moira gently scolded. "You've been in the Sidhe. You understand that when it comes to this sort of thing, the only rule is that there are no rules. Besides, you've always been able to see things the rest of us can't see. You have Eithne's eyes."

Morgan shot a surprised glance at Moira—it was the first time he'd heard her mention the name of Eithne.

"I agree," said Peter Alcuin. "Look at me, Eny. I know you're not crazy, and I know that you always tell the truth. So I *have* to believe you. Seeing and believing aren't necessarily the same thing. It's trust that counts, and the relationship that fosters the trust. Some see and some don't. Others have their eyes opened only once or twice in a lifetime. Once is more than enough for me."

"But it *isn't* enough!" said Eny with abrupt intensity, her eyes flaring. "Not at a time like this! Simon Brach is lost! The Morrigu has Lia Fail! Don't you see what that means? She can do anything she wants now!"

All fell silent under the weight of these solemn words. But then, very quietly, Morgan spoke up and said, "No. She can't."

Moira's brow arched upward in an expression of mild puzzlement. Rev. Alcuin's eyes narrowed. George's face was a mask of blank bewilderment. But Eny's fierceness dissolved at once, as if in the light of a sudden realization. "Of course not!" she exclaimed, gripping Morgan by the arm. "You're absolutely right!"

"Why?" asked George. "Why is he right?"

"Mrs. A said it," answered Morgan. "Eny has Eithne's eyes."

Moira bent forward, her own face reflecting the illumination in Eny's countenance. "So I did. And that means—"

"The maiden of perfect purity," said Rev. Alcuin. "I see."

"I don't," said George. "What are you talking about?"

"The Morrigu may have the Stone of Destiny," said Morgan, "but it's of no use to her. She can't use it. Not without your daughter."

"*My* daughter?"

"Yes. And you have no idea how close she came to getting her!"

"That's one of the most important pieces of this whole puzzle!" said Eny. "I was so upset about Simon and the Stone that I almost forgot! That's why the Morrigu lured me

319

into the Sidhe in the first place. She thinks I'm the girl who unlocks the power of Lia Fail. She wants *me* as much as she wants the Stone!"

"Which means that the danger is far from past," observed the Reverend.

Moira nodded soberly, but said nothing.

"You tried to warn me, Eny," Morgan said sheepishly. "But I laughed at you. Now that it's too late—now that she already has the Stone—I know that you were right. She tried to get me to betray you. She kept asking me to bring you to her shop. I came *that* close to doing it, too." His voice faltered and he looked down at the floor between his feet.

"Why, Morgan?" said Rev. Alcuin.

"You know why," he answered huskily. "It was because I wanted Lia Fail. I needed it to finish my work on the Philosophers' Stone and the Elixir Vitae. I was trying to help my mother! I wanted her to get well! But in the end I couldn't turn Eny over to that woman. Not even for that!"

Tears were burning in his eyes. Eny leaned over and hugged his neck. Moira reached out and touched his hand.

After a long pause he wiped his face and said, "So I guess it's all over now."

"How do you mean?" Peter gently prodded.

"All over for my mom. I tried to save her, but I failed. I know I was an idiot, and I guess I'm only getting what I deserve. But it still doesn't seem fair. Why should *she* have to suffer for *my* mistakes?"

Rev. Alcuin smiled. "Do you know the parable of the workers in the vineyard, Morgan?"

"I don't think so. What is it?"

Peter laughed. "Suffice it to say that hardly anybody gets what they deserve. That's the good news."

Morgan rubbed his nose and scratched his head. "I've already told God that He can have my mom if He wants her. She was right all along. She kept talking about prayer and faith. She told me that today is all we've got, and that we should be happy just being together. She wanted me to get rid of my father's things and give up my quest for the Philosophers' Stone. I know my mom at least as well as I know you, Eny— even better. I should have believed her. I should have trusted her. But I wouldn't listen. Now all I want is to see her and talk to her one more time."

Without warning, Rev. Alcuin got to his feet and reached for his coat. "In that case," he said, "let's get going. If you've had enough to eat, that is."

Morgan stared up at him. "Right now?"

"Right this minute. I spent most of yesterday afternoon with her. She begged me to bring you just as soon as I could lay hands on you. I think you'll find that we're expected."

Chapter Twenty-Eight

MORE THAN ENOUGH

The glare of the midmorning sun spilled in through an open window and rippled in waves of white fire down the long polished floor. At the far end of the corridor a hint of the morning breeze stirred the edge of a curtain. A door opened, and an orderly emerged and hurried away. Overhead hummed the faint cool blue of the fluorescent lights.

Morgan walked in silence behind Peter Alcuin, his eyes lidded against the dazzling sunlight, his ears captive to the tap-tap of the minister's heels on the tiles, his mind mechanically ticking off the numbers of the rooms as the doors slipped past on the right hand and the left: *208 ... 209 ... 210 ... 211.* The air at this end of the hall was deathly still, redolent of alcohol and sterile cotton.

I'm not going to cry, he told himself, biting his lip and lifting his chin. *The time for crying is past. This is the time to say what needs to be said. That's why I came.*

"You're lagging behind," Peter observed mildly as they approached Room 215. "You're not getting cold feet, are you?"

"Me? Cold feet?" he said. "I asked you to bring me here, didn't I?"

"Of course," Rev. Alcuin smiled.

But Morgan's steps were sluggish as they continued down the corridor—as slow and heavy as his thoughts were firmly resolved.

You were right, he'd tell her. *You knew all along. I should have listened, I should have believed you, but I didn't. I know I was stupid, but I did what I did for your sake. Please don't hate me.*

"Your mother thinks the world of you, you know," said the Reverend, glancing over his shoulder. "I wish you could hear the things she says behind your back. Caring. Responsible. Trustworthy. That's how she describes you. She calls you the light of her life."

Morgan dropped his gaze. "She's my mom," he muttered. "What do you expect? Besides, she doesn't know the whole story."

"None of us knows the whole story, Morgan. Not yet."

They made an odd pair talking there in hushed and solemn tones: the gangly boy with unruly yellow hair, the short, bald man in coat and clerical collar. If anyone had been on hand to watch them, he might have considered it a strange and unusual scene. But there was no one to see, no one to judge, no one to comment or offer advice. They were all alone as they proceeded down the long, empty hallway, step by step by step. *Room 222 … 223 … 224.*

I had so many dreams and schemes, Mom. I think you know. Good dreams and bad. The good ones were all about you and me together, in the days before you got sick. I realize now how much you did for me back then. I wish we could start over. I want to make it up to you somehow….

Again and again he ran through this little speech inside his head, arranging the phrases first in one way and then another, visualizing her gentle gray eyes as the words passed like marching soldiers through his mind. He imagined her as she used to be when he was a little boy, her hair tied up in a blue scarf, a blush of pink in her cheeks. He closed his eyes and saw her bending over his bed to kiss him good night. He smelled the scent of her hair, her perfume, and the fresh white linen of her blouse. Again he felt what it was like to be small and helpless and blissfully dependent.

I guess the bad dreams won out in the end. I don't exactly know why. I was trying to help you, but it was never good enough. My experiments went wrong and my plans fell through. I almost betrayed my best friend. Now the Stone of Destiny is lost and Eny's in danger and you're still sick. So it was all for nothing in the end. You asked me to forgive you, but it's me who needs your forgiveness. I don't deserve your love….

He was picturing her now as she'd looked on the occasion of his last visit: a dim yellow light tangled in her diaphanous hair, her skin white and papery, her cheeks pale and hollow. He wondered what she'd look like when he stepped into her room for the last time. Blindly he stared at the floor tiles, knowing that she was drawing nearer with every step. In the last remaining seconds he rehearsed his confession once again, and an image of her face, twisted with disappointment, flitted through his brain. He flinched and closed his eyes.

One day. One day is more than enough. You were right, Mom. It's more than enough to tell you the truth. Before it's too late.

Rev. Alcuin came to a stop. Morgan shook off the shroud of his dark musings and glanced up. They had arrived in front of Room 247, but the door was closed—a circumstance that seemed to have caught the Reverend by surprise. Peter hesitated a moment before lifting his hand and rapping lightly. When there was no reply he knocked again. Then, very quietly, he turned the handle and stuck his head inside. Pushing the door wide, he beckoned with his fingers and walked straight in. Morgan followed.

The room was empty. From over Peter's shoulder Morgan could see the vacant bed, tightly made, neat as a starched collar, fitted up with crisp new sheets and white pillowcases. The bedside tray had been cleared off and rolled aside, and the ever-present water pitcher was gone. Gone, too, were the flowers and cards and potted plants that had filled the corners and crowded the windowsills during his last visit. An odor of detergent and disinfectant hung in the air, as if the floor had been recently mopped and scrubbed.

"I thought you said she'd be expecting us."

A crease appeared on Rev. Alcuin's forehead. "I did, didn't I? You're absolutely right." To Morgan's dismay, the minister appeared to be at a loss for words.

"So where is she?"

"I'm not exactly sure at the moment." The Reverend tugged at his collar and cast his eyes around the blank room as if in search of the missing patient.

"You don't think—"

"I'm certain there's a reasonable explanation. They've probably transferred her to a new room. A different unit."

"What do you mean by that? Intensive Care?"

Peter frowned and knitted his brows. "Let's not jump to conclusions. Remember what you said up in my office?"

The boy looked away and shook his head. He was fighting hard to hold down the sick, panicky flutter rising in his stomach.

"Something about faith, wasn't it?"

He bit his lip and nodded.

"Didn't you tell me that your mother was right, and that you should have listened to her all along? If you really believe that, this is the time to show it."

Morgan felt light-headed. He fell against the wall and covered his face.

"She *was* right! And I was wrong. But that's not *her* fault!"

"Listen to me, Morgan," said the Reverend, grasping him by the arm. "Your mother has taught me a great deal through all of this. She's shown me that when we're at our weakest and lowest, that's when we're really strong. She's proved to me that hope shines brightest in the darkest night. I've been a minister for a long time, but she taught me what it really means to believe in God! If I can learn, so can you!"

Morgan twisted and moaned. "I could have had Lia Fail! I could have figured something out, but I didn't! I could have cured her! I should have taken that chance while I had it!"

"No, Morgan. I know what you're thinking, but that Stone wasn't your only chance. More often than not the true cornerstone turns out to be the very stone the builders rejected. Something everybody overlooked. It's happened time and time again. In any case, you *had* to let Lia Fail go. If you hadn't, it would have destroyed you. Your father knew that!"

Morgan blinked at him through tears. "My father?"

"Yes. That's why *he* chose to give it up in the end."

For a long moment the boy stared at the minister's round, rubicund face, straining to understand the meaning of this latest revelation. Had John Izaak known that the last stone step on the tower stairway was actually Lia Fail? If so, how far had he been obliged to go—what had he been forced to sacrifice—in order to gain that knowledge? Did he know about the Morrigu? Did the Morrigu know about *him?* Something like a bolt of frigid lightning flashed through his overheated brain. He remembered what his mother had said to him about his dad: *He was taken.*

"I've got to find her!" he said, jerking away and making a move toward the door. "I've got to talk to her before it's too late! You can wait here if you want to, but I'm going! Somebody around this place must know what they've done with her!"

He turned to run, but found the way blocked. Skidding to a halt, he stumbled backward just in time to avoid a collision with a tall figure standing just outside the door—a figure dressed in a white medical smock.

"Excuse me," said the doctor, looking stunned and apologetic. "Are you Morgan Izaak?"

"Yes," stammered Morgan, rubbing his eyes and backing away.

"And the Reverend Peter Alcuin?" the doctor added, looking over the top of Morgan's head.

The Reverend stepped forward and took the doctor's hand. "We came to see the boy's mother," he explained. "He's just a bit confused. About not finding her here, I mean."

A sort of pained expression crossed the doctor's face. "I'm terribly sorry," he said, flipping through the papers on his clipboard. "We regret the inconvenience. I'm afraid none of us were expecting this. I certainly wasn't."

Morgan turned cold and darted a glance in Rev. Alcuin's direction. Peter shrugged and raised his eyebrows slightly.

"The situation changed so rapidly, you see," the doctor went on, taking out a pen and writing something on one of the sheets of paper. "We were quite taken by surprise." He glanced up and gave Morgan what appeared to be a look of sincere pity. "I'm really very, very sorry to have upset you."

"Doctor," said the Reverend, moving quickly to Morgan's side, "if you have something to tell us, perhaps it would be best if—"

"As I believe you already know," the doctor continued, almost as if he hadn't heard him, "Mrs. Izaak's cancer had metastasized. We found spots not only in the lungs, but on the liver and in the spine. One very recent test uncovered a questionable mass in one of the lymph nodes. I'm sure you can understand our concern at that point."

Rev. Alcuin nodded. Morgan said nothing, but simply stared down at his feet with a hollow sinking feeling in his heart.

"In light of the situation, you will also be able to appreciate the feelings of deep shock we experienced upon completing our last test. That was yesterday evening. Just prior to all the ruckus with the earthquake and the storm. Though we checked the results over and over again, we were unable to detect even the slightest sign of cancer."

With that, he turned the clipboard around and thrust it up against Peter Alcuin's chest. Morgan could make out only a single word at the top of the page as it passed from hand to hand: Discharge.

"Gone. Completely gone," said the doctor with a tired smile. "The most extraordinary case I've seen in twenty-seven years of practice. I honestly don't know how to account for it. Nobody does. You're probably aware that oncologists rarely use the word 'cure.' It's safer and more sensitive to speak in terms of 'remission.' All I can tell you is that, in this instance, I'm sorely tempted to ignore such protocol. A most remarkable case. Now if you'll be so good as to get these papers signed and turned in to the business office, I'll be off. You'll have to forgive my abruptness. It's been a long night." And with that he was gone.

"Morgan! I'm so glad you came to meet me! Thank you, Peter, for bringing him!"

Together they turned and saw Morgan's mother standing there, as big as life and as alive as she could ever be. She was dressed in her street clothes: a denim skirt, a plain white linen blouse, and a light beige sweater thrown loosely over her shoulders. In one hand she held her purse, in the other a canvas shopping bag that bulged with a miscellany of personal items. Her sparse, whitish hair, which had thinned considerably, was mostly hidden beneath a big blue scarf, and her high, narrow cheekbones were still alarmingly prominent beneath her transparent parchmentlike skin. But there was a rosy glow in her cheeks and on her forehead that Morgan had not noticed during his last visit, and her gray eyes sparkled with life.

"Forgive me for keeping you waiting," she said. "I was just getting my things together and saying good-bye to the nurses. They've been so good to me here!"

Morgan ran to her and hugged her neck. "I don't understand," he said through a fresh set of tears. "I did everything wrong! And you *still* got well!"

Mavis laughed. "What a funny thing to say! None of this is about you or anything you've done! It's about grace! What else can I say? Grace is enough."

Morgan smiled up at her. "It's more than enough," he said.

Peter Alcuin stepped up and threw his arms around the two of them. Morgan hugged his mother again and again, pressing his wet face tightly against her shoulder. Laughing in his embrace, she dropped her canvas bag and lifted a hand to stroke her boy's unruly yellow hair.

"Isn't it wonderful?" she said. "We're going home!"

Epilogue

There were deer on the Point—four dun-colored does and a spotted fawn—when Eny, fiddle in hand, came over the footbridge and took the path down to *La Cueva de los Manos*. They kept to the shadows under the spindly pines as she passed, cropping the thistles and chewing the lace lichen off the low-branching trees. Lithe, sleek, and majestic they seemed, but not in the least uncanny. Not one of them had red ears or fiery eyes.

A warm, dry breeze was blowing off the land and sweeping out over the ocean. It tossed the spray around and fluffed up specks of foam on the crests of the waves. Not a shred of mist nor a puff of cloud obscured the blue dome of the sky from the hills to the violet horizon. No engulfing sea of fog rolled toward the shore, no stalking shadow bent its head beneath the arch of stone. There were no green islands winking out through sudden windows in the west.

Sea lions barked between the echoing cliffs as she tramped along, groaning and grumbling at one another as they lolled across the rocks and sported in the surf. Eny laughed at them, wondering how sailors could ever have mistaken such awkward brutes for mermaids. Blackbirds twittered among the branches and bracken, calling to her distantly from the steep wooded heights above the emerald lagoon. But they did not know her name, and their song, though lovely and lissome, was innocent of enchantment.

Down through the breakers she waded, the sun hot on the back of her neck. Up over the rocky terraces she trudged, splashing and dripping with brine. Standing on the lonely strip of sand below the Cave she saw hermit crabs go scuttling over the black rocks. Bright blue anemones and orange starfish glittered in the tidal pools. Shoals of mussels shone like ebony beneath the shimmering surface of the water. But nothing even remotely like a human shape could she discern anywhere along that gray and empty stretch of sea-washed gravel. Cormorants dived, gulls wheeled, kestrels soared. There was not a single crow among them.

Within the Cave of the Hands she found no tracks. No sign that coracles had been dragged across the sand. No slings, no stones, no forgotten leather bags. The whole place looked exactly as it had always looked: intimate, friendly, ordinary. She cocked an ear to listen but heard no muffled voices, no rasping croaks and caws among the shadows, no strains of harp music beckoning to her from the depths of the earth. She searched but found no doorway between the boulders—only a wall of solid, dripping stone.

Seating herself on the sand, she took out her fiddle and rosined the bow. She lifted her chin and turned her eyes toward the wall. There before her rose the familiar swarm of red-ochre hands, like an upwardly sweeping cascade of pure sacrificial flame. Lowering the violin, she reached out and touched them, running her fingertips softly from hand to painted hand. The words of Simon Brach came back to her: "Perhaps as if it were through fire."

Outside, the breakers were crashing on the shore just as they had crashed on the pebbly strand at Luimneach. The wind was singing as it had sung in the hills of Beinn Meallain. Eny closed her eyes and tried to remember. When she opened them again, there was something bobbing over the surface of the waves far out on the ocean. But it was only a commercial fishing boat.

"I saw Tory Island," she said to herself, "and the ships of the Tuatha De Danann. I fled from giants, fell into a whirlpool, and escaped from the Morrigu. I was there when Jacob's Ladder touched the top of the tower stairs. I fiddled with one of the fairy folk, lived with the Fir Bolg, and handled the Stone of Destiny. Why am I neither ecstatic nor dead of fright? Was it just a dream?"

But no sooner had the thought passed through her mind than it was followed by a prayer—the very prayer she had prayed when last she pressed her palms against these same silent hands. That's when it occurred to her. What if the visions and enchantments were over and past? Mavis Izaak had come home. So what if the tower of St. Halistan's had fallen amidst storms and terrors? Morgan had his mother back again. A smile came to her lips. She bowed her head against the wall. "Thank You," she murmured into the close and holy darkness.

For a moment she paused to exult in the music of the waves. She sat very still, breathing in the salt sea air. She savored the delights of sunlight dancing on the water.

And then, with a flourish of her flashing bow, she picked up the fiddle and played.

... a little more ...

When a delightful concert comes to an end,

the orchestra might offer an encore.

When a fine meal comes to an end,

it's always nice to savor a bit of dessert.

When a great story comes to an end,

we think you may want to linger.

And so, we offer ...

AfterWords—just a little something more after you

have finished a David C Cook novel.

We invite you to stay awhile in the story.

Thanks for reading!

Turn the page for ...

An Interview with
the Author

This is your first novel, but not the first time you've told stories. What's the difference between your previous story writing and writing a novel?

As a matter of fact, this is my fifth work of fiction. I've done three Kidwitness novels for Bethany House/Focus on the Family—*Crazy Jacob* (about the son of the man possessed by the "legion" of demons), *Dangerous Dreams* (a slave girl in the house of Pontius Pilate), and *The Prophet's Kid* (the son of Isaiah)—and *Canyon Quest,* a prequel to Focus on the Family's *Last Chance Detectives* video and audio series. Even my nonfiction books have been primarily concerned with the quest for deeper meaning in *stories* (for example, The Lord of the Rings, *The Hobbit,* The Chronicles of Narnia, and traditional fairy tales), so there's a natural overlap between the two.

What's the difference between writing a novel and a shorter piece of fiction? I guess the answer would have to be that it's a much longer and more intensive discipline. There are more details to keep track of, more balls to keep in the air, more plates to keep spinning. It takes a lot of work and concentration.

What's your favorite story you've written prior to The Stone of Destiny?

I've always been rather partial to *Dangerous Dreams*. There's actually a connection here with *The Stone of Destiny*: Livy, the heroine of *Dangerous Dreams,* is Celtic—she's a slave girl from Gaul—and her knowledge of Celtic myth and lore plays an important part in the story.

Did you invent Santa Piedra, Punta Lira, and La Cueva de los Manos from your imagination or base them on real places?

Santa Piedra was inspired by a couple of different locations in California: first and most important, Monterey and Carmel on the Central Coast (notice the rocky coastline, the crescent-shaped bay, the steep streets, the Mission, and the perpetual mists); and secondarily the Balboa Peninsula in Southern California (the Balboa Fun Zone looms large in my memories of childhood vacations). Punta Lira, like Stevenson's Treasure Island, owes a lot to Point Lobos State Reserve, "the greatest meeting of land and water in the world." As for the Cave of the Hands, it was suggested to my mind by a small grotto I found beside the emerald green waters of China Cove on the south side of Point Lobos—though details were provided from my readings about a similar cave which, as I understand, you can find in the Santa Lucia Mountains near Esalen, California.

Is all this stuff about alchemy real?

Not "real" in the sense of "factually true." But it *was* believed in and practiced for centuries by some extremely intelligent people. Even today there are some folks "out there" who are pretty serious about it. The methods and techniques employed by Morgan in his experiments are based on the documented methods and techniques of famous medieval and Renaissance alchemists—people like Edward Kelly, John Dee, and Paracelsus. And the natural philosophy or "science" behind those techniques goes all the way back to Aristotle.

I feel like you've got more stories of Lia Fail *hiding away. Are there more to come?*

Ah! That would be giving it away, wouldn't it? But without revealing too much, I can tell you that there are a few definite Facts and a number of shadowy Possibilities floating around in the back of my mind, waiting for me to give them closer attention.

What part of The Stone of Destiny *is your favorite, and why?*

That would be hard to say, but a couple of parallel incidents come to mind immediately: Morgan's initial encounter with Madame Medea, and Eny's first meeting with Simon Brach. Each of these episodes attempts to depict an encounter with

Unseen Realities breaking into our world in the form of visible, "normal," everyday people and experiences—in the one case the Reality of Darkness, in the other the Reality of Light.

What inspired you to write this story?

In the first place, my admiration for all the great imaginative writers—George MacDonald, C. S. Lewis, J. R. R. Tolkien, and many others—who have so effectively used the vehicle of fantasy to lead readers into a new experience of timeless truth. We learn and grow by imitation, and my book represents my own feeble attempt to emulate the great masters. Second, I believe it was G. K. Chesterton who once said that a landscape is meaningless until it's linked with a story. An inspiring place needs an inspiring tale. I wanted to create a narrative to go along with a couple of special locations that have always been deeply meaningful to me on a personal level.

Morgan seems to do a lot of things wrong—that's not typical of a book's hero. Why did you choose Morgan for this journey?

I guess the simple answer is that I didn't "choose" Morgan. Morgan is simply *myself* under another name. Like everyone else, *I* do a lot of things wrong. Like everyone else, I need to understand how, by God's grace and providence, all those wrong things can be taken up and woven together into a beautiful tapestry in which all things work together for good. In my opinion, the really good fictional heroes are always bunglers. It's their journey from ignorance to understanding, from vice to virtue, from selfishness to sacrifice—the *transformation* they undergo as the story progresses—that makes a book powerful as well as interesting.

You've written books about fantasy worlds—what was it like creating your own fantasy world? How did those nonfiction books inform your own world creation?

It was far more difficult than I supposed. But in the midst of the hard work I found myself on a journey that became an adventure in its own right—a trek along a road marked by twists, turns, and sudden drop-offs I never could have foreseen or predicted. In that sense, writing *The Stone of Destiny* was a lesson in letting go and allowing the creative process to have its own way. Did my nonfictional analyses of fantasy stories help me in this process? I suppose so—but only in the way that a very basic trail map aids a backpacker in the high country. It can give you a good idea of the direction in which you should be going, but it's no substitute for actually *being* there.

PRONUNCIATION GUIDE

For some of the more difficult names in
The Stone of Destiny

Badb—*Bibe*

Baile—*BAY-la* or *BAY-lee*

Beinn Meallain—*Ben MEL-lane*

Crimthann—*CREE-van*

Crucha—*CROO-cha**

Currach—*CUR-rach**

Danaan—*duh-NAY-un*

Daoine—*DEE-na*; **Daoine Sidhe**—*DEE-na SHEE*

Eba Eochaid—*AY-ba YO-chid**

Eire—*AIR-ya*

Eithne—*EN-ya*

Eny—*EN-nee* or like the word *any*

Eochy—*YO-chee**

Fedelm—*FAY-delm* or *FAY-del-um*

Feth fiada—*Fay FEE-da*

Fionn MacCumhail—*FINN mac-COOL*

Fomorian—*Fo-MOR-ee-un*

Geis—*gaysh*

Genann—*Ge-NAWN*

Inisfail—*IN-is-fall*

Lia Fail—*LEE-a FALL*

Lugh—*Loo*

Luimneach—*LOOM-nyach**

Macha—*MAH-cha**

Mag Adair—*MAHG ah-DARE*

Morslogh—*MOR-slow*

Muir Mor—*MOOR MOR*

Niamh—*Neev* or *NEE-uv*

Oisin—*o-SHEEN* or *u-SHEEN*

Ollamh Folla—*O-lav FOL-luh*

Rachra—*RACH-ra**

Sengann—*SHEN-gan*

Sidhe—*Shee*

Tuatha De Danann—*TOO-uh-huh de DAN-nawn*

*ch indicates hard ch sound as in German *ach*.

GLOSSARY

These definitions are adapted from Websters-Online-Dictionary.org, Merriam-Webster.com/Dictionary, and Dictionary.Reference.com. Please check the dictionaries themselves for correct pronunciation.

admixture	something added by mixing
akimbo	set in a bent position
alembic	an apparatus used in distillation
apparition	an unusual or unexpected sight
arroyo	a water-carved gully or channel
astrolabe	a compact instrument used to observe and calculate the position of celestial bodies before the invention of the sextant
athanor	a furnace that feeds itself so as to maintain a uniform temperature; used by alchemists
aura	a distinctive atmosphere surrounding a given source
besmirch	sully, soil
bole	trunk
bougainvillea	any of a genus (*Bougainvillaea*) of the four-o'clock family of ornamental tropical American woody vines and shrubs with brilliant purple or red floral bracts
bulbous	resembling a bulb especially in roundness
cacophony	harsh or discordant sound

calcine (calcination)	to heat (as inorganic materials) to a high temperature but without fusing in order to drive off volatile matter or to effect changes (as oxidation or pulverization)
censers	a vessel for burning incense
chancel	the part of a church containing the altar and seats for the clergy and choir
coagulation	to cause to become viscous or thickened into a coherent mass
colonnade	a series of columns set at regular intervals and usually supporting the base of a roof structure
confect	to put together from varied material
congeal	to change from a fluid to a solid state by or as if by cold
congenial	pleasant, sociable, genial
cucurbit	a vessel or flask for distillation used with or forming part of an alembic
cupola	a small structure built on top of a roof
dilapidated	decayed, deteriorated, or fallen into partial ruin especially through neglect or misuse
discomfiture	disconcertion; confusion; embarrassment
dissolution	the act or process of dissolving
dun	an Irish word meaning "fort"
effervescent	giving off bubbles
emanation	something that is emitted or radiated
erubescent	red or reddish
etheric	the rarefied element formerly believed to fill the upper regions of space

facade	the front of a building
furze	gorse; a spiny yellow-flowered European shrub
gesticulating	making gestures especially when speaking
gingham	a clothing fabric usually of yarn-dyed cotton in plain weave
globular	having the shape of a globe or globule
gyrations	a single complete turn (axial or orbital)
heel	to lean temporarily (as from the action of wind or waves)
hempen	composed of hemp
hermetic	of or relating to the Gnostic writings or teachings arising in the first three centuries AD and attributed to Hermes Trismegistus
immolation	to destroy, often by fire
incandescent	strikingly bright, radiant, or clear
inexorably	inflexibly
iridescent	having colors like the rainbow; exhibiting a play of changeable colors
lichen	any of numerous complex plantlike organisms made up of an alga and a fungus growing in symbiotic association on a solid surface (as a rock)
luminous	softly bright or radiant

lummox	a clumsy person
maelstrom	a powerful often violent whirlpool sucking in objects within a given radius
magnanimity	loftiness of spirit enabling one to bear trouble calmly, to disdain meanness and pettiness, and to display a noble generosity
manto	a Spanish word for cloak, coat, robe
megalith	a very large usually rough stone used in prehistoric cultures as a monument or building block
mellifluous	having a smooth rich flow
miscellany	a mixture of various things
mortar	a sturdy vessel in which material is pounded or rubbed with a pestle
negligence	the trait of neglecting responsibilities and lacking concern
oscillate	to swing backward and forward like a pendulum
panacea	a remedy for all ills or difficulties
pennon	a long usually triangular or swallow-tailed streamer typically attached to the head of a lance as an ensign
perennial	continuing without interruption
pestle	a usually club-shaped implement for pounding or grinding substances in a mortar

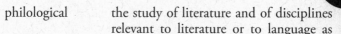

philological	the study of literature and of disciplines relevant to literature or to language as used in literature
phosphorescence	luminescence that is caused by the absorption of radiations (as light or electrons) and continues for a noticeable time after these radiations have stopped
pinnacle	an upright architectural member generally ending in a small spire and used especially in Gothic construction to give weight especially to a buttress
plaintive	expressive of suffering or woe
portent	something that foreshadows a coming event
profusion	great quantity; lavish display or supply
redolent	exuding fragrance
refulgence	a radiant or resplendent quality or state
renunciation	rejecting or disowning or disclaiming as invalid
roseate	resembling a rose especially in color
rubicund	ruddy
scimitar	a saber having a curved blade with the edge on the convex side and used chiefly by Arabs and Turks
scree	an accumulation of loose stones or rocky debris lying on a slope or at the base of a hill or cliff
seethe	to be in a state of rapid agitated movement

sibilant	having, containing, or producing the sound of or a sound resembling that of the *s* or the *sh* in *sash*
sojourner	a temporary resident
talisman	an object held to act as a charm to avert evil and bring good fortune
tangible	capable of being perceived especially by the sense of touch
tincture	a substance that colors, dyes, or stains
torque	a usually metal collar or neck chain worn by the ancient Gauls, Germans, and Britons
translucent	permitting the passage of light
transmutative	the conversion of one element or nuclide into another either naturally or artificially
tremulous	such as is or might be caused by nervousness or shakiness
undulation	a rising and falling in waves
vacillate	to move or sway in a rising and falling or wavelike pattern
verdure	the greenness of growing vegetation
vermilion	a vivid reddish orange
westering	to turn or move westward